THE CULT LEADER
BY MARIA SEA CHANNELS

MERIGOLD INDEPENDENT

THE CULT LEADER
BY
MARIA SEA CHANNELS

CONTENTS

CHAPTER ONE:
THE CULT LEADER

In the beginning, he overloaded me with information. I couldn't keep track of what was true and what wasn't.

I can't remember whose idea it was first. Did I make him that way? Did I want him to be that way? All I could remember was a conversation.

"What are you writing?"

"I'm writing about you."

"You should make it a book."

"It already is."

"What's it called?"

"*The Cult Leader.*"

Cash had always been a cult leader, a businessman, a CEO. He and I both knew there wasn't much difference between business and the occult.

His mom said he was a loner in high school. He didn't have any friends until later in life; a true social butterfly. He told me he spent most of his time alone in high school, studying. When I asked him what he studied, he said money.

He was born in the year of the dragon in Daytona Beach, Florida. He said his grandma liked him the most out of all the grandchildren. Whenever one of the kids made trouble, she always found him alone, away from the group he had been playing with, as if guided away by an angel. I met that grandmother at dinner once. She wasn't impressed with me but fawned over Cash like he was the last man on earth. At her side, her husband told stories she must have heard 1000 times that made her look like she had a mouthful of bad soup.

Cash started selling drugs as a kid in junior high when he realized his mom couldn't afford anything he wanted. He bought gold chains, diamond studs, and nice clothes. The thugs loved him because he was articulate but mostly because he never got high off the supply. They called him "smooth with two 'o's." From then on, he always had a lot of money.

The only job he ever had was working at an art supply store so he could get free art supplies. He thought art supplies were too overpriced to pay for and he liked to paint. His boss loved to fuck with people. Cash was the only person he didn't fuck with.

He got his high school girlfriend pregnant and she gave the son up for adoption. The son lived somewhere on the other side of Florida. The adoption family told Cash that the baby never cried. Cash said he never cried when he was a baby either.

A self-made millionaire by 21, he earned his first million selling motorcycle parts for the Chinese. Then he started his own motorcycle parts business with his brother. Then he did a lot of things that made him money that I don't really know much about. Real estate, Amazon fulfillment businesses, stocks, whatever.

When his business partner wouldn't go out on the town with him one night, he pulled a bible out of the drawer at the hotel that changed his life forever. He became a man of God at 23. For a week, he lived in complete service to other people, without thinking about himself at all. When he went back to his girlfriend she could barely recognize him.

He invested in his women like his companies. He got his first girlfriend to run his motorcycle business for him when he left to travel and study Muay Thai fighting in Thailand. When he came back she went off and started her own motorcycle business out of spite. His baby mama, Stacey, did the same thing with their candle company.

He brought out power in people, fucked the potential out of his women, his magic with them forever. He never left anyone worse off than when he found them.

He tried to get me interested in starting a business with him.

"We could start a little café on the beach. Super dope, super hip, with cool events that bring all the right people in."

"I've already been a barista. I don't need to do that again," I said. I reminded him I was writing his book.

He wanted to control me. He flickered into it sometimes out of nowhere like he'd forgotten that was his main objective.

"Woman!" He'd snap at me when we argued, as if suddenly remembering he placed himself hierarchically to me, not equally.

"Men ripen. Women rot," he said when he thought I was getting cocky or cool.

He didn't follow any rules. He paid his employees under the table and put his cash into jewels. He said we'd go and smuggle emeralds out of Colombia one day.

In the older photos I found of him on the internet he looked chubby, rounder, thicker, softer. He was nothing like the fit, lean, muscular man that I knew him as with rippled abs, a broad chest, big muscles, and a chiseled jaw. His hair style used to be a dweeby side part, and he wore nerdy polos with cargo shorts and flip flops. When I met him he had a permed sun-blonde mohawk and wore whale sperm cologne. Only wore linen, silk, and cotton.

He was redneck. He was actually the color red. Sometimes he was just tan. But if you get the light right, you can catch the red.

He talked of reptiles and secret societies and knew what was coming. Knew that the government would come up with aliens next and then the floods or, possibly, vice versa but definitely both. Of course not until after World War 3 happened.

He was into sex magic. He would cum inside me and then move around like he was trying to dig it all in deeper, groaning, contorting his mouth and twisting his eyeballs around.

"Maybe my love is too much for you. Maybe I give too much love to you," he'd say. Sometimes I believed him and worried I wasn't enough. But most of the time I saw right through his words. I could see the manipulation, a means to gain more control and power over me. I stuck around because I was so in awe of that power. I couldn't blame the crows when they ate the bread crumbs I left behind and I found I couldn't get back to reality, had lost track of where the fairy tale ended and I began.

It was like I told him, usually my sister and I don't go for players. We don't go for the show and pony. He got so mad when I told him that. He didn't like being called a player, though that's what he was. Of course he didn't like that. He denied any reality that was not his own making. And that's how he was so powerful.

We all wanted to believe in something and he knew. He became the religious fervor that we missed, that we had all been looking for- the magic we had been promised as kids. He had it in stock all the time somehow, gave us tastes and gulps, sometimes shoving it down our throats. He put meaning into a world devoid of meaning, where any meaning left was dripping, leaking out and if you didn't clamp onto something you could fall right into an existential pit. When I met him I thought being saved was just believing in something. So I believed in him.

He gave us a movie in his own genre. He gave us more than we ever gave anyone else. We never waited, we danced. We never walked, we flowed. He showed us there was never any reason to hurry, never any reason not to enjoy and celebrate. He made us see all the ways life spoke to us subconsciously.

After I left, Lucci and I talked about everything he gave us- so much beauty but so much evil. Maybe we would stay enamored with him for the rest of our lives. Maybe we could help him.

Lucci still called to tell me about the trance he was in, the trance he was coming out of. The same one that I had been in, that I now missed, that I searched for in other realms. Lucci wanted to leave Florida and move to Colombia.

I often thought about how easy cracking the literary code was. How you could easily entangle the literary inclined into believing your bullshit by using all the values they held to charm them: romance, heroics, tragedy, adventure. I knew this was how he enthralled me, how I let myself be enthralled. He put in the effort like I'd never seen it done before. His devotion to the cause made me devoted, made everyone devoted.

I didn't want to see his untruths, so I hid them from myself. I simply looked the other way as if each of his lies were small dust balls I didn't want to acknowledge until one day I was drenched in dust. Sooner or later I would become the dust.

But even so, ever since I met him, everybody else is just another stranger.

CHAPTER TWO:
THE IUD, PANDEMIC POLITICS, FLORIDA, AND MASCULINITY

In the beginning of Covid-19, I came up with a hundred plans for what to do with the rest of my life. I told them to my sister on our walks around the neighborhood.

We were living at my parents' house in a small, one part suburban one part country town that was settled by the Gold Rush. A little red bubble of Northern California nestled in a basin between the state capital and the Sierra Nevada mountains.

It was late spring 2020. I spent most of my time asking questions and looking for answers about what was going on.

In early spring 2020, I left the studio apartment I shared with my boyfriend in Oakland to return to Suburbia with all its empty gray space and quiet grass greens and chirping birds. Oakland sucked when the corona hit. For a month and a half we quarantined in between cement apartment buildings until our lease was over. We were paying 850 dollars each to split a box atop boxes amidst a sea of boxes. Whenever we sat on our roof all I could see were more apartment buildings.

On the same morning I got my IUD removed the day after I read, *Blackfishing the IUD,* I got laid off from my start-up job along with 80% of the sales team, a few days before shelter-in-place began. A journalist called to discuss the mass lay-offs that happened at my company. He believed the company had some insider information in regards to the burgeoning pandemic.

Week one of shelter-in-place I remember waiting in line at the grocery store behind a girl in an encapsulated plastic suit and gas mask who had a grocery cart packed full of large dirty carrots with the tops still on.

Week two of shelter-in-place I panicked at my boyfriend when he came home from playing basketball. "How could you?" I yelled at him. "You could kill us!" That was the only time I lost my cool about the pandemic.

Week three of shelter-in-place I kept running around Lake Merritt but I stopped surfing at Pacifica. On one of my runs I read, "Sanitize your minds. Fear is the virus," spray painted in graffiti on the side of an electrical box. It imprinted on me like a stamp and became my take on the pandemic.

Before I saw the graffiti I kind of figured the pandemic was a cover for the global consolidation of the world economies anyways. The perfect scapegoat the world leaders could use while governments printed money and resources diminished. I always wondered what would happen when the resources ran out. I thought this might be it. The pandemic felt like something I'd been waiting for my entire life.

I was more shocked about what people were turning into on social media. Hysterics, blaming, shunning, shaming all became normalized behavior. People became outraged when others did not comply with their standards of safety or whatever standards the medical institutions were enforcing. I didn't understand how people could trust "medical experts" when I thought we had all realized western medicine was corrupt and Big Pharma was not to be trusted. It was like people didn't realize they trusted a medical establishment that ran a country where more than half the population was either deathly fat or deathly ill. But I was used to being confused by the behavior of people.

I guess it started in high school, when my class was assigned to write an essay on the USA. The next day, when we read them aloud, I was surprised to learn that everyone else had written positive essays. My essay was scathing. That's when I first learned most people slept through life with little to no sense of interest aside from their own immediate circumstances.

The pandemic felt like another level of what I went through in college when I realized how shallow and self-absorbed most people were, how limited their thinking. As far as I knew, everything was unprecedented and no one had any right to tell anyone else what to do.

"People need to adjust their expectations of how many people in their life are going to die," my best friend tweeted. People were turning into authoritarian experts at a shockingly quick rate and the grossest part was how easily they slipped into these roles. It was as if they enjoyed freaking out and making sure everyone else was freaking out too.

When I made the return to suburbia I felt psychically safer, especially in red suburbia. We were armed, we were calm, and I could breathe normally. I didn't have to wear a mask. We were free to distrust and condemn the state and its medical institutions. My dad ignored the covid guidelines while my mom was obedient but watched all of Governor Newsom's speeches with a sardonic attitude. "Let's see what ding dong has to say today," she'd say as she did her leg exercises in front of the TV.

Eventually, in fall, I went with the first plan I came up with: fighting human trafficking for Americorps in Southwest Florida.

I was pretty end of my rope, uninterested in doing anything except what I could muster up a pulse about. I had been working in tech startup sales for the last couple years and was tired of bullshitting people about data driven equity and trying to change the world through software.

Last summer, the Jeffrey Epstein scandal had reignited my outrage about human trafficking, which I had first encountered when working in foster care at a group home for teenage boys. On the job one night, my manager told me that one of the boys I had grown close to was grooming other boys to be trafficked. I organized trainings in human trafficking awareness for my coworkers and then I left the job to travel in South America to escape a relationship and improve my Spanish. And then I went into tech startups because I was curious about the way money was being tossed around at half-baked ideas and I thought tech was changing the world in a good way. But it wasn't.

The Americorps position would pay almost nothing. I would go from making $4000 a month doing nothing on pandemic unemployment to $1050 a month. I was beginning to feel increasingly useless to society and thought I needed to grab onto a purpose fast, before the depression deepened. I felt like I was sinking into an abyss of myself, having left my parents' home that summer to wander around Eastern Europe, doing little else but follow a boyfriend around while everyone else in the world struggled with the socio-economic outcomes of Covid. Plus I was tired of arguing with my boyfriend about whether white people could experience racism on white sand beaches in Turkey. Admiring the remains of the Ottoman Empire, I decided to catch what might be final glimpses of the American one.

When I landed at the airport in Southwest Florida in the middle of October, I cried. Lee County, Florida was gruesome. Even the sunlight felt cheap, like it came from stagnant air that got trapped in the 80s, made of strictly synthetic material. The people walked around in sad family beach clothes.

But it was also wild, wrapped in jungle and swampland so voluptuous it was like part of the prehistoric era stayed behind its own extinction, the ultimate topographical haunted house of the living dead, where people talked themselves into feeling murder close by: swampy, muggy, covered with roadkill, and loud with animal noises. It took a half hour driving to get anywhere. To get places faster, I started speeding like crazy and when my mom visited she begged me to stop driving that way. I took photos of the strip malls, the art deco buildings, the neon signs, and the birds.

For weeks I was so focused on seeing an alligator that the people I saw walking around the white sand beaches started to look like alligators. I dreamt I was running away from them.

A man at a farmer's market showed me his collection of megalodon teeth he found on Florida's west coast beaches. I picked through the multi-million year-old teeth, rubbing their serrated edges with my fingers, marveling at the smokey tie-dye on black phosphate.

I said, "fucking Florida," to myself a lot. Hurricane Eta passed us by, my first hurricane. The sunsets were spiritually transcendent. It's not like you had to point them out to anyone either since it was so flat the sun went down right smack in your face every night, no obstacles, more sky than land, answering every single question you ever had. No wonder there were so many believers around. Jesus freaks.

I was supposed to spread awareness about human

trafficking in three different counties of Southwest Florida: Lee, Hendry, and Glades. I had to drive an hour out to a sprawling town called Lehigh Acres where it was rural like I'd never seen before.

Lehigh Acres was a town that got slammed by both the '08 housing crisis and the opioid epidemic. Housing developments built an hour away from the nearest grocery store in the middle of nowhere.

One afternoon, after presenting at a housing appraisers office, a coworker and I got lunch at a restaurant she knew of that she used to frequent when she lived out there. I ended up getting grouper tacos. Grouper was a hideously monstrous-looking Floridian fish that tasted divine. It fit right in with Florida's prehistorics. I couldn't get enough of it and ordered it everywhere I could.

We had just gotten our meals when she realized her ex-husband and his family were there. She was married to him before she became an anti-racist feminist who worked in nonprofit.

"What are you doing out here from the big city, city slicker?" Her ex's father asked when she went up to them to say hi.

The "city" he was referring to was Fort Myers, more of a town than a city and hadn't even reached its first 100k in population. But it was so rural out there that Fort Myers was like a city to them.

Her ex wheeled out an alligator in a crate without saying anything.

"Is that your companion pet?" I asked, joking and giddy to see my first alligator in Florida.

"Uh, no," he said, without looking up at me, wheeling the reptile away.

After they left, my coworker explained how it had been a rude awakening for her ex and his family when she started studying critical theory and taking online college classes.

The southern mentality was traditional. I found it exotic, having only lived on the progressive west coast.

A whole new world of fully embodied and dichotomized masculine and feminine forms as opposed to the gender fluid world I was used to. Women were considered innocent and naïve; barely any different from a child.

"Would you like me to walk you to your car? Do you need help finding it?" A handsome married man once asked me after one of my presentations. It was custom, not creepy. And I liked feeling cared for, protected, precious. Men were more liable to hit on me and approach me but I didn't mind. It felt like time travel.

I moved into a house on Dolphin Street in Bonita Springs, a little town on the edge of Lee County in between the cities of Fort Myers and Naples, where two divorced Gen Xers lived together as roommates named Karen and Dexter. Karen ate a lot of frozen pizza and watched a lot of Survivor. Dexter considered himself a socialite and was passionate about dating trans women.

The house sat on a canal where I once saw a dolphin swimming. I bought a stand up paddle board and paddled it down the canal in our backyard, through the other neighborhood canals and into the Gulf of Mexico. It took me seven or eight times before I got bored of paddling on the flat water. Karen asked me how I didn't get lost in the canals and I said I looked for things like chairs and lawn ornaments.

The house looked shabby and small on the outside but inside it was huge, with long, mansion-shaped rooms. You walked into a giant, two-part entryway to walk through a large dining area into a spacious kitchen which led into another dining room and then a bar area and then the giant lanai. I counted eighteen ceiling fans. The house echoed, it was so spread out. Each of our bedrooms was like a separate wing.

We all worked from home due to the pandemic. My room was tiny so I moved around a lot in the house, working in different spaces. I liked to take long breaks out on the lanai, drinking coffee and watching the flora and fauna.

Both my roommates ran their own businesses out of the house, something I was beginning to aspire towards myself, having seen so many people less smart than me running successful businesses. Dexter had his own medical equipment company that supplied and installed parts to medical professionals for their geriatric patients. Years ago, Dexter cheated on his wife a bunch of times so now they raised their kid divorced and states apart. He flew out to Indiana to visit his kid every other weekend.

Karen's business was called the Grief Goddess. She wrote and sold books, cards, and workbooks for people dealing with the grief of losing a loved one to death. She also facilitated workshops and retreats. Her son had died from an OxyContin overdose a couple years ago, at nineteen. She still had her daughter, Violet, fifteen, who lived most of the time with her dad and his wife. Karen had been married five times: to Violet's father, the safest of the bunch; her son's father, a meth head; a sex addict; an alcoholic; and a prescription drug addict. But her misfortunes in love didn't prevent her from encouraging me to date.

I tried to break up with my ex I lived with in Oakland on the telephone when he was in Mexico. The whole time we were in Eastern Europe I had tried to get him to go to Mexico since I knew Europe was going to go into lock down. But he didn't go until I left for Florida. That was my last straw. He was so adorable but his lack of foresight and maturity drove me nuts. But he wouldn't let me break up with him and instead, he flew out to visit me in Florida.

When he said he didn't think Florida was a southern state I told him I felt that way the week before but assured him it was a southern state, just with more outsider influence than the other southern states. I mumbled something about biscuits and how people talked so slow and so insignificantly that they'd learned to talk over each other. We looked it up: Florida had been in the confederacy, signifying its "southerness."

My boyfriend wrangled me into going to Fresno to spend Thanksgiving with him and his family.

Since the pandemic, it was getting harder and harder to follow the news. Every event was separated into two disparate realities: Democrat versus Republican and people *still* bought that shit as if corporate entities hadn't purchased all the political power already. For example, in the news, Hunter Biden, the son of the brand new but very old president, had something to do with leaked emails and a corrupt relationship with China. I observed the usual split of a reaction between the two parties in my close relationships.

In Fresno, since my boyfriend's family didn't have room for us, we stayed with his friend who talked to his three large, neurotic Australian Shepherds like they were very naughty children. Whenever we visited him, he always had the news on. He was a big Hilary Clinton and Margaret Thatcher fan. MSNBC was covering the election results. He thought the Republican Party was becoming obsolete though the 2020 election had just churned out nearly 50/50 results.

"Did you guys hear about the Hunter Biden thing?" I asked. My boyfriend and his friend both responded that it was nothing. They said it with conviction. They didn't even look at me.

Just a few days before, my dad told me on the phone that it was the biggest corruption scandal we would ever see in our lifetimes. I asked my boyfriend and his friend one more time about the Hunter Biden scandal, thinking they were confusing it with something else. Again, they refuted that it was nothing. They were so quick and assured. I wanted to know what source they used that brought them so much assurance. They had none to give me.

I wanted to be that sure, as sure as them. But most importantly, I didn't want a crazy dad who believed crazy things. But at this point, we were all crazy. But some of us were more far gone than others. Some of us believed they could actually know things.

The news continued to distort economic analyses that even less people could understand then people could understand the political war bullshit. I heard people parroting back sound bites they'd heard from the news and then reacting suspiciously when they heard sound bites they'd been programmed against. So I just stopped reading and listening to the corporate news. I listened to political commentary podcasts less and less frequently; my only means of staying informed. Politics was bad juju, or, at the very least, a complete waste of time. And that was back when the Covid-19 death count was still on the news, before they started rolling out vaccination counts.

I lost a best friend during this time, not to the virus but to politics. It all started when I refused to vote for Joe Biden, refused to vote at all, and it ended months later on a phone call.

"Yeah I'm just grocery shopping. I went to this thrift store today and found this incredible dress," I babbled to her, looking at different boxes and bags of sugar as I tried to decide which kind I should use to make purple potato donuts.

"You are thrifting during a pandemic? Don't you want to protect people?" She said from her quarantined apartment in Portland, Oregon.

"Oh. Yeah. I mean, it's Florida. No one really cares about the pandemic here. It's sort of a group effort to ignore it and live life as usual."

"But what about the elderly? The immunocompromised?"

"I think they just stay inside. You probably won't like anything I'm going to say about this so maybe we shouldn't talk about it."

"You know, it's really not that hard to stay inside."

"Yeah, if you don't have much of a life to begin with." I didn't realize I struck until I felt the buzzing in my tongue.

She stuttered from the impact. Then, with a mouth full of venom she said, "You don't care about your community!"

"Look, you are obviously upset... I'm going to hang up now." I hung up on her again for the second time that year.

But what did I expect? People still worked way too hard to buy evil products from evil companies and pay evil taxes to evil rulers. I got upset when the Superbowl continued to run during the lockdown while all the little venues across the country had to stay shut. At the Superbowl, the poet laureate dressed in Moschino and read a stupid poem about the heroic front line workers. She was celebrated for being the first poet to perform at the Superbowl halftime show. That sounded like bad news for poetry to me.

And then there was the televised spectacle of inauguration where all the politicians wore designer clothes and watched Lady Gaga sing. This time the poet laureate wore Prada. People celebrated because the vice president was, for the first time, a woman of color. But she was totally evil, with a track record for punitive justice and criminalization.

It was a time when people assumed you shared the exact same opinion as them and, therefore, a time for listening and being careful with whom you were speaking. Most people couldn't handle anything you had to say if it diverted from what they'd been told to think by the mainstream narrative. Questions were not only frowned upon but could be ridiculed and considered offensive and inflammatory. And no matter what, if you were talking to a liberal, the conversation got driven to the concept of white privilege somehow. You'd be talking about one thing and then the next thing you knew you were discussing police violence or the oppression of black people. It was like people's brains were broken.

Everyone's version of events blended into copy-pasted opinion and hearsay. People preferred to demand a co-opted form of racial justice while there was no such thing as global justice. Maybe sometimes there was, incrementally, and that made all the difference to some people, even if those increments never progressed past the symbolic. People thought "having a conversation" would change the world though the conversation had been happening long before it was trending. It was impossible to tell whether any of this was helping black people but the infiltration of academia hyperbole into the layman's word bank sure was weird to watch.

There was nothing to know but yourself anymore, nothing to do but gain complete control of your own mind, to think critically and independently. But most people didn't think that way. They listened to the news vividly of the times, alive in the now, ambivalent to history. Some thought the United States was keeping everyone from enlightenment and freedom. Others thought it was the only thing standing to protect enlightenment and freedom. I always felt better when I remembered the United States was just an experiment after all.

I started to occult myself, digging into Colin Wilson. I was obsessed with understanding systems of power. I learned about the slave-military-coin complex, coined by David Graeber, and read books like *Weapons of Mass Instruction*, written by John Taylor Gatto. I studied the true power behind American government like the Federal Reserve, Koch Industries, McKinsey, the Rockefellers, Robert Moses, and the Sacklers. I even read Wikileaks.

Since covid started, people who read conspiracy theories got shamed though I couldn't understand why when as children at school in America we were told Colombus heroically "discovered" America. How could you not be a conspiracy theorist when you grew up on that story? I couldn't understand how my people could continue constructing the world in the same violent, punishing, dominator culture. So I made the fairy tale choice to fight the Nazi state and began to practice intuitive therapies like astrology, herbology, and tarot. America was a cult I wanted nothing to do with.

And then there was the mushroom trip I had a few days after Fresno Thanksgiving with my boyfriend, our final consummation.

Sitting in his mini cooper, we ate some mushrooms. I was hesitant because my mental state had been unstable but he urged me to trust him. We wandered around a forest. We crossed a street and ended up in an orchard. It was beautiful to trip in the orchard in the middle of fall; reds, oranges, yellows, greens moved and swerved into us, seducing us, staying inside us as we huddled our bodies together in the cold fall air, watching the sunset and playing music on my iPhone, swaying to the sounds together. Then the full moon rose. We laid down on the leaves. He wanted to take all my clothes off to fuck but I wouldn't let him since it seemed impossible.

The next thing I knew, I was underground, beneath the earth. The orchard could tell that I wanted to die, that I wasn't enjoying existence on earth- that I was totally over it and ready to move on into the Great Beyond. But by forsaking the earth, I would go to hell, the orchard said as it pulled me down to hell. And then I spent the next phase of time believing I was in hell, believing I would be raped by the forest entities in the cold dirt forever. And as my boyfriend kept trying to have sex with me, I realized that once I surrendered to the masculine, I could leave hell.

So in the middle of the orchard, at the bottom of hell, I surrendered to the masculine. And to embody the divine feminine, the shrooms told me I needed to be a mother, or they awakened my desire to become one. As he fucked me, wolves started howling. So then I thought he was the wolf prince of Fresno. I told him to cum inside me so that I could be the wolf queen and raise another prince. He did.

Walking back to the car, still tripping, I thought about how the masculine was the creative force that made everything happen and the feminine was supposed to be impressed by all this power. The masculine wanted acknowledgement and admiration from the feminine and in reciprocation she would be worshiped and provided for with structure and luxury. I was so relieved to have gotten out of hell that I wanted to express my gratitude by total submission. And so, my new life path began: surrender to my boyfriend to honor the divine masculine.

We went to get plan B the next day. As the trip melted off, my boyfriend and I proved to be just as incompatible together as before the trip. It wasn't necessarily him I needed to submit to, just the masculine force in general, which could be embodied by a different man, one more capable of provoking and earning my submission.

CHAPTER THREE: SUGAR DADDIES, CULTURAL APPROPRIATION, AND GOD

My roommates had a friend named Troy who was famous for being rich and getting laid by young women. Dexter and Karen had been grooming me.

"Oh, he's going to fall in love with you," they would say. "You're just his type."

But I think they were just excited about being excited because his "type" was just "young." That was pretty much it. Though I was somewhat intrigued as I had been nursing an attraction for older, wealthier men since college. And after a couple months at Americorps, I was tired of working. After my colleague interrupted my two hour presentation on human trafficking with a hysterical cry of, "The Republicans are storming the Capitol!" I realized I was engaging with the wrong polemic.

It couldn't hurt to be open to the sugar daddy idea. It had always been a plausible situation if all else failed. The fantasy of not having to work aside from going on a couple dates here and there was appealing and seemed like it could be easy for a person as charming and personable as I.

From my roommates, I learned that Naples, the city on the coast line below Bonita Springs, in Collier County, was rich and teeming with the discreet but overt arrangement of sugaring. The neighborhoods had huge glossy gates and all the cafes and bars were full of glossy girls with glossy highlights.

One day, after sauntering around Naples in a mini skirt with high heels, stealing from places like Whole Foods and Nordstrom Rack, a sugar daddy asked me out at a café. I considered the offer. He was ugly, fat, old, and a foot surgeon. He offered me $200 for a lunch date. After giving it a couple days' thought, I turned him down. There was no way I could make myself have sex with him. But when I opened myself up to that energy, and created a requisite for sexual chemistry, what I ended up with was Cash. But before we get to him, I need to expand on other factors.

Post breakup, in the middle of Florida winter, my new roommate, Karen and I decided to go out to a bar for our first roommate hangout. I asked her to take me to the best dive bar in the area. I figured the people would be an interesting mix and I'd get a good look at the local population.

She didn't know where to go so Dexter told us to go to a place called Sneaky Pete's. Like all of southwest Florida, Sneaky Pete's was full of Boomers, and the Silent Generation, with a few Gen Xers here and there. And like all the bars it had an island theme. We sat ourselves at the bar and after our first drinks we started playing a game the bartenders taught us. We had to guess random people's names.

That was when I first spotted Khalif, another millennial. He had this white beanie on that caught my eye. Karen said it made me think he was more intelligent and hipster than he probably was. Both my roommates had warned me about the low IQs of all the people I was about to meet and that I'd be smarter than all of them.

I was undeterred by Karen. Maybe it was his curly hair. I'd always had a thing for curly hair. He was playing pool with another guy, so I went over and asked if my friend and I could play the next game with them. Karen was impressed. "I love how you just give no fucks," she said.

So that was how I met Khalif. He was a caddy and a snowbird that spent his warm weather months in Maryland. He was raised as a Santeria shaman back in Puerto Rico. Karen thought this was freaky. But I didn't think it sounded any worse than the freakiness of the cult of America and our business of war.

The other guy was his roommate, Charles. Charles believed in aliens and liked talking to animals. They both talked like they had only been talking to men for a long time, all jokes and big laughs, big riffing, big ego games. They both had skin browned from caddying all day in the sun with big beer bellies from constantly drinking.

I pretended to fall in love with Khalif that night to entertain myself, to heighten the dramatics in the air because I was already so bored in Southwest Florida. Karen and Dexter thought I was serious and tried to talk some sense into me. I told them I was just playing around. Dexter was confused. Karen laughed.

Most of my personality went over Dexter's head. Karen and I bonded over our shared distrust of the state while Dexter and I argued about mine. One time I overheard Dexter arguing with one of the many dates he brought over to the house.

"I just want everything to be open!" I heard her say.

Dexter argued with her vehemently. He watched MSNBC and listened to NPR daily, without the capacity to recognize the components of the military state propaganda embedded in these media programs. And apparently without the awareness to recognize his own hypocrisy as he frequently went out in public.

Karen and I found him a lost cause, an ignorant Joe, a deluded robot. He used divisive political buzzwords regularly.

One night he took us out to dinner for Karen's birthday, as he did have good intentions, and truly wanted to be our friend. Just kidding, he wanted to fuck us. He took us to a ritzy restaurant in downtown Naples.

After dinner, we walked down the street and stopped to look at an art gallery window. There was a giant Buddha statue covered in Swarovski crystals. I commented on its beauty. Dexter said it was "cultural appropriation," buzzword number one.

I told him I thought cultural appropriation was bogus as nearly everything could be considered culturally appropriated. And who was he to decide which people could do what with what anyways. He wasn't even Buddhist.

He told me I had white fragility, buzzword number two. I asked him what he meant by that, if he could please explain. He quickly changed the subject.

I thought he must have black fragility but I didn't say anything. I didn't want to offend him further. He was already hurt by the fact that I liked the Swarovski Buddha.

Eventually Khalif invited me over for dinner. I said yes even though I already knew he wasn't "it." Karen was still trying to get me to date him. Again, I think she just wanted to be excited about something. Or she still thought I really was in love with him instead of just playing around.

Karen and I had long kitchen talks on our work breaks where we plotted our manifestations and wondered about GOD and men. We both wrote until we slept and wrote right when we woke up. We were writing our lives down so we could live them as we wished. We shared our dreams as they changed and shape shifted.

Karen could be brash like when I had to tell her to stop calling me "bitch." I think it was just a Minnesota thing. She also said cool spiritual stuff like how GOD showed her how to bend time or when she talked about seasonality: the rhythm to our individual living patterns that we can tap into and use to our benefit. Occult sort of shit, though she didn't know what the occult was. But she sure knew her bible. She taught me a lot about how to talk to GOD. She was pretty lost when it came to men though.

I told her that I was trying to unbury myself and get to the root of my desires, the bottom of my own soul before I connected it with another's again. Karen suggested Khalif could help me do it.

"He's even more buried than I am!" I told her, thinking about his beer belly.

"You can unbury each other!" she said.

She didn't get that I was just using him for romantic attention. But even I only understood that in hindsight- at the time, I had no clue what I was doing. I thought it was as reasonable to go on a date with someone you weren't interested in as it was to water a plant. I thought it was akin to a healthy chore. Now I know I was "getting attention" like some kind of parasite.

Before the dinner date, Karen and I went to Troy's BBQ fundraiser. He had his whole posse there and then some. There was some big boat show going on and people were driving their boats around the marina blasting the 90s and making lots of noise.

Karen called all the people at the BBQ white trash. But then she noticed the moon in the sky during daytime for the first time in her life. I definitely could not trust her. She was a 40-something-year-old noticing the moon in the daytime sky for the first time in her life.

We took two rounds of shots with Troy and his posse. Troy was hitting on me heavily. The group found out I had a date that night. They wanted me to go clubbing with them and skip the date. That's exactly what I should have done, since my interest in Khalif was sparse.

In the middle of the group conversation, Troy turned to me and asked, in front of everyone, "What do you want?"

I stuttered then deflected and told Karen to answer for me. She laughed and said something unserious. Troy suggested I be his personal assistant. I turned it into a bit for the rest of the party, joking with the men that hovered around, rolling my eyes with the other girls.

Karen had Charles come over to our house that night while I went to Khalif's. A few nights before, Violet recorded a strange noise on her sleep tracking app so Karen was having him investigate the house for spirits. The recording captured a squeaky, dark, creature-like sound in a creature-like language. We all thought the noise sounded demonic and Charles agreed. He said the house definitely had paranormal activity. It was an old house, like most houses in Lee County.

They spent the evening talking about demons. He told her that they can get addicted to emotions. They will try to urge these emotions onto humans so they can feel them again through their human hosts. They can get addicted to masturbating, for example, and make us want to masturbate more by using strange smells like marijuana or trash. Florida must be rampant with demons.

Khalif and I stayed up all night watching movies, drinking whiskey, and smoking hash. The salmon dinner he made for us was delicious; he had been trained as a chef. We cuddled on the couch and I went home in the morning to sleep: untouched, angelic.

But a week later, I started to get horny. Maybe it was the demons. Finishing up my work, I texted Khalif to see if he was around. He invited me over. He warned me that he was going to want to jump my bones. I figured it could be good for me. Sex: another healthy chore, like watering a plant.

I decided to stop at the grocery store for a bottle of wine to take to his house. Thinking deeper, I stopped myself. Why was I going after a man for sex instead of prioritizing my writing, my creativity, my manifestations? I thought about how I left my adorable but annoying boyfriend behind in Eastern Europe and now I was considering a man I found even less appealing. I considered grabbing Cheetos, my comfort food, instead of wine and going home to write.

When I pulled into the parking lot at Publix, I was still undecided about whether I would buy Cheetos for writing or wine for sex. I walked into the store and saw an answer from GOD: Cheetos on the walk-in display. Who puts Cheetos on display at a grocery store? So I bought the Cheetos and went home.

GOD; another factor I should explain before Cash.

During the beginning of Covid-19, I went through several epiphanies in my childhood bedroom as spring ended and summer began. I spent hours alone feeling enlightened, whole, and close to GOD.

Part of my occult studies was reading a book actually titled, *The Occult*. I had picked it up months earlier at a thrift store in a Bay Area suburb. But I didn't start reading it until I was back at my parents' at the beginning of the pandemic.

From the first page I knew I had discovered my own version of the bible. I tried to come up with a way to say that so I sounded less fanatical in my secular group of friends. We never talked about GOD or the occult. But I got really close to GOD that spring.

For weeks, I stayed up until the early morning, taking hits off my weed vape, reading, and contemplating the secret knowledge the author wrote about. I'd wake up and go on hikes in the Sierra Nevadas, listening to birds, walking with baby deer, spotting bald eagles, seeing the little symbols and patterns and rhythms made just for me, answering all my questions.

Maybe all those epiphanies and awakenings occurred because of the strand of weed I was smoking but I felt like a changed woman. Maybe it was the government money I was getting for pandemic assistance that made me feel so whole. Maybe that's just how rich people who don't have to work feel. Constantly enlightened and close to GOD.

It was a time of letting go of that which did not serve me, in order to get to the core of me. I began to see through more of the state propaganda. Once a leftist, I realized I was being used by the system with this ideology- with any ideology.

At 29, it no longer bothered me to be called, "idealistic." People who labeled me that way were just on a different frequency. My dad called me that and so did Dexter- both men, both older, both corporate news watchers.

Everything I ever did in my life was for the experience: to follow my heart and do anything but conform to normalcy and a false sense of security. I didn't want to compromise. Ever.

And that's how you fall in love with a cult leader. They know how to meet you at the perfect moment – how to be exactly what you're looking for, at just the right frequency. Of course it's the wanderers they're after. He spoke the way I needed someone to speak and he was the way I needed someone to be. Romance is a cult.

CHAPTER FOUR:
TAROT CARDS,
ZOLOFT, AND
CACAO

I started reading tarot at the same time I started seeing Cash.

I pulled a 9-card pyramid spread after our first three dates. He was out of town for the weekend and I hadn't heard from him yet. I wanted to feel something about the relationship.

As I read the cards, I realized how much I wanted his devotion. Karen was watching. I had to convince her that the tarot wasn't satanic or evil. It only took about a minute to change her mind.

"Well, not gonna lie, it looks like the cards want you to date him," she said, after I turned over all but one card left at the top.

And then my phone rang. It was Cash. I felt nervous but giddy. I picked up the phone.

"Is now a good time to talk?"

He was just saying hi. Asked me to dinner when he came back into town.

I hung up and turned over the Ace of Swords. Just like the dangling silver sword earring he wore in one ear.

Cash was different from the other guys. When I threw him a bone he didn't just chew on it until his strength or focus was diminished, he devoured it. He tore it apart then put it back together. Didn't just sniff at it or lick at it, he fucking annihilated it then mass produced it and didn't break a sweat.

One time, on the drive to one of our float tank sessions, he was trying to get me to explain my reasoning to him about an abstract concept, something about why I thought it was funny the way he had expanded the craftsmanship of his joke through the use of time. I was failing to explain myself clearly and I accepted he just wouldn't get it; that it wasn't even that important, that, as was common for me, I was being too abstract, too cerebral.

When I came out of my float and went to meet him in the lobby where he waited, lounging on a sofa, always finished before me, he eloquently explained my reasoning to me. He figured it out during his float meditation. I was amazed that he cared so much. No one else had ever put that much concentration or care in understanding the intricacies of how my mind worked.

Not even the mental health start up I subscribed to.

I was on my second round of a foray into the phenomenon of antidepressants. I subsisted on a daily dose of 50 milligrams of Zoloft paired with 15 milligrams of Buspar. The start up was based in San Francisco and doled out SSRIs like wedding cakes after a 10-minute phone call with a nurse practitioner. I had to lie about which US state I was in when I resubscribed and started taking the pills again in December once I was in Florida after a short lapse when I was in Eastern Europe.

My first round of the SSRI foray lasted from April to August before I ditched both the pills and the US for Turkey with my ex. He was pretty pissed when he learned I'd left my pills behind. He was the one who wanted me to get them. When we broke up I replaced the pain with the pills and started taking them again.

"How's your mood?"

The nurse practitioner started every conversation the same, looking so bored and tired in her little room on my computer screen.

"Yeah so my mood has been good. It's hard to wake up though. I have a hard time getting out of bed in the morning. I'm thinking I need something more high energy."

A podcaster I liked said she was on Wellbutrin so I wanted to try that. Zoloft really did make it hard to get out of bed in the morning. Though I had never been a morning person in the first place. I googled ahead of time what I should say to get a Wellbutrin prescription.

"Okay so what we're going to do is slowly taper you off the Zoloft and start you on a small dose of Wellbutrin. And then we might find that you don't even need the Buspar and we can take you off that."

"Okay."

"So just keep me updated on your mood."

The startup was called Mood.

Wellbutrin or Zoloft, I had an unlimited supply of serotonin coursing through my bloodstream. I was always happy. Sometimes all I could do was sit completely still without moving, feeling the strong, pulsating waves of happiness. It was like I was so happy I didn't know what to do with myself, like when I took MDMA or LSD.

Maybe that's why I thought I could handle Cash and his two-wife-cult vision. What did I have to lose with an endless supply of happiness? And it was 2021 after all. A two-wife cult sounded better than the boring corporate illusion I found most people living in. How big is your magic if you don't experiment with reality?

We met on Valentine's Day at a heart opening ceremony on the lawn at the Cape Coral Yacht Club. Cape Coral was a chunk of a town on the peninsula across from Fort Myers. If you weren't coming from the north, you could only get to Cape Coral by two different skyways.

Southwest Florida had miles of skyways all over, skinny highways that hovered along the crack between sky and water that reminded me of a recurring dream of driving a highway straight up into the sky where I only wake up once my tires leave asphalt and I'm falling through the sky.

The lawn overlooked a beach where people dozed on towels in the sand and waded in the water. There was a dock where some people dumped their boats into the gulf and others fished.

On the lawn, the heart opening ceremony event had four or five booths offering free kombucha, vegan snacks, and gluten-free desserts from different local vendors. There was an eclectic mix of deep Burner hippies who had dreads and homemade clothes all the way up to people wearing Lululemon yoga pants and summer dresses from Banana Republic. A lot of people had the same tie dye t-shirts on.

My friend, Ashley, was organizing the clothing swap. We became friends immediately after I took her yoga class at Neenie's House, a community arts nonprofit where all the hippies gathered. Ashley connected me to all the hippie programming in the area. She was always running around going to events and I followed her sometimes, meeting her friends who were interesting, alternative people. She included me in her permaculture club that met every weekend.

Ashley had also just gotten out of a break up and we bonded over that, quickly becoming each other's replacement significant other, having sleepovers, taking road trips, and talking every day. We gushed over each other with compliments. We both knew the world was full of shit, same wavelength.

I stood next to Ashley's friend, Leslie, during the cacao ceremony.

Most of the people at the event gathered into a large circle and passed paper cups around until everyone had one. There were about 40 of us. We each got a pour of warm liquid cacao into our cups. Someone gave a little speech about love and connection and then we all drank our cacao.

Drinking cacao in ceremony can be a powerfully transformative event. It can connect you to situations and people that you need to transcend your current level of consciousness. I didn't know that until nine months later when a medicine woman told me so.

Leslie and I partnered up for the next event: eye gazing. She also knew the world was full of shit.

We sat on blankets and stared into each other's eyes for three minutes. I was disappointed by her lack of seriousness, making silly faces and winking instead of maintaining eye contact. I thought she was spiritual enough to take it seriously. I always took meditation and spiritual practices seriously as that was the only way they could be beneficial. I guess that's how some people feel about democracy.

Then some large spray-tanned blonde woman stood up on top of a picnic table and gave a speech about being unafraid and choosing love over fear. She proclaimed that "they" wanted us to feel afraid and alienated, that "they" wanted us to feel powerless and weak.

"But," she said in a booming voice, "we will not be beaten down! We will remain strong and brave. We will not give in to fear but we will keep living in light and love!" She threw in the words, "cosmic fam" a bunch of times too but I didn't understand the reference. I enjoyed her speech but when I started thinking about the type of person it took to say things like that in the way that she did, *sociopath* crossed my mind.

Next she announced there would be a free candle giveaway and someone placed a heavy pink pyramid candle in my hands. I took it to where Ashley was talking to some guy wearing the same tie-dye t-shirt that many others were wearing. Some guy he turned out to be. It was Cash.

I showed them the candle. "Look what I got. What is this?" I asked, laughing. I laughed a lot in those days. It was probably the Zoloft. Everything had an amusing tint to it.

"Aw! I've always wanted one of those! They do so many free giveaways and I've never gotten one!" Ashley whined. She whined a lot.

Cash took the candle from my hands and, holding it, explained what it was.

"It's a Cosmic Candle. In ancient times throughout many ancient cultures, scent was used ceremonially and ritually to engage with spirits and visions. These candles can be used as tools to empower individuals to manifest their dreams and create their ideal worlds. And there are crystals inside too. You can get a reading from us based on what kinds of crystals you find to apply the meaning to your life."

I found his enthusiasm odd. How awkward to be so passionate about a candle company you work for. It was just a candle. But he had good eye contact. We chatted a little more and he got my Instagram handle so we could golf sometime. I was happy to find someone to golf with. I told him we could even share the same size clubs because he wasn't that much taller than me.

"Hey now," he said, a little miffed. I found this amusing.

When I told him I worked for a nonprofit in anti-human trafficking for Americorps, he laughed and said, "Like you really do much work."

How this stranger already knew this was a curiosity but mostly I liked his candor.

Ashley told me he was the CEO of the crystal pyramid candle company called Cosmic Candles that was running the event and that the speaker I thought of as sociopathic was his business partner and baby mama. The "cosmic fam" she was referring to was their cult-like following of customers.

"But they're separated," Ashley explained. "It's a lot of drama. I was kind of worried that she'd be pissed at me for eye gazing at him."

Cash and a girl he introduced as his assistant helped us put Ashley's stand away at the end of the event. I felt a little anxious. He was trying to be a gentleman. He was showing interest in me.

Standing by Ashley's car, he asked if I was going to the after party at the kava bar. I said I was and we agreed to talk more. He drove away, his lifted Ford F-150 truck a meaningless shade of Crayola blue. I felt wary about all his drama. But Ashley had a penchant for drama and jealousy, and could have been making something out of nothing. Or maybe she was cock blocking.

Kava bars litter Florida. I got excited when I passed one on my way to the beach for the first time. I had been to one in San Francisco and liked the earthy, laid back vibe of the place and the numbness the kava gave my mouth. However I learned that in Florida, kava bars were nearly as rampant as Dunkin Donuts. Kava bar customers were mostly hippies, and high school kids, with a lot of former drug addicts, former alcoholics, and the odd businessman or girl boss or two. All the kava bars were decorated in a tropical island vibe like every other bar in Florida.

Kava is a tea made from a plant. The Pacific Islanders have been making it for centuries, though their tradition involved chewing on the root and spitting the substance into a bowl, thus creating the drink for all of their friends. At the kava bars in southwest Florida, kava is brewed. They pour it into coconut shells which get passed around to take like a shot as everyone cries, "Bula!" Bula is a Fijian word that can be used in multiple ways: as greetings, expressions of wellbeing, celebration, etc. They also Americanize the drink by adding coconut milk, bubbly water, and syrups.

Kava bars also serve Kratom, another tea made from a plant from Southeast Asia. Kratom was a lot more controversial since it binded to the same receptors in the brain as opium, and was debatably addictive. The strength and outcome of the Kratom depended on the type of strain which was dependent on how long the plant was grown before it was picked. You could choose to have stronger effects like relaxation or sleep or lighter ones like social lubrication or joy.

At the Cape Coral kava bar I hung around Ashley's second stand of the day: a table covered in magazines and poster board for people to make vision boards. And of course, as always, she peddled her moon phase ritual kits she carried around everywhere. I told Ashley I would make a vision board but once I got started, I stopped after a couple minutes. People kept talking to me. I never liked making vision boards anyways. I preferred writing my shit down. And I used Tumblr, the online version of a vision board.

"BULA!" I took a shot with everyone at the kava bar. The workers, who were always high school kids, occasionally handed out free bula shots to people.

I met a bunch of other hippies: a girl who gave henna tattoos and did murals who said that she was "called to speak to me," as she handed her business card to me, a couple toting their baby around whom I spoke to about their at home birthing experience and how the baby wouldn't come out in the bathtub for hours but came out right away when she drank some Kratom, and a guy who was reading a book by Carl Jung that I liked.

I eventually strolled over to where Cash was sitting at the bar to say hi before I left. Ashley came over too and started babbling at us. She became performative in group social situations.

When we could get some words in edgewise, we chatted a bit about traveling and surfing. He said surfing was his favorite activity, same as me. He liked to go on surf trips to

Puerto Rico. Out came the first shimmer of attraction. Well-traveled surfers were a hot commodity in southwest Florida.

A friend wanted to fly me out to Arizona so I couldn't make a plan with him for the weekend so we agreed to Wednesday night golfing. He asked if I was going to the singles event that night at the kava bar.

"Probably not," I said. "It's a long drive from Bonita Springs."

He scoffed, as all people accustomed to the drives in Southwest Florida did, and said, "That's nothing."

"I might be too tired," I added. But really I just didn't want to attend their very first singles event which could have been terrible. And aren't all singles nights terrible anyways?

Ashley and Leslie went. Later they told me it was lame as I had expected. They said Cash showed up in a limo with two girls and another guy asking about me. Then he asked them if they wanted to have a threesome with him. It sounded Lynchian. Ashley was worried I would be offended but I didn't care, he wasn't mine. He was just some guy that was going to take me golfing. What did I care if he tried to have threesomes? Ashley was such a Cancer.

His Instagram bio read, "Just another character in your dream." His handle was "Cash2create."

"What do you create?" I asked him via DM.

"Magic."

"What kind?"

"You have to see it in person." We exchanged phone numbers.

Cash didn't text me that Wednesday so we never went golfing. I think I ended up going to yoga though I was disappointed getting blown off.

He messaged me that Saturday asking if I was in Arizona like I had said.

I told him I didn't go because I didn't feel like traveling.

He asked me to get kava near my house that afternoon.

I accepted then blew him off minutes later to go thrifting with Karen and Violet.

So then he invited me out that night.

I accepted but then I remembered I had my online improv class and had to cancel on him again.

"Well, fine then. I give up."

I thought that was interesting so I asked him to kava the next day.

He invited me to have dinner on the beach instead. I agreed.

"I'll wait," he texted me, obviously expecting me to cancel again.

I liked his snark.

Once again, just like with Khalif, I was thinking a date would be good for me, as water is for a plant. The spark of attraction was tiny, compared to my anxiety about his dramatic life and douchebag potential. I thought of him as a practice round. I had to stay adept at dating because who knows when the right one would show up.

He sent me an address to meet him at. I drove the half hour there and it turned out to be a Mexican restaurant.

I was early so I decided to walk to the beach across the street to see the sunset. I texted him to say I was there just as the sun went down at dusk. He called and said he changed his mind on the restaurant. He said he'd swoop me from where I was.

He was driving the lifted bright meaningless blue Ford F-150.

My world shifted when I stepped up into that truck. The vibes were strong. I wasn't ready.

"I forgot how big your truck is," I said.

I knew that the Ford F-series was the deadliest vehicle in America but one of the cheapest to insure. Also, the most popular truck ever made. Very American.

In an attempt to gauge him, I said something about how I always dressed ironically. He asked how I was being ironic in my Tommy Hilfiger button up. I told him that I stole it. He laughed.

We bantered back and forth. He was witty and not just a stupid douchebag as I had suspected.

"Just so you know, I want two wives," he said out of

the blue, driving slowly, coolly maneuvering through tourist traffic.

"Well I was raised Mormon so that's nothing new to me," I responded, amused. I couldn't tell if he was kidding.

"Really?" he said, sounding intrigued.

"Yeah, I mean it's 2021. Things have to change. Why not start with monogamy?"

"Oh we'll have plenty to discuss at dinner."

"I think so."

"I'm an aristocrat, you know." He was wearing loafers, khaki shorts, and a button down. Had gold chains on. Rings. Hair styled. He looked preppy and my thoughts went to old money, a daddy's boy.

"So that means you're paying for dinner?" I asked.

"Sure," he said slowly but good naturedly. "I suppose I can pay for dinner."

His voice sounded like he just woke up from a beautiful dream.

At the restaurant I went to get cuter in the bathroom. This date was not just a scrimmage like I had thought. No, this was the real deal. He could banter, this wasn't some thoughtless bloke. He actually had a brain that he actually used, real thoughts of his own that he shared easily and confidently. He played with life, experimented, and had passions.

So I fixed up my unwashed hair, took off the dumb shirt I had on underneath my button up, and walked back into the dining area thinking that I may have met my match. I had never had that thought that before.

He said he didn't usually drink but he would for me. The waiter asked for our IDs when we ordered wine and we found out we were both Libras. That's when it felt like game over. The connection was stark. We were both brilliant, illuminated, sparkling with charm and controversy. Libras were hard to come by.

He was dexterously callous and morbidly playful. There wasn't a single moment I felt bored. We drank each other up.

We talked philosophy, sociology, literature, history, biology, physics, religion, on and on. The conversation was richer than I'd had in years, possibly ever. I had never been so stimulated. We both wore philosophies like jewelry and used religion to rule. Religion didn't rule us. We were spiritual hackers.

"Hindu, Buddhist, Christian... why not be everything for more spiritual power?"

"Exactly," I said, beaming.

We talked about how human thoughts, feelings, and imaginations were so big and powerful that entire gods were created just to contain them. If you do not make a GOD then you have to fight against your own emotions alone. Believing in GOD was necessary for survival or, at the very least, extremely advantageous.

He told me he was "kind of codependent," but I found his admission to be self-aware, honest, instead of worrisome. I considered myself pretty codependent anyways, so what did it matter if we both were? Maybe our codependencies could each cancel each other out.

He talked about theories I'd read about on the internet, back in early stage rabbit-holing during high school and college. He was the first person I had ever heard speak about these things in real life. He told me that blue-eyed people like us came from Atlantis, that everything in the media was not what it seemed, that there were deeply sinister powers of evil running the world.

He didn't live in the logos so much anymore, as most others did. He chose to live in the mythos.

"I don't see what you see. You haven't experienced what I've experienced. I see aliens, demons, angels, gods. They give me visions. My reality is different from yours. I see entities. Everywhere."

He said he had only just started opening his eyes to the world this way. It all happened recently, when he began to suspect that his ex, the mother of his children, didn't have a soul. It was like a thought experiment for him at first: perhaps some people didn't have souls. It took him a long time to arrive at this hypothesis. They had dated seven years but he didn't start recognizing the darkness in her eyes until this past year. He started noticing how she fed off of bad energy, how she preferred him when he was in a bad mood and became irritated if he was happy or something good happened to him. She became energized when he suffered. He said they started dating when he was more feminine than now, that he used to be a completely different person, and that she used that to her advantage, controlling and manipulating him. She lied and said she couldn't get pregnant until she did. Twice.

"It all happened back when I was a vegan. Have you ever been vegan?"

I shook my head no.

"Good. Bad for the brain."

His last relationship catalyzed him to dedicate his studies to the divine masculine and feminine. He considered himself an expert.

It was like he was picking up on where my mushroom trip had left off, where the mushrooms told me to worship the divine masculine in order to become the divine feminine.

He said he had a theory that children should be primarily raised by their mother from birth until the age of 6 when they begin to inquire into the nature of the world. Then the father would introduce the child into the ways of men and traditions. The mother fulfilled the nurturing, caretaking role while the father led them into society. I thought this made sense.

My own lack of studying masculinity and femininity felt criminal. How devastating to be so disconnected from basic human nature, ancestral knowledge, and cultural traditions.

He told me GOD had spoken to him. That having two wives had come to him in a vision from GOD. He wanted to save masculinity. He thought feminism was destroying the world. Personally I knew few happy women, and none of them were feminists. Before Cash, I already thought feminism had gone too far and had never identified with the cult. Once the masses got ahold of anything, they destroyed it. Ideology was always mutilated by the mainstream.

"I'm going to be on the cover of *Wired* someday," he said.

"Why *Wired*?" I asked, though I had the feeling it was because he was a shoot for the moon type guy.

"Because that's the plan," he said. "Trust the plan." Maybe he *would* land on the moon. And it turned out he wasn't just a daddy's boy. He made his own money.

He was one of those hard hippies, an elite group of burner types that radically lived in the present, never bothered by anything as they had mastered absolute self-control and dressed like they weaved in and out of different timelines and eras with little effort and a surplus of coolness; the type I had always wanted to date or at least get to know.

I asked him what he meant when he said he was an aristocrat. He told me he loved fine dining but that there was more to it, I'd see. That's when I noticed we were at a fine dining restaurant. He showed me how to put my silverware down to indicate I was finished with my plate, how I should only use my fork upside down, how I mustn't cut with my fork, only my knife. Then he ordered escargot and insisted I eat it with him. I found the food to be rubbery and disgusting. But I ate it to please him.

We got tipsy off the wine. We flowed into one another like the wine flowed into our cups.

He was profound, deep, and mystical like me. I hadn't met many people like that. They were usually strewn around in other countries and I only found them on my travels. We always had to part.

"I live a lot," Cash said. "You'll see." His most recent ex told him she lived more in the four months she knew him than she ever had in her entire life. I told him I already lived a lot on my own, had my own adventures, and made my own magic. Yet, I confided, I had always felt like an outsider.

He slid happily ever after into my mind. "We're going to procreate," he said before turning around on his way to the bathroom. My heart swelled. This was my calling! This was my time to be a mother, just like the mushrooms had said. This was a man I could submit to, one who was in charge of his own mind and destiny.

He tried to kiss me outside the restaurant but I told him I didn't kiss on first dates. He rolled his eyes. "Seriously?"

I stepped up into the passenger seat of his truck. He stood next to me, lighting a cigarette. I tried to kick it out of his hands.

"Prickly legs!" He said, grabbing at my calves. "Look at my legs. They're immaculate. Look at yours. Like ew, what is that?"

He pointed at some slightly wrinkled skin above my knee. I didn't mind. I knew I had amazing legs. He was probably worried about them.

"Why are you smoking cigarettes? They're so bad for you," I said.

"Let me show you something."

He got into his truck and put on a YouTube video on his phone.

"Watch this."

He started to drive while I watched the video.

It was a music video. Pretty acoustic music played as a cartoon animation showed a woman looking in the mirror. She saw herself in the reflection; mousy, pale, average, chunky, and then she turned red. She got pulled into the reflection and she became the devil. She walked through a hellish jungle, pulled along by impish monsters. Then she flew up to a heavenly paradise, pulled along by birds.

It made me think about how everything started in the mind, that reality is made by the individual, that humans can be whatever they want to be, that they have total power. Our destiny is to create and we create our destiny.

They tell me "good things come to those who wait"
To speed the process along, I came to tempt fate

"So it doesn't matter if we smoke - because we control our destiny?" I asked.

He just smiled and handed me a cigarette. He seemed to know so much more about the world than I did. So I smoked my first cigarette in five years.

Cash took me to a bar on the beach where there was a band playing to a full crowd. He bought us gin and tonics. We danced to 80's covers, Florida music. He was a good dancer. Everyone smiled at us. I kissed him on the cheek so he would hold my phone. He took a video of us under the rainbow Christmas lights. He sent it to me the next day. I watched it over and over again.

Outside the bar under the moonlight by the water with more drinks he asked, "You're looking for a sailor aren't you?" and pointed to the anchor crest on my Tommy Hilfiger button up.

"Yeah, I guess I am," I said, giggling.

"Well, I'm a sailor. I'm going to buy a yacht and sail the whole ocean," he said. "Maybe I'll even bring you. Will you kiss me now?"

"I can't kiss you. It's a boundary."

"Oh, come on," he said. I felt a little silly.

"I'm trying to get better at setting boundaries. I have to set them so I get good practice."

I knew the boundary thing was sort of arbitrary. I had only heard or read somewhere that it was good to set boundaries. It didn't culminate from my own brain, so I didn't entirely buy it. I wasn't totally devoted to the cause because I wasn't sure it was more than just a trendy buzzword. But I suspected I had a problem. And maybe setting boundaries was the solution.

I liked blending into people. I was very open and I connected on a deep level more often than not. But I also got into difficult situations, falling in love too fast and too hard, losing myself in the group, or flirting when I wasn't interested. I welcomed a lot of energy into my space that didn't belong there. Sometimes I felt uneasy after giving too much of myself away too fast. People started to expect things.

Cash took me to another bar on the beach.

"There's Venus," he said, pointing up into the sky.

"Yeah," I smiled. I'd been watching her rise that whole year.

"That's where we came from," he added.

I stepped behind him to get past a crowd. I took a deep breath and exhaled deeply. Most men would call it a sigh.

"You ok?" He asked.

"Yeah, just processing. It's a lot."

I had to stay grounded and not float with him all the way up to Venus.

The next bar had dollar bills covering the walls. Cash took out a dollar for me and wrote "Libra love" on it. He told me to write something on it and then he left to go to the bathroom.

I crossed out GOD and wrote Bitcoin so it said, "in Bitcoin we trust." I asked the bartender for a stapler so I could put it on the wall with the other dollars. He said it was broken. Then Cash came back. I told him the stapler was broken and at the same time the bartender pulled out a stapler and stapled the dollar bill on the wall. Cash nodded at him.

"What was that about?" I asked Cash.

"They see so many tourists here they don't have room for strangers," he said, shrugging. I forgot I was in a place where most of the people were tourists. I was here randomly. Cash belonged.

We talked and joked about currency and finance. He was still trying to get me to kiss him.

"Maybe I should just make you my assistant," he said.

"You would be so lucky," I said.

"Why won't you just kiss me then?"

He was determined. He said he wasn't going to end up friend zoned like another guy I told him about.

"Well look at how much more of you I've seen now," I told him. "How much more of your personality I've seen. I've seen what you're like when you don't get what you want."

But eventually I gave in and we kissed. I don't remember the first kiss because kissing Cash felt as natural as breathing. I just know that we kissed a lot once I finally gave in.

We agreed to a sleepover. We didn't want to separate yet. It didn't feel like there was even a thought process about splitting up, the decision already felt made. Whether it was destiny or alcohol, no matter how much I drank, the night remained vivid.

"But no sex," I said.

"I'm not having sex right now, anyways," he said. "It's a pact I made with my brotherhood."

He was in a mens' group which, he added, Alex Jones may or may not be a part of. They met and discussed tradition, ancient masculinity practices, rituals, and the occult. They kept each other up to date on the current events and trends that mattered to their masculine causes.

We drove to his house, thirty minutes away, taking turns playing songs back and forth on his iPhone, dancing in his truck.

His house was warm, painted dark with dark floors, and dim lighting. The rooms were small like a little bungalow. Three black cats played in the front yard.

"They just showed up one day."

He had a friend staying with him named JT who was sitting on a couch in the front room when we arrived. He wore a backwards baseball hat, and was very quiet. He started rolling a joint for all of us. I cheered.

Cash left the room to make drinks. I picked up a guitar and started strumming.

"You play guitar?" JT asked.

"A little bit. Just chords, really."

Cash came back into the room with glasses of whiskey.

"I think JT is falling in love with you," he said with a chuckle. He picked up another guitar and started playing alongside me.

We stayed for hours in his living room playing music together, him on guitar mainly, with me freestyle singing and rapping with JT as our audience. I immediately felt comfortable around JT. It was like I'd known them both a long time.

"You learn that all from improv?" Cash asked. "Can I hire your team?"

I laughed. "We're just learning."

When I went to use his bathroom, I found a book called *The Wall Speaks* sitting on his toilet. I flipped through it reading passages, and took it with me into the living room. I sat on the couch and read about the chaos in women, their raw, emotional power, their need to be contained, and their hyper focus on details as opposed to man's long term vision. Men had a role, a responsibility to correct that feminine chaos through the masculine frame. There were instructions on how to tame and curtail this energy in women, how to appeal to their needs and senses, the wild emotions that ran their programming.

Cash came from the kitchen with mixed drinks. He handed me one.

"This book is fascinating," I said. "Where'd you get this?"

He set down his glass and snatched the book out of my hands.

"What is it?" I asked.

"Some things are not meant for little girls," he said.

"Oh come on," I said.

"Go look at the art in the hallway," he said, giving JT a look. JT started laughing.

Hanging on the wall near his bathroom was a large framed print with the title *Babylonian Marriage Market* printed on the bottom. I had never seen the painting before yet it looked familiar.

In the foreground of the painting, twelve young women, barefoot and dressed in gowns, adorned with gold jewelry and beads, sat in a row behind an auction stage, presumably awaiting their turn on the stage. They sat atop rugs of leopard, zebra, and lion skin in various positions, looking young, whimsical, and naive but also haughty and mischievous. One girl cried with her hands covering her face. Behind them, on the stage, one of their own stood beside an auctioneer, facing a crowd of men. These men were posed in various positions- some spoke at or gestured to the auctioneer, others talked amongst themselves, and others stood silent in thought.

The painting came from 1875. Edwin Long, the artist, was inspired by the writings of Herodotus from 400 BC. *Babylonian Marriage Market* collected the most amount of money ever paid at the time for the painting of an artist still alive.

I liked the dark mystery and how I didn't quite understand. Were women meant to serve men and find their own meaning through mens' success? Cash was so powerful, I could feel his control of himself, of his life, of his world, emanating and pulsating through him. I immediately felt a desire to be in his circle and do whatever it took to keep seeing that power manifest. I could serve a man like him. Like the shrooms had foretold, I must submit to the masculine.

I was enthralled by Cash's commitment to an alternative value system. Like the music video he showed me and the book I found, the painting embodied this commitment. In the age of men playing video games and evaluating data in spreadsheets, there weren't many men living with a set of values I could revere or respect. Most men I knew were lukewarm about their lives and had little passion for anything besides watching sports or getting promoted.

Maybe women were supposed to stay at home and be submissive instead of out in the world striving for achievement alongside men. Maybe their success and independence was why men turned into passive dweebs. Maybe there was something unnatural about women competing with men. Maybe there was a delicate balance and a woman's ambition subordinated the ambition of men and obfuscated their true purpose. I wasn't a fan of the most recent developments in feminism which scapegoated men for the toxicities inherent in our culture.

I went back into the living room. Cash brought out glasses of port. In our drunkenness, I remember him pulling me close, saying softly, "What are you doing here in Florida?" He was just as surprised to have found a mind like mine as I was to have found his. Gold mines. Bingo.

That night I told him, from the deepest depths of my heart, "You're the most powerful person I've ever met." And then we fell asleep in his bed, no lust. He took me back to my car the next morning in front of the Mexican restaurant where I parked.

Driving we passed a man skipping down the sidewalk holding a sign that said, "Love others! Be happy!" He had a big smile on his face.

When I got home I wrote in my journal: *Falling in love is better if you just relax. Don't hold back. Just let yourself go. Don't tense up because that's how you hurt yourself. Just like in a car crash.*

When I started work that afternoon I found I could no longer take any of the work seriously. Cash was the first person who didn't make me feel as if I needed to apologize for my stark indifference to the world nor did I have to disguise my pure apathy of society because he felt and thought the same way. I didn't have to pretend I didn't see through the illusions anymore. Cash showed me it was okay to see the small-mindedness of others and to be honest with one self instead of feeling guilty for being judgmental or too critical. Now I couldn't unsee the matrix at all. All it took was a single night with Cash. I couldn't fake it anymore now that I knew I didn't have to.

Cash told me he had already tried empathy, of feeling for others' struggle, of trying to curtail himself to meet others where they were at and see it from their perspective.

"But it doesn't get anyone anywhere. And it is far too late for that."

One part of my role was to change the perspective of the community to view prostitutes as victims not criminals. However, the nonprofit didn't want to push the victim narrative anymore. Political correctness and recent psychology had decided "victimhood" was more debilitating than helpful. My boss wanted to move towards using empowerment-based language. But most people in Southwest Florida hadn't even gotten to the victimizing part of social progress and were still on the criminalizing part.

At the end of the day, we were trying to fix a symptom of a broken system. I wanted it to crash so we could start over. Back in my first week on the job, I learned that most human trafficking victims were trafficked by their own family. Whatever actions taken were either miniscule or not productive at all when the main issue stemmed from the most biologically fundamental aspect of human civilization: the family. The forces of destruction ran deeper and darker than I'd thought.

The nonprofit spent most of its time establishing policies and procedures that bureaucratized the issue. Money and resources got funneled into structures and systems instead of directly helping people.

During a meeting, a coworker once said, "Bureaucracy is the backbone of democracy," and I wanted to jump out the window. How idiotic to do a bunch of work we hated to try to fix a system we hated. On days I showed up to the office, I watched coworkers watch the clock until it hit 5. I didn't blame them. The office was disgusting. Centipedes dropped from the ceiling.

I started to believe we were all being trafficked. Everything wrong with the world stemmed from our relationship to work. There were too many people working way too hard at bullshit jobs. Systems were over, but many people still didn't realize this. Even my coworkers at the nonprofit worked at their jobs in unhealthy ways: long hours, skipped lunches, too much screen time, downing sugary Dunkin Donuts drinks every day, too much sitting- all to "help" other people. But they themselves were sick. The sick can't help the sick.

Since I didn't have a lot of experience with human trafficking, I started watching a YouTube channel called *Soft White Underbelly* where people living on Skid Row in Los Angeles are interviewed, many of them prostitutes and pimps. I decided to call the journalist who created the channel and conducted the interviews to get his take on changing the title in his videos from prostitute to human trafficking survivor. He laughed at me then lectured me.

After his monologue, we chatted for a while, mostly about the disparity and hopelessness of the situation. He said there was too high a cost of resources to ever completely recover the vast majority of individuals out of the trafficking life. Even with the best, most expensive resources, most prostitutes and human trafficking victims ended up back on the streets hustling their bodies for money or back on the worst kinds of drugs or, most commonly, both.

It was a time of letting go of that which did not serve me. And meeting Cash heightened all of that. I couldn't bear to attempt to fix the old world anymore, the world I didn't believe in. I wanted to make a new world, one that I believed in.

I called my dad after work that day just to chat. I noticed the way I spoke had completely changed. I was infinite, unfiltered, brilliant, eloquent. I was finally speaking my truth.

"Chase me, chase me, chase me," Cash texted me.

For our second date, I put on a mini skirt, a strappy black long sleeved top, and high heels. I chose my outfit like I was preparing for battle, like I was going to fight for something I cared about more than my own life. I slid on a gold chain and my black cat eye sunglasses too.

This time, Cash told me to meet him in the parking lot outside Twin Peaks for lunch, a restaurant just like Hooters. I think it was a test to see how I handled his "fondness for women" as he called it. But I was in the throes of taking pole dancing classes. Who was I to get upset at a restaurant that promised sexy waitresses? I'd dreamt of having my own strip club run entirely by women. I even had my own name picked out: Eighth House Strip Club.

When I found him in the parking lot, he was playing his guitar in his truck. He told me the electricity had just gone out in the whole town and that we'd have to find somewhere new. On my phone, I found a California-style café in the next town. He told me to jump in the truck and we were on our way.

It wasn't a long drive, but we struggled to find it until we realized it was a café inside of a gas station. I felt on edge, like I was disappointing him. But he stayed calm and cool. My other boyfriends would have gotten anxious or annoyed that it took so long to find.

"You've had a profound effect on me," I blurted out right after we sat down and ordered. "No one has ever impacted me so strongly, so quickly. My entire perspective is different now."

"I tend to have that effect on people," he said.

"I normally don't show this level of seriousness to other people. They usually can't bring this out of me."

"I feel the same way about you, little lady."

"Do you really think everything is going to fall apart? I sometimes think things are getting better. I hate seeing the world as decaying. It makes me feel miserable."

"If you can't see society as decaying then you have a small mind."

What I had said was I didn't *like* seeing society as decaying, though of course I saw that it was. But Cash wasn't there to listen to people talk about their feelings or preferences. He wanted to get to the point: society was dead.

He called them normies: people that didn't think for themselves. Those who lived by the rules, followed the status quo and didn't question where everything was headed or wondered who made the rules for their lifestyle or choices.

After we finished eating he tossed me his credit card and told me to clean everything up and pay while he went to the bathroom. He was abrupt and unapologetic in his command and spoke precisely.

He was definitely testing me. I could follow directions.

We walked to a forest nearby. There were forests and lakes all over Lee County in between the parking lots, shopping malls, and neighborhoods.

We were smoking cigarettes. Cash flicked his butt into the field next to the forest. We talked about how this forest would soon be destroyed.

"Have you ever heard of accelerationism?" He asked.

"No…" I said shyly.

"It's letting everything fall apart, even adding to the collapse to make it collapse faster. Accelerationism is the belief that the faster things collapse, the sooner we can start over again."

We kissed in between trees. He picked me up and carried me over the short fence. We got back into his truck.

He drove me back to my car. He kept looking at my legs.

"I love those little blonde hairs all over your thighs. They're so sexy. I want to say something dirty, but maybe I shouldn't."

"No, say it," I said.

"I can't wait to see my cum all over them."

My heart thudded but I said calmly, "That's not dirty. I like it. I'd love to have your cum all over my thighs."

"Let's get dinner before I leave town," he said.

"Okay," I said coolly, though I was burning up inside. He had this daddyness to him that killed me, a knowingness of women and their girly ways. I blossomed so easily for him.

After I got home I texted Troy to hang out. I had been trading him my homemade kombucha for weed. He called me his "weird friend." I would go over to his house, hit his bong, make the trade, and then he'd order sushi for us and we'd watch *Twin Peaks*. Then he would try to convince me to have sex with him.

I told him I met my soulmate. He asked if I loved him enough to let him have two wives. I said that I would.

"Lucky bastard," he said.

Troy couldn't have known about the two-wife thing because I hadn't told anyone, especially not my gossipy roommates. It was like everything was all up in the ether, hovering there for anyone to grasp, my whole life laid out on an accessible plane.

Troy told me he was my guardian angel once when we were drunk at one of his parties. Maybe he was. Maybe we had a soul connection where he could tap into my life and know about things. Or maybe it was all just a coincidence. Like watching *Twin Peaks* and then getting asked to go to the restaurant in the same month.

That was the last time I saw Troy. The next time I asked if he wanted to do a trade he said he didn't need my services any longer and we never talked again. He wasn't the first man to step off. Once I was with Cash, no other man ever got too close to me.

CHAPTER FIVE: MAGIC MUSHROOMS, LIES, AND THE LANI KAI

Back at home I looked at old photos of myself on the internet to remind myself what kind of girl I was.

Cash texted me: "Meet me at the kava bar by the beach. And wear comfortable shoes."

I found him out back of the kava bar, talking to someone. JT was there too, floating around off to the side. Another guy hovered around with Cash's assistant, Jackie.

Walking towards him, I tried to figure out how to greet him but he made it easy. He asked for a kiss on the cheek so I gave him one. He handed me a cigarette as he lit his own. Then he lit mine. I only smoked cigarettes when I was with him.

He was talking to a guy named Josh, a geologist who had just moved to Fort Myers for work. Cash and I started asking him questions about the corporation he worked for and the specifics about his line of work. We teased him about his scientific paradigms. Josh had a good sense of humor. He didn't get worked up.

Cash had Jackie drive his truck to where we were going. He told JT and the other guy to go with her.

Cash and I went with Josh in his car. I still didn't know what we were doing as everyone shuffled around under Cash's command. I didn't care. I just liked being around Cash.

Cash drove since Josh had some sort of sports car he wanted to try out. Eventually we pulled up to a bar called the Nauti Parrot. Grimy dubstep bumped from inside.

"Let's get weird!" Cash's assistant said.

We got checked by the bouncers and walked inside. Cash led, dancing as he walked and we all followed suit. I felt powerful, like I was in a sphere of Cash's influence.

It was called Wub night. Artists, hippies, and burners gathered to dance to EDM at this bar by the docks in the smooth warm Florida night. It was a mixed scene but mostly Gen Z.

As I danced on the floor in front of the DJ, Cash floated around, talking to people, walking around. His crew orbited around him, keeping watch, as if they were looking for something or someone.

I noticed JT watching me, like a security guard. It felt mysterious and strange. I got the sensation that I was being tested again.

Cash brought me a drink.

"You like to dance."

"Of course. And it's been so long," I said, taking the drink.

"The DJ is an alien."

"What..." I said, staring at the DJ who had brown, grungy dreads.

"He's also a genius," Cash added.

He walked away to talk to some other people.

I saw Khalif sitting at a table with Charles and some other guys, probably other caddies. I blew Khalif off a week ago. We had plans to hang but I never texted him back. I went over to them.

Charles saw me first and with a big grin called out, "Hey girl!"

"Hey guys!" I hugged Khalif.

"I'm sorry about blowing you off," I said.

He smiled, shook his head.

"No, it's all good." That was the last time I saw him. I could feel him watching me as I walked back to Cash.

Cash was standing on one of the docks talking with Josh.

When I got to them, Cash grabbed my ass and asked where I went off to. A part of me wanted to protest but I knew that wouldn't be following the rules of the game Cash wanted to play.

"I ran into a guy that was sort of suiting me before I met you," I said.

"Oh?" Cash said.

"Yeah but I wasn't impressed by him," I said.

"Did you hook up?"

"No. We didn't even kiss."

"Are you sure?"

"Yes! What are you guys talking about?"

"Which bars have the best women and which bars are the most fun," Cash said.

"Women here are so slutty," Josh said.

"That's Florida," Cash said.

Pre-Covid, I probably would have said something about the problematic concept of sluttiness. Post-Covid, I didn't care about feminism anymore. I found it trite and morose; just another vapid means of virtue signaling. In the last decade it was just another status symbol co-opted by institutions of power to divide the masses against one another.

We were in swampland where it was wild and always warm. Skin was always showing. Of course the women were sluttier. Everyone was. The sensuality of the lush greens, the vibrant flowers, the mating sounds of birds and animals running around in an Eden so many scorned. Even the elderly slept around.

Maybe Floridians were so wild because they never had a winter to confront their shadow sides. They never saw everything die around them so they thought themselves invincible. The fun never stopped. The summer never ended. No winter dread being stuck inside dealing with yourself, dealing with what your soul had to say about you when no one else was around. So the Floridians' shadows ran rampant, uninhibited. Or maybe their shadows were completely integrated and the people in the cold were the fucked up ones. Everything can always go either way.

"Do you want to take her home with us?" Cash asked when he saw me staring at a young girl dressed as a unicorn with a dog collar on.

"Um... no," I said. I was not into her look or her vibe, especially as she was so young, maybe not even 20. Wasn't it too early for her to be into that stuff? But the kids these days were different from the kids in my days. I didn't want to judge but I also didn't want to deal with it either.

He laughed at my nervous reaction. "Let's go," he said.

We left the Nauti Parrot and went to another kava bar. The other guy hovering around introduced himself to me.

"I'm Dash. Cash's brother."

"I didn't know he was your brother!"

Cash shrugged. "I'm bad at introducing people."

We walked through downtown Fort Myers down a brick alley and smoked a joint. The boys tried to get me to flash them and I refused. Was this a Florida slut trick? At the kava bar, we all went into the back room. I played Josh in chess.

We talked about the pandemic. Cash and I tried to explain the politicized, corporatized paradigm of science to him. Josh said he wasn't like us people. That he didn't worry too much about stuff like that.

"Us people..." Cash and I said, looking at each other. We barely knew each other yet our minds worked the same way. We were cast from the same mold- adventurers, scientists, priests, poets. Geniuses.

Cash left the room and after I beat Josh, I left to find him. He was sitting in a chair near the bar on his phone.

"Hey..." I said, wondering what he was doing on his phone. He looked up at me and smiled.

"You sure like Josh," he said.

"What? I mean sure. He's your friend. Do you want me to be less friendly?" I had this burning need to make Cash happy, to make him proud of me.

"No," he said. "Shall we call it a night?"

Cash paid for the drinks, like he paid for everything.

We debated about whether I should stay the night at his house again. He told me his mom was staying with him. She just got out of a break up.

"Well, I don't want your mom to think I'm some slutty girl," I said.

He laughed and said, "Up to you."

The pull was strong and I didn't want to leave him.

"I'll see you tomorrow night," I said, cruising down the safer route. He was taking me to dinner, his favorite French restaurant. He told me to wear a dress. He thought women should only wear dresses.

Back at home the next day, I tried on outfits and showed them to my roommates.

"He's pulling out all the shots," Dexter said when I told him Cash was taking me to a French restaurant that night.

"It must be the Veranda."

Dexter was right.

He had me meet him at his house. He was wearing a suit and fine leather shoes. He looked like he just came from a mafia wedding. Maybe it was the gold chains. I sat on his lap.

He had a blue sapphire ring on his pinkie that matched my pink star sapphire ring I wore on my middle finger. I grabbed his pinkie.

"Blue sapphire! Like my pink one," I said, excited.

Unphased, Cash said, "Let me see."

He looked at it, saw the star and said, "Alexander the Great wore pink star sapphire."

"Really?"

"Come on, let's go."

He opened the door for me and I climbed into his truck.

Driving he asked, "Should we drink tonight?"

"Sure. Why not? It loosens you up," I said.

"You think I'm too serious?" He asked.

"A little bit, yeah," I said, teasing.

The restaurant was in an elegant house built by the Fort Myers founder's son over a hundred years ago. Later we learned Fort Myers was founded exactly 155 years before our first date.

"1+5+5=11 and 1+1=2. Twin flames!" Cash said, excited.

I was unfamiliar with numerology but I was quickly catching on. The synchronicity made my head spin.

Tablecloths, a piano player, waiters in tuxedos, chandeliers. At dinner he ordered escargot again. I chewed the bite he gave me quickly, hiding my disgust.

I told him about the avant-garde crowd I followed online who lived in New York. I was trying to impress him.

He sneered at me, "What use is the avant-garde? The avant-garde is everywhere! I went to the top of a mountain in Peru and you know what I found? A whole town of people with rat faces walking around. Who only ate popcorn! You don't need to go to New York to see the avant-garde."

I did a 180 in an instant and agreed with him. He could change my mind like that, with quick, cutting words. He opened portals for me, unlocked places my brain had closed off. I had idealized a scene in New York that I could create myself. The avant-garde *was* everywhere. I didn't need a specific intellectual group to embody that world for me. I could do it with Cash.

I ordered the Chilean Sea Bass and he got the Pan Seared Jumbo Scallops and then he told me his ancestors were slave owners. He paused for my reaction. I simply shrugged. It was the south after all. His family's history wasn't going to do anyone any harm. At least he knew his heritage. My black Ethiopian friend's family had black slaves back in Ethiopia too. It wasn't even a white thing.

Cash didn't only think society was decaying. He thought it was going to collapse. I once believed things would get better. Not easier but better. But Cash had me believing it was all going to end soon. And that's why he wanted to start a cult. "I've always been a cult leader," he said.

Nearly my whole life, I had sought the ideal path to get people to break away from the dominant culture. This could be the answer to the inherent dullness of the inertia of sticking to the status quo.

And he was serious about the two wife thing. Again, he brought up his vision where GOD showed him two wives. I didn't necessarily believe him. But I liked the idea, the myth, and that he was serious, committed. It was 2021. Fuck it. I was open to anything. We had to have something to attract people to the cult. In order to change society, you must make it extremely compelling. You have to make reasons for others to join. Having two wives was extremely attractive.

The world was dead. It was time to begin anew, and what did monogamy matter? What with all my Buddhist meandering and Mormon upbringing, I could detach from the cultural and ego-driven desire of a husband all to myself. And I liked the irony of breaking away from the Mormons at my father's dismay only to later become one of somebody's two wives.

Covid happened and now everything was even more trippy. How little the material world meant to me, the meaning dripping out of it slowly over the years until Covid happened and meaning gushed out like a waterfall.

Nobody could agree if we were going backwards or forwards anymore. Everyone wanted to move forwards of course. But we weren't all sold on the concept of progress anymore, especially since democracy got outed as a scam. But we all wanted it- progress, that is. We just weren't sure anymore that it was actually happening. And everybody wanted enlightenment. No one in my generation would take anything less than enlightenment.

"It's just an experiment," he said, planting a seed of mystique in my mind, an incentive to get him all to myself one day.

Once I made him see that he didn't need anyone else the two-wife experiment could end. He became something to acquire, to achieve. I liked the challenge of being flexible, adaptive. I would become stronger in destroying my preconceived notions of love and romance. And I liked games. This was going to be a long one.

He told me I was going to have his son. It made my heart flutter.

"What if I don't have a boy?" I asked.

"Then we'll try again," he said simply.

My whole body fluttered. It was like the mushrooms left butterflies inside me to twirl around when the main objective came within reach.

"It's like you know what page of the story I'm on," I said.

"What page of the story you're on…" he trailed off.

After a bottle of wine, he tried to get me to flash him at the dinner table.

"No way," I said. We giggled at each other.

Leaving the restaurant we noticed the address numbers hanging in gold on the outside of the building: 2122 Grand Avenue. Cash's lucky number was 22. Mine was 21.

"Isn't it incredible that our lucky numbers are next to each other?" He asked. Another magic detail of the magic world we were making.

Walking downtown he pushed someone's door closed for them with his hip.

"Smooth move," they said.

He always had the vibe.

"Have you ever had your heart broken?" I asked him as he walked along a brick ledge, balancing effortlessly.

"Of course. I have a big fucking heart," he said.

Turns out the baddest kingpins have the biggest hearts.

We went to a cigar bar downtown. I had never been to a cigar bar before. I sat down and looked at a magazine called "Cigar Snob" while Cash flirted with the woman selling cigars. He asked her if he could play his guitar there. She told him he could. He told her he wanted to be a performer. Said he was going to call himself Mr. Swanson.

Lighting the cigar, outside the bar, he told me I could be in the act too sometimes. He offered the cigar to me and showed me how to smoke it correctly. It was the first cigar I ever enjoyed. I had tried to smoke them plenty of times and always found them disgusting. But Cash's cigars were good.

I fell in love with Fort Myers that night. It was a beautiful little town, where it was easy to just be and move around and meet new people. Empty enough to never be crowded but full enough to stay interesting.

On the walk to another bar, Cash talked about the night watcher, the man on the border between the two worlds who guarded downtown. "Can you see him?"

I couldn't see him.

"Maybe you'll see him later."

Being with Cash made me more observant as he showed me how to slow the world down. I began to see people make moves that didn't make sense, as if they existed between worlds. A couple times I saw a man walk straight through traffic.

In the next bar, we played pool and made out like we owned the place, like no one else was around. When he bought the drinks, whenever he bought anything, he made me sign the receipts. I asked him why.

"Receipts have estrogen. Kills sperm."

I beat him at pool after he showed me how to get closer to the table and see the angles at eye level. Maybe he let me win. He didn't seem to notice. That was the only time I ever beat him at pool.

I slept over again and in the morning he showed me his factory. He told me he didn't show it to many people.

"My business is an entity itself."

He was in the process of moving into a bigger factory across the bridge in order to triple production. He said he was already making a hundred thousand dollars a month. Every week, his candles sold out within the first ten minutes of restock.

In the morning after I left, I texted him that he made me feel so goddamn real. I just wanted to fall deep and not hold anything back anymore. I wanted to feel everything and meld into him.

"You've turned my words into gold."

"The alchemist," he responded.

Cash made everything expand. He awakened my true nature. I suddenly smelled the ocean in the air. Maybe it was the changing wind patterns but I knew I didn't have to be simple minded any longer. I didn't have to dumb myself down. I didn't have to make reservations, excuses, compromises. He made me feel free to go against the grain and integrate with the gods.

He made me think deeper about how people made me feel, how I made others feel. Showed me how others used their emotions to pull you in, bring you down where they lived. He told me I was stronger than I knew, that I affected and influenced people. I began to hold myself to a higher standard, a gold standard.

He told me I needed to stop being a people pleaser. I should embrace the way people gravitated toward me but I had to be careful not to let them pull me into their story. I was on a higher plane. I flew closer to the sun, and that was why Cash and I belonged together.

He was my master, my mentor, my mystic, my magi, my merlin.

He taught me first, to accept myself, to understand myself as gifted, different, bright. He was the first to tell me to trust my own intuition.

"Your soul will tell you when the vibes get sour. And it will keep you safe," Cash said.

He didn't shun my interest in dark realms as so many others had done before. He walked me down there, hand in hand.

He allowed me to see the world as I had long seen it. He allowed me the space to demand superiority, excellence, godliness.

As times got worse and worse, as people got lost even deeper to conditioning and brainwashing, everything stood out in starker contrast. I was surrounded by stupidity, conformity, mediocrity. I didn't tell myself it was all in my mind anymore; it wasn't a debilitating perspective I had to wrestle with. It was the way things were and Cash saw it too. Even before the Pandemic people had been under more control than ever. Their thoughts and emotions came to them in instructions from a crystal mirror. They stopped experimenting, stopped changing, stopped growing.

I used to chat up the tourists and ask about their respective cities.

"How are things over there? Opening up?"

"Oh yes."

"Oh great!" I used to say, but then I learned to hold my tongue.

I once assumed people traveling sought a more mild-mannered approach to the covid virus since they didn't mind spreading it around themselves in other peoples' cities with lax approaches. But then I learned to wait and listen for their potential to gripe and complain about the irresponsibility of opening up, even as they were on an "irresponsible," in their logic, vacation.

"Dance, monkey, dance," Cash liked to say. All these dancing monkeys. What a circus.

"Before Covid, I used to think maybe 80% of people were smart. Now I know it's even less than I thought. Less than half," Cash said.

"Yeah, I've known that a while," I said.

"Okay, cool kid."

In my journal I wrote: *I would wake up in hell if this were ever to be only a dream. Ah, but of course it is. Just enjoy it. Hell only catches up to you if you look down. Like a bat out of hell I'll look anywhere but down.*

The next day I was at Ashley's house. Cash and I texted each other poetry back and forth.
I kept my cool for maybe ten minutes and listened to her life updates which were mostly mundane complaints before I gushed to her about how strong and intense my connection with   Cash already was.

"Okay. Woah. This is happening," she said, looking at me wide-eyed.

"Uh huh," I said.

"Are you guys going to fall in love and change the world? Everyone is finding their twin flames and uniting to save the world."

Again it was like my life was on some etheric plane for everyone to interpret. I'd never heard of *twin flames* before but how did she know that was exactly how it felt?

Ashley knew all the spiritual buzzwords. On our second hangout she told me I might be a *sapiosexual.*

She said I was eons better than his baby mama, Stacey.

"Less materialistic. Less concerned with the superficial. Happier."

That weekend, while Cash was out of town, I went on a camping trip to go free diving with Ashley and Leslie. As I drove they told me they could see my crown chakra illuminated. They said I was a queen.

"You love your story!" Leslie grinned.

"You can't compete with a Libra," Ashley said solemnly.

We made flower crowns in the forest, got visited by a cat, and stayed up late under the full moon. We woke up early for dives in the clear blue Florida spring.

"Send me some lyrics," Cash texted me.

I quickly typed:

"My minds so wide open
I live out ten lives
All the time you're talking shit
I take 50-foot dives"

He sent me a recording of himself playing guitar and singing my song. I could hear people in the background. I wished I was there. Did he ever spend time alone?

I invited him to my house for dinner to cook for him when I got back from the camping trip.

When he came over, the first thing he did was sit down at our piano in the front entrance. He played "L'Amour Toujours," a haunting song I had heard before, several times. But I never got the name or composer of the song and I always forgot about it until I heard it again somewhere and fell in love all over again.

"A dreamy song," I said. "It has haunted me for so long."

I led him towards my kitchen. Walking behind me through the dark, empty entryway and dining area, he said, "You know you're pretty dreamy yourself."

When we walked past my bedroom, I gestured to indicate where it was and he walked right into it, going straight for my pile of notebooks.

"You write a lot?" He asked, as he pulled one of my notebooks out.

I nodded.

"That's good. Can I read?"

I nodded again.

He began to read aloud. No one had ever read my writing before. Some of it sounded good. A lot of it was bad.

In one of the passages he read, I wrote about how I felt bad for black people. It was during the black lives matter protests last summer. He said I had a good heart but that there was no reason to get caught up in politics.

"I know, I know," I said, my mind always ready to be polished by his.

"I like your simple little bohemian vibe," he said, looking at my mattress on the floor, my piles of books, the yoga mat, and the candles.

We ate on my backyard patio. He seemed nervous, which made me feel giddy. How could I have that effect on him? Did he have any idea how he affected me?

He ate everything quickly, asking, "What is this sauce?" I wouldn't tell.

He told me I enthralled him. I poured us some wine and we toasted: I to freedom, him to liberty.

He was wearing a different ring on his pinkie. I touched it.

"This was the ring of the man that used to run Studio 54. You ever hear of Studio 54? The disco club? The gangsters gave it to me."

He winked. It was an opal band encased in gold. Our birthstone.

He pointed to the trees in the canal.

"That's Spanish moss right there. I haven't seen it grow farther south than my Ocala house before, how cool. Do you like it when I tell you these sorts of things?"

"Of course," I said.

After dinner we walked back inside my house. We stopped in the living room.

"The guy that used to live here ran a casino," Cash said, crossing his arms and looking around the room.

"See all the fans? They kept the cigarette smoke moving. He had tables over here, over there, there, and over there."

He motioned around the room and then stood, deep in thought.

We walked around my neighborhood. He told me

to make friends with whoever lived in the big house at the end of my court. The house had four vehicles out front and a hand painted "no trespassing" sign covered in ivy. We stood looking at the property for a while.

"He must be a powerful man."

He pointed at the ways the different cars were parked.

"See? The one that's backed in with the front facing at us is the man's. The two with their rears facing us are the wife's and the kid's."

There was some ultraviolet light pouring out from a window where you could see the ceilings were high like in a warehouse.

"What do you think that is?" Cash asked me, grinning.

Walking, we discussed whether we should prioritize our genius or our romance, like astronauts discussing the logistics on a trip to outer space.

Secretly, I had already put all my money on romance. I was all in. But I played the game. Played tough. A little aloof. I was very quiet. Didn't say much but talked with my eyes, my body.

Before Cash, no one had ever returned my gaze before. I could hold a whole look out to him and he'd read it and know exactly what I was saying. He caught everything and always said something back.

We saw rabbits hopping around in the streets and through the yards.

"That's a good sign," Cash said. The animals became accomplices to our crime.

He was mindful of time, like he was using time to cast a spell on me. Before going back inside he said we had to wait. He played his guitar in his truck bed, checking his watch a couple times. He played a song he wrote for his daughter.

"Okay," he said. "We can go inside now."

He did some yoga on my mat. He said yoga was supposed to be for warriors, not women. He said women learning yoga was a sign of the dark ages. He didn't trust any man who didn't do yoga. Men were the sages now that women had taken rule. Men had the gift of prophecy now that they were the oppressed ones.

"There is darkness in you that I like but I'm kind of afraid of," he told me.

He said the woman was the conqueror, the predator. The woman seduced the man.

He lit my candles and we stayed up for hours in bed talking. He had strange parallels to my dad's life: both high school quarterbacks sent to juvenile hall as teenage thieves. Both grew up in Utah.

And then we found our own parallels. We both dreamt the same deaths a long time ago: by gun. He told me to never tell anyone else about it. We were both the oldest with one sibling lost to death.

He told me he oscillated between getting land or getting a boat to prepare for the apocalypse.

"If I get a boat will you go with me?"

"Of course."

I told him three auspicious things happened that day before he came over.

First, in the morning I woke up and remembered my dream from the night before. I was living with Cash and his family on a boat, including his mom, his baby mama, and his children.

Second, Karen told me about an ugly statue that used to be in the entryway of our house that she hated. Dexter told her she couldn't move it because it was the homeowner's but she put it in the closet one day anyways and he never noticed. Just from the way she talked about it, I knew I would like it. I went to the closet to find it. It was the statue of Kuan Yin, the Chinese bodhisattva of compassion. I thought she was beautiful and put her in my room. She was bronze and heavy. She looked a lot like the tattoo Cash had on his back that he got from a Buddhist monk when he was training as a Muay Thai fighter in Thailand.

Third, in the afternoon, I was lounging on the kitchen counter, pulling out gems and charms from Cash's candle, blabbering about how infatuated I was with him. From the hallway Karen called me a smitten kitten at the exact same moment I pulled out a kitten charm.

Cash was quiet for a while.

"I can tell you get fixated on things."

"Of course I do, I don't let things just fly by," I said.

"You have a lot of layers. Is there an onion underneath?" He asked, cuddling me. We laughed.

After talking until nearly sunrise, we fell asleep in my bed.

In the morning, he said he had a dream about me where I drew a rectangle and told him he could have anything he wanted. And then the statue asked him what he wanted.

Before he left, as he got dressed, he told me to pray to understand what I really wanted. I asked if I could borrow his gold opal ring. He said if I wanted it I had to show him my breasts. I flashed him from the mattress and he tossed me his ring.

"I already know what I want."

"Just pray about it." He kissed me and left.

He was going out of town for the weekend.

Later, he texted me a picture of a notebook page where he scribbled the words: *And I retreat into the comforting darkness of my room so that my dimmed light can once more burn bright and be seen. The constant veneer of so-called huemans is a game I get tired of playing. I dream of being on a green island and teal blue fishing holes with the one girl who can see truth and gives my weary searching rest. I find a single strand of her hair on my pillow and contemplate storing it until the mothership returns and I'll clone her and drop her off in the many parallel universes so my other selves can see the best tits in the infinite.*

But then he disappeared. March was half over. He hadn't called or texted me for three days after we talked every day for a month.

Dexter thought it was a power grab. I told Karen what Cash said after dinner, that he could get over me fast if he needed to. Karen said I should tell him how that made me feel, ask him what his intention was when he said that.

But I knew it was to program me. I knew all his actions were to program me. I wanted to be programmed. I believed in Cash. I believed in his power, in his system. I wanted to be his. But I knew earning his love would be no small feat. He was brilliant. I would have to play his games. The ignoring was a test. I spent years studying power. I had found the most powerful man. And he lived in the mythos. That's the only place I'd find him. I couldn't use logic anymore. I knew what a labyrinth was.

But by day four, I was angry. I sent him a poem:

I can't stop thinking about you
Whether it's true
Whether the things are true that we are meant to do
Everything is lesser now that I know that you're better
Will you ever answer
Or are you leading me on and might as well be cancer?
I know I'm precious and that I've been looking for you
But are you as aware as me and are your eyes as blue as they seem?

He texted me: "Do we need to talk or should we call it quits now?"

I responded: "I've practiced the thought of losing you so many times I'm becoming quite adept in fact."

He called me on the phone. "Okay, so you need more contact," he said, like he was diagnosing me.

"Come see me on the beach when I get back."

I agreed.

It was our first tiff. Cash later told me he thought it something more significant; thought we'd been close to ending it. I thought it was just another part of the game.

I wrote in my journal: *just remember the stakes are as high or as low as you want them to be.*

When I went to meet Cash at the beach after he got back, I spotted him when I was still driving. He was walking with his friends on the boardwalk, bordered by neon lights and tourist crowds. I found a parking spot and walked in the direction I saw him walking. I got to the boardwalk and he was walking towards me, through the crowds, still with his friends. I walked straight up to him, wrapped my arms around him and kissed him. "Get a room!" a stranger yelled at us.

We walked to the beach with his crew. Again I got the sense they were looking for something, eyes scanning, watching everything, noticing everything. Was this Cash's influence or command?

His friend, Stone, introduced himself to me. Cash had told me about him before.

"I like to collect icons," he had said. "Stone is an icon."

Stone had long dreads, tattoos on his face, and a southern swampy way of talking with lots of "Ooo-eee!'s." He told funny stories about his adventures in drinking, mudding, fucking, and fighting.

We got a standing table on the sand in front of the Lani Kai, a big happening spot right on the Fort Myers white sand beach, where locals mingled with tourists. It was a 40-year-old resort covered in murals and bright colors where there was never a quiet moment. Like all of Fort Myers, the Lani Kai was a testament to vacation romance and free spirited fun.

Cash pointed one of the murals out to me, "See that? The owner had that mural made for his wife, that little airplane writing out, 'RC loves GC' right on top of the building for everyone to see. Isn't that the sweetest thing?"

Cash adored the Lani Kai. Said it had soul.

"But," he added, "There are the darkest of energies awaiting exploitation in every corner."

He got a phone call from Stacey, his baby mama. He walked off to talk to her.

"I don't know if you know yet but Cash's got a crazy baby mama," Stone said.

I feigned shock and surprise and ran away in the sand towards the boardwalk. Dash ran after me, shouting, "No, Princess!" He grabbed my arm, and pulled me back to the table. We laughed at each other.

Cash told me Dash was on the spectrum but I never saw anything like that about him. He was very funny and genuine and I liked him a lot. He lived in the mythos like Cash. He felt like my little brother already. We understood each other on a soul level.

I pulled out the last of the weed I got from Troy and

JT pulled out a swisher. I threw a football back and forth with Dash with a cigarette in my mouth while JT rolled the blunt.

I ran up to Cash when I saw he was finally off the phone. He was sitting on a dock swinging his legs and watching me. I edged my way in between his legs.

"You're a heartbreaker," he said.

"What?" I said. "No, I'm not."

"I've already decided I'd stop talking to you four times."

"That's why you disappeared?"

"Yeah."

"But why?"

"Because you're a heartbreaker."

"No I'm not!" I said, displaying anger to hide my pride. Every woman feels empowered when told she's a heartbreaker. It's another way of being called beautiful.

"Let's take a walk," he said. The others were standing around smoking the blunt with a group of people they'd met.

We walked towards the ocean. The tide was low, giving us space under the stars.

"So this is why you stopped talking to me last weekend." I repeated.

"You have a lot of red flags."

"Like what?" I wanted to know them but he wouldn't tell me.

"I'm not going to hurt you," I said.

"I can see the love in your eyes. And I'm afraid of what I see. I'm afraid of how real it is."

"It's real. This is real. Of course it's real! We're soulmates."

I had already devoted myself to him. The signs were clear to me. His hesitancy was amusing. He'd see.

We sat down in the sand and he told me the story of how he was cheated on by his high school girlfriend with his best friend. How he had never trusted another woman since her.

"What a dumb bitch," I said.

"I have a lot to lose, you know."

"I know."

"I can't be with someone I can't trust completely. I have a lot of work I'm doing. I need someone who won't add to my stress. I have daughters."

"Can I recite you a poem?"

"Sure."

"The only poem I ever memorized was about a ship. I never understood why this poem always meant so much to me," I said. "But now that I've met you, I think I know."

I kneeled in the sand and faced him. I took a breath and began to recite:

I wanted to be sure to reach you;
though my ship was on the way it got caught
in some moorings. I am always tying up
and then deciding to depart. In storms
and at sunset, with the metallic coils of the tide
around my fathomless arms, I am unable
to understand the forms of my vanity
or I am hard alee with my Polish rudder
in my hand and the sun sinking. To
you I offer my hull and the tattered cordage
of my will. The terrible channels where
the wind drives me against the brown lips
of the reeds are not all behind me. Yet
I trust the sanity of my vessel; And if it sinks
it may well be in answer
to the reasoning of the eternal voices,
the waves which have kept me from reaching you.

Just as I finished his brother came over and sat down next to us. "Stone's getting drunk," he said, then proceeded to describe everyone's state and what they were doing.

"Okay, thank you, soldier," Cash said. He kissed my forehead.

We all got up and joined the rest of the group again. We decided to go to another bar. The one covered in dollar bills.

On the walk, Stone begged me not to take Cash away, to let him have a little more time with him.

"And then what will I do?" I asked.

"Join a convent," he said.

"Okay then I guess you won't get to meet any of my friends."

"Okay, wait…" he said.

We all laughed.

On date number six, Cash took me to another fancy French restaurant. We drank Prisoner wine and I tried shark for the first time. And of course, more escargot.

After dinner, when we got back to his truck, Cash gave me a mushroom wrapped in a napkin folded like a little flower. He pulled out a naked mushroom for himself. We ate them. And then Stacey called.

He let me hear the phone call. She was telling him about all the evil people she had to deal with in their business, the people without souls.

"You won't believe these people!" She whined. "I don't even know what kind of creatures they are."

She had a watery cartoon voice. She would have sounded annoying but the animation in her voice made it attractive. She would have made a great voice actress.

When he called her sweetie, I felt a jealous pang.

After he hung up, I asked, "Why do you call her sweetie? I thought I was your sweetie."

"Aw, hey, you're jealous? I won't call her that anymore," he said.

He said it was a good sign I was jealous.

Later I realized that "sweetie" was just another southern word people threw around at one another, like "beautiful" or "honey."

Cash took me to a beach off the side of the road underneath a bridge. The stars were twinkling and we started making out by a canal. He took me out on the sand and tried to take my clothes off.

"No!" I said. I walked into a tunnel under the bridge away from him. I could tell he was frustrated but still happy from the shrooms.

Cash was the first person I knew who looked cute on

drugs instead of creepy or tweaking out. He looked like a little boy, full of wonder. Underneath all that power, all his success, all his drive, there was a playful little golden boy, endlessly mischievous and innocent. For everything I knew that he wanted to do to me, for every lustful thought I knew he had, my heart went to him for his purity of spirit, his true love for life.

But I didn't want to give him the upper hand quite yet. I wasn't ready to lose my power, my footing.

He coaxed me away from the tunnel where it was dark and damp and pulled me back near the canal. I walked alongside him on the beach. He started grabbing me, caressing me. I pushed him away again, staring him down. I told him I was afraid he would disappear again if I had sex with him, that I didn't trust him yet.

"We're in this so far already," he said, pulling me close again.

I pushed him away, hard. We wrestled like lions, rolling around in the sand, pushing each other down until he pinned me. We looked at each other, breathing hard. We stood up. I had cuts on my arms and legs. My hair was in knots. I felt refreshed and alive.

"Why do I always bring out the goddess in girls?" He asked, speaking to the blue velvet sky.

We drove back to his house. When we pulled up, we started making out again in his truck. I crawled into his lap, kissing his neck hard.

I pulled away and looked at him right in the eyes.

"Have you had sex with anyone else recently?" I asked.

He told me he hadn't.

"Let's take a shower," he said. "Get clean."

We were both covered in sand.

He kept the lights off and brought flickering candles into the bathroom. In the shower, I saw his penis. It hung long and soft, the biggest penis I'd ever seen. I had to have it inside me.

"Wash my feet," he said. Slowly, mindfully, I washed

his feet, scrubbing between his toes and up to his ankles.

"You'll have me marrying you in no time with that work," he said.

Back in his room, my desire hung heavy, breathing in the air. He started to finger me. He made me cum quickly and wiped my cum on his forehead with his thumb. Then he entered, no condom. He came inside me after a couple minutes. I felt the danger of it all, the most dangerous game. But I had already jumped off the plane.

Lying there in bed, we tried to fall asleep. The sex was… not sexual. It felt like bodies rubbing, not our bodies, not our magic. Without words, we both knew something was off.

In the dark he said he forgot to bless the mushrooms. He said we must have been inhabited by mushroom demons. He said a prayer but a dark energy still lingered.

I never told my friends about any of it. Only the sweet and sappy stuff; the poetry, the gifts, the dinners. I didn't tell them how after we had sex, he told me he had lied to me.

"I have to tell you something," he said.

"What?"

"I lied when I said I haven't had sex with anyone else recently. I had sex with someone else."

"Who?"

"My ex. Mary."

I had expected this. I knew he wasn't to be trusted. He was too good at romance, knew all the right words, all the right moves.

I turned to ice and asked him how his relationship with his mother was. He laughed at me and said I was doing the same thing he would do. I told him I didn't have time for this type of bullshit. I asked him to drive me back to my car. He pleaded with me to stay. I stood up, went to another room and took a couple breaths. I came back.

"No. Take me home. Now."

He drove me back and kept trying to get me to kiss him or hold my hand. But I was frozen.

"Do you still want to go to Key West?" He asked.

"No. I never want to see you again," I said.

He still tried to get me to hold his hand. I ignored him. We got to my car and I got out.

"I'm going to quit you like cigarettes," I said to him before I slammed the door shut.

He sat there, waiting in his truck before I drove away.

I drove to my house. He sent me a song at the same moment I pulled into my driveway. I didn't listen to it, didn't even look. I called him. He answered on the second ring.

"Where did the magic go?" I asked.

I felt horrible, like everything good that had ever happened to me was leaking out of my body.

"I don't know," he said. "Let's sleep on it and check in when we wake up." It was 4AM.

When I woke up the next morning, I felt broken, powerless, destroyed, empty; all my energy depleted. I knew he was a player, had sensed the danger from the start. I knew what I was risking – a player was always more likely to fuck up. But I didn't think I would feel this bad after only a month of the game.

I couldn't get out of bed. My friends were texting me in a group chat about the following weekend plans but I couldn't respond. I missed all my work meetings that morning without sending any emails, frozen in cold reflection; spasms of thoughts tearing lightning quick through my brain and body. Did I want to suffer now and try to piece myself back together or did I want to keep going, resulting in either my complete destruction or my complete illumination?

I called my most recent ex. "Can we please be together?" I begged. I was drowning and grabbing onto anything that might keep me alive.

"What?" He was surprised, disconcerted by my sudden turnaround. We had been texting every week or so but since dating Cash I had broken off contact with him.

He said he needed to go, that he had to think about it.

I was desperate. I hated myself for using my ex as comfort, as salve. It was parasitic, vampiric, sociopathic, but I didn't think I could make it otherwise.

I pulled a tarot card. My eyes fell upon the ace of swords. My mind fell on the dangly sword earring in Cash's left ear. I went into a trance. It had to be him. I had no other option but to return to Cash. I had to follow the magic. Trust was irrelevant. Of course I didn't trust him. I never would. He was a player and brilliant at the game. But we weren't in the logos anymore. We were in the mythos and I was under his spell; there was no need for trust. The story was too good, the adventure too real, our connection too raw. Maybe all players are poets.

I texted Cash: "You're still my king."

"Key West?" He responded.

I texted in the affirmative.

Like Cash said, it was an experiment. The only reason I was going to Key West was for my writing. The main thing is to keep the main thing the main thing. Once the relationship ended, as he was sure to fuck it up being a fuckboy, I could write a book about him – channeling my fascination with his love spell into artistic endeavor. I wouldn't get hurt because I wouldn't take the romance seriously. I would never trust him.

In this case, love was not the answer. I'd be all intellect. I'd put on a show. Like all men, Cash was just a boy and I could have everything I ever wanted if I just played my cards right.

But I fell in love with him anyway.

CHAPTER SIX:
KEY WEST, AND MDMA

Have you ever been to Key West? People called it the island of misfits. And misfits we were, always had been, and always would be. But we were misfits who had found each other. Being misfits became our power, our strength. Our multi-lifespan connection magnified this power and gave us great energy. We were there to save the world together. We were together to save the world. Everything in our lives had been leading us to be together.

I turned all my thoughts and feelings off about the lie he told me. He lied to me but it didn't matter. I was in love with our future. Not him.

The next morning, I met Cash at the dock where we got on the Key West Express.

We smoked cigarettes on the stern and told each other stories about ourselves. Dolphins jumped in the bow waves.

"A good sign," he said.

I told him about the liminal space, where the dolphins rode in the waves, the places between darkness and light, the edge, the border where life grows quicker, bigger, bolder.

We moved to the deck. My eyes always flashed bluer by the ocean.

"You're really pretty," Cash said, looking straight into my eyes. I allowed myself to swoon. I fawned. This man was taking me to the Keys. Upon moving to Florida a trip to the Keys was sitting high on my to-do list.

We sat at the bar and ordered coffee. The man sitting next to us told us about his family and why he was visiting Key West.

"You're a lucky guy," he said to Cash, nodding at me.

"I know," he said.

He put his hand on the back of my neck.

We got to the island and on our walk to the hotel Cash pointed out all the reasons, "Key West has soul." Chickens, iguanas, and roosters roamed the streets. Everyone was there to celebrate and take it slow, making art out of themselves and their rides whether bicycle or car. Masters of their own lives. Makers of their own dreams.

We passed another man who told Cash he was lucky.

"I know," he said.

It was like we were bathing in the light from GOD's smile.

Cash's assistant had drawn up an itinerary for us. We had the afternoon free.

When we arrived at the hotel, we made love on the bed. At first I tried to stop him.

"I knew you were going to try something like that," he said, pushing my arms down. He took my dress and panties off with his teeth. I loosened the grip on control and it turned to sand.

It was the best sex I'd ever had in my life. I went places.

We finished and there was blood on the sheets. I wasn't on my period.

"Virgin blood," Cash said.

Everywhere we went I felt Cash looking, observing, absorbing everything. Life dripped and he drank. It was like he had a Bluetooth synced into a device I couldn't hear. He told me how men sized each other up, the unspoken war and brotherhood they were simultaneously engaged in with each other at all times, the awake ones anyways.

Cash's mind was constantly preparing for battle. He exchanged sacred nods and matched subtle flexes that I didn't notice but that he described later. Interactions I missed where whole worlds were communicated and fought over. I was left to enjoy myself, luminescent as the moon, vibing, thriving.

That evening, after an afternoon of wandering we sat down at a bar and he gave me a little box wrapped in ribbon. I opened it and found a pale blue stone necklace. It was Larimar, the stone of Atlantis.

"We better find you a dress to match my suit tomorrow night," he said, pulling me into a boutique before we went to our dinner reservation that night.

The next day we rented a motorbike and roamed around the island, stopping at bars, drinking and dancing. Cash blessed all of our drinks and drugs, intentional in every moment. He took me to see the busts of the artists and writers and other great thinkers who had lived there. I put a cigarette in Tennessee Williams's mouth. He took me to the Hemingway house. He told me it was where we would get married. Ever since he was a little boy he had wanted to get married there. And then he met me. I had loved Hemingway since I was a little girl.

I told him the famous myth about Hemingway at a bar, how he said in a bet that he could write a story in six words. Nobody believed him and everyone bet against him until he said, "Baby shoes for sale. Never worn." Cash loved it and had me tell it to everyone we met.

We bought a book of Hemingway's short stories at the Hemingway House. Cash started to read it on the beach while I read Balzac. I told him to start with "Hills like White Elephants." He read it once, twice, three times but didn't understand it. We read it together a fourth time and I coaxed him to get the meaning: an abortion. The man wanted the woman to get one, but she didn't want to.

Five hours later Cash made up his mind that it was a clever story. We referenced the text in our conversations when we talked about the second girlfriend.

"It'll just let a little air in," Cash said, just like the man in the novel.

He became so passionate about the story. I'd never met someone who got as riled up as I did over language and literature. I saw myself in him, mirrored back at me. Indeed I had finally met my match.

The three nights we were there, we floated through all the different scenes: cowboy, hick, hip hop, bluegrass, heard the best local bands, talked and bantered with dozens of people, and at Captain Tony's Saloon, he showed me how to stand backwards and flick a quarter into the grouper's mouth that hung on the front of the building for good luck.

Cash knew how to interact. He also knew how to take drugs and made sure we stayed supplemented with glycine and magnesium.

We bought coconuts off a street vendor and guzzled

them down. I tried to break mine apart so I could get to the meat.

"Knock it against something," Cash said so I threw it hard on the ground but it didn't break.

"That's right, babe, don't waste any time!"

He picked the coconut up and jammed it against a wall in one move. It broke neatly in half.

A man walked up to us from behind and passed by, turning to us and said, "I just wanted to let you know, I saw all of that and that was the coolest thing I've ever seen."

We got approached a lot. Like we were on stage for the world, the stars of the coolest movie. Cash was so smooth with his Key West blue eyes. He said mine were like the Atlantic, the deep sea. Ever since we met on the 14th and had our first date on the 21st, my favorite number, I'd been living in 7s, seventh heaven.

He asked me if I told my friends about the two wife thing. I told him I hadn't and he laughed.

It was during this trip he began to prepare me for Mary, the other woman, his ex. I had thought we were going to find the other woman together, someone new, someone that we both liked. But it turned out he was just going to include his ex-girlfriend.

"She submits to me," he said.

"Well then why did you break up with her?"

"I was dimming her light. I don't want to do that to you."

"You could never dim my light. But how can you know you were dimming hers?" I asked.

"I can just feel it. It's in her power. She's losing her power, her strength. She wants to be something for me that she can't be."

I wanted to ask why he didn't just leave her alone. I knew that she was struggling with being one of two, that she didn't want it, that it must be difficult to go from being the only one to including another. I was told from the beginning that I would be one of two. Her uneasiness made me uneasy. She called Cash throughout our trip.

"I can feel her here. I feel sorry for her," I said.

Cash didn't say anything.

"Why don't we just find another who actually wants to be one of two?" I asked.

"Maybe we will," he said. "You have to understand. We are too serious, the two of us. We need someone to lighten our seriousness. She is that way."

"But how's it going to even work?" I asked. "What about if I want to have sex with you? We will just send her away?"

He laughed. "It's an experiment. Maybe I'll get over it someday. I'm the king anyways. You must obey me."

We took MDMA and went to see a psychic. She told us we were soulmates and that we would have three children; two boys and one girl. The daughter would rebel from our lifestyle and become a doctor. One of the sons would be a businessman, like his father. The other son would invent something. She said I'd have my first at the end of 2022. She told me that I would always live by the water.

"You are mostly water, in fact," she said. I knew this was true as I was mostly made up of Scorpio and Pisces.

We met our first followers at midnight. We had just walked out of a raucous country bar to smoke a joint outside. We were sitting on top of a table – the times were in transition – customs were increasingly null and void. And with that random act of timelessness we opened our first portal.

Lilith and Jack entered the scene. They were both shorter than us, mousey, out of shape and dressed in island clothes. We offered them hits off our joint. They had been living on the island in a 1988 Mustang until someone stole it.

"Oh no," I said.

"Easy come easy go," Lilith shrugged.

"Who steals around here?" I asked Cash.

"The Cubans from Miami," he said.

I couldn't tell if he was joking.

"You wanna jump off the end of Duval Street with us?" They asked.

"Hell yes!" We said.

On our way there Cash wanted to make a stop at the Garden of Eden. The bouncer wouldn't let Lilith and Jack in because they were too drunk so Cash paid him off and the four of us went up to the rooftop.

There were topless women and fully nude men standing around, swaying to the DJ.

"It's clothing optional?!" Lilith screeched and stripped out of her clothes.

Jack couldn't stand up straight and was escorted out by another bouncer.

"Jack! Nooo!" Lilith screeched again and tore out of the bar butt naked into the street after him.

Cash and I looked at eachother.

"Let's have a swim then shall we?" He said, giving a final glance around the bar.

We gathered up the redressed Lilith and the stumbling Jack and made our way to the end of Duval Street, picking up a few more stragglers who decided to join our motley gang.

We got to a dock at the end of the street. The group of us stood, looking at the moonlight sparkling on the water.

Somehow, Cash popped up out of the sea, having already jumped in.

"What are you all waiting for?" He shouted.

In an instant I slipped off the pink silk dress Cash bought me that day to match his pink suit. He was already wading onto the shore.

I ran down the dock, got to the end and dove, slipping into the water without a splash. I swam to him at the shore. The water was perfect. The stars were bright.

"You can tell me you love me now," he said, pulling me in to kiss him.

"I love you," I whispered, like I was letting out a sigh.

"Come on then!" Cash yelled at the others. Lilith and Jack jumped in next.

When they were making out in the water, Cash turned to me and said, "I've changed my mind."

My heart nearly stopped and the butterflies started moving again. Was I victorious already? Did he finally see the magic I saw?

"Really?" I beamed at him.

I thought he meant he only wanted me and didn't want another girlfriend anymore.

"You can still talk to your ex-boyfriend."

"Oh," I said, deflating.

He knew what I thought he meant. It hung in the air, a phantom of hope. Maybe he did it on purpose. Was he toying with me? I could play. He'd see.

Lilith ran into the bushes and came back with a sparkly lava lamp. She presented it to me like an award, a better seal to any other deal I'd ever been a part of; the seal of our love.

Lilith and Jack and the rest of the gang stopped too many times to talk with other friends so we left them to get hot dogs and get to bed.

"Nothing good ever happens after midnight," Cash said. It was 11:29.

Walking back to our hotel with our hot dogs, we heard a mob of drunken singers inside a bar bellow, "Sometimes wish I'd never been born at all!"

"How funny," I remarked, thinking the odds were unlikely that anyone in the bar could hold an existential conversation around the lyrics of "Bohemian Rhapsody."

"That song summons demons," Cash said.

"Makes sense to me," I said. "How do you know about this kind of stuff?"

Once again, Cash's brilliance overcame my pathetic normie literary analysis. My mind went to existentialism which I was beginning to reconsider as a tool for distracting the masses through dismal meaninglessness. What had once been Kierkegaard's greatest contribution and Sartre's brilliance was now denigrated to a design of thought that led American college students to nihilistic perspectives, self-absorption, dreary outlooks, and useless ponderings. Hell I was thinking I had some sort of gambit upper hand because I could consider satanic ramblings to be a sort of sophisticated philosophical musing but I was only disoriented. Nearly all the classic rock singers were the sons and daughters of prominent international bankers and diplomats. And the radio stations had been playing those songs on repeat for decades now.

"Think about it. Beezlebub, at best, a GOD of the mob and I'm talking about the messy mob not the organized mob- the Philistine mob. At worst, that's Satan himself. The singalong goes, 'Beezlebub has a devil put aside for me! For me! For me!' Three times? You're learning your numerology. And you know your words. Words and numbers hold immense power. Those fools are cursing themselves. And even worse, you think they're blessing their drinks? Their spirits? They're summoning the devil and they don't even know it."

"Nothing really matters. Nothing really matters. Nothing really matters... to me."

Their drunken singing cascaded off the streets along with the lullabiac notes of "Bohemian Rhapsody."

Key West was also the first time Cash slapped me. It was the first time I ever got slapped. Cash left me outside a bar to go to the bathroom. He told me not to move. I realized I left the lava lamp back at the hot dog stand so I went back for it. When I returned to the spot in front of the bar, Cash was looking for me down the street. When I got to him, he slapped me with his palm, quick and light on the face, like he was trying to wake me up. But he was angry.

"Why did you leave?"

"The lava lamp!" I said.

"Oh okay. Don't do that again." His anger dissipated as quickly as it had come.

I felt refreshed.

After I bitched someone out in passing who told Cash his suit was ugly, he told me to bless people no matter how rude they were. "Just wait and watch. GOD will always reveal himself to you in people."

"And how do I bless them?" I asked.

"Like this," he said, holding his palm up, facing it away from himself like a bodhisattva statue.

In the morning I woke up to an entrepreneurial Cash deliberating over whether a software platform or a phone app could be used to prolong the magic of last night. How could we continue the movement that we started in a single night? How could we continue contact with our followers? How did we create assets out of these strangers who so quickly followed our lead in revelry and rambunction?

"Through software?" I asked with disdain.

"Yeah, I don't like it either," Cash said. "But I have to get on the cover of *Wired* somehow."

We fooled around and made love.

With my head on his chest, he said, "I like how Lilith called Jack 'daddy' whenever she wanted a cigarette. But at first it threw me off."

Cash? Thrown off by something? I stroked his firm pecs, and abs. Brushed my fingers along the veins of his strong arms. He had the softest skin. I was fascinated that he could ever be thrown off. He was so in sync, so in rhythm, so in the flow with everything.

Of course he admired the outward display of submission. He was preparing me to be this way.

I said I'd call him daddy whenever I asked for a cigarette. With Cash, submission was easy. I liked embodying a submissive philosophy to dance alongside a king. I already embodied more tradition than I had ever allowed a single soul to see, awaiting the one man who was man enough to turn the key.

He told me a woman's role was to serve her husband. He said it to me cautiously like he wasn't sure if I got it or how far I could take it, gauging me.

On our last day on the island, Cash surprised me with a helicopter ride around the island. Usually I didn't like overt displays of wealth. I found it stupid and obnoxious to get into a helicopter just to look around but I kept my mouth shut and Cash made it fun. He made everything fun.

Cash said we would sail across the world to Maine, the rest of the Keys, Argentina, Costa Rica, Panama, Cuba, Puerto Rico, Indonesia, Japan. Everywhere would be ours to visit. We would find cult members all over the world. He wanted to marry me in every country. I couldn't see any other way to live, couldn't believe I hadn't thought of this before. The apocalypse was coming and we needed an escape. He said we would go by the end of December.

The waters were rising. It was going to be time to hit the ark. The culture was so rotten. It was time to find your tribe. Build your commune. I wondered what it would feel like to miss land.

When Cash said he wanted to stay another night and I agreed, I realized he wasn't kidding. He was dead serious. We would have stayed another night but I told him I had work to get back to.

"You should just quit," he said.

"I don't know about that," I said.

But again, he was dead serious.

"I probably should."

"You will."

He gave me more confidence than I ever knew I could have. Anything he told me to do, I did it without fear. Even cutting dozens of people in line, if my man wanted it, I did it. If he wanted a certain seat, we'd get a certain seat. So I cut the line for the return ferry so he could sit where he wanted to sit and didn't blink twice. Waitress didn't hear him? I'd yell at her loud and clear what he needed so he didn't have to repeat himself. Someone in his way? I'd make sure they knew to excuse us.

Riding back on the Key West Express, Cash asked why my last relationship ended. I told him how, during covid, my ex would disappear from our apartment for days at a time and ignore all my calls. Then he'd show up out of nowhere, apologizing. I never got over it. Plus, he was corporate.

"I'm not going to leave you," he said. "I'm going to move into you."

"I never knew it could be this easy," I said, again like I was releasing a sigh.

He leaned in to me and whispered in my ear, "Dance, monkey, dance."

I pulled away, humiliated. But it was also kind of funny and I laughed.

CHAPTER SEVEN: TRAD, CULT LOGIC, HILARY DUFF, AND LANA DEL REY

When we got back to the mainland, he went back to her, his other girlfriend. I asked him to make love to me in his truck one more time before he left. Before he came he looked me straight in the soul and asked me if I surrendered to him.

"Yes."

"Say it. Say you surrender."

"I surrender."

"To who?"

"To you."

"And who am I?"

"My king."

After he came, he said he had a vision of a talking sun.

"What did it say?" I asked, lighting a cigarette, trying to keep him to myself longer.

"Be cool."

Was he cool enough to have two of us? I asked what she looked like and he showed me her picture on his phone. He looked at me solemnly as he held up his phone. She was beautiful.   I was relieved. That made it easier.

I had a dream about her that night. She and I went back and forth to Cash, telling him he had to pick one of us. In the dream she seemed really cool but later I learned that I was the cool one.

Maybe the best men deserved more than one woman. Cash was the first man I met who walked in GOD's light. If a man like that wanted two women then he deserved them. Society needed more men with that much greatness, enough greatness to attract two wives. Too many men were "soy boys" as Cash called them, complacent to slave away at bureaucracy and participate in dominant cultural hegemonies like sports watching, video games, pornography, and the humiliating ritual of voting.

I could be sanctimonious about the second wife. I got a sexual buzz thinking about the three of us, the taboo of a romantic threesome. It could be holy, sacred, cool. Some people watched porn and some people got multiple girlfriends. It was an adventure.

Cease to resist, come on say you love me

Give up your world, come on and be with me
I'm your kind, I'm your kind, and I see
Submission is a gift; give it to your lover
Love and understanding is for one another
I'm your kind, I'm your kind, and I see

Charles Manson wrote "Cease to Exist" for the Beach Boys but they renamed it and called it, "Never Learn Not to Love." Manson had the Beatles for prophets. I had Lana.

I love you the first time, I love you the last time
Yo soy la princesa, comprende these white lines
'Cause I'm your jazz singer and you're my cult leader
I love you forever, I love you forever

Her latest album dropped that week. I played it back in the bedroom at Key West. Like all my boyfriends, Cash didn't like it. It was too sad. Straight men didn't get it, thank goodness.

Just like the greatest of cult leaders, Lana del Rey was a channeler of energies. She put her followers in a trance. I knew most of her songs by heart and rarely went a month without playing her music. Going to a Lana concert it hits you that you're in a cult. You look around and see everyone singing every single word to every single song just like you. Lana's power was transcendent for the modern American woman; she transmuted the sexual objectification of our youth into art, beauty, and power. Through the romantic, she made our horror, our abjection, even our American consumerism beautiful again. And then we could transcend the trauma and pain.

I suppose that shows how my mind goes. I'd like to know how many Lana fans started under the first Disney teen queen, Hilary Duff. I know I did. I used to take notes of what she wore on *Lizzie McGuire*. American tween culture carved my soul out early at eleven years old.

And now Cash and I were two philosopher mavericks like Dean and Kerouac. Best friends and lovers, we weaved in between roles for millennia, summoned by the universe, ambitiously bored with the mainstream. We would write a cult treatise. He, the entrepreneur, artist, engineer; me, the writer. He had the visions and I kept track of the details.

He showed me a sketch he made of me from a selfie I sent him in the mirror. He used a stylus on his iPad. He created his company logos the same way. He was a master marketer.

"I want to study cults with you."

"Let's go to a different church every Sunday."

"We can make out on the pews."

"Let's make everyone love us and lead them."

Key West's Duval Street became our code for the initiation rite in our cult. Each member had to "take a jump off Duval Street."

When I talked about the 1920s with a golden age lens or of any of the other time periods with nostalgia or respect, Cash reminded me we were in the age of Kali Yuga, the dark ages. Everything was going to get worse before it got better.

I wondered if I was really going to get pregnant like he said. I knew how badly I wanted a child, how ready I felt to be a mother. The fun was all over. The fun was just beginning. I was powerful, could do anything. I was with a GOD.

In my journal I wrote, *I think Cash could teach me about true love and take away all my anger and give it to the poor.*

He talked about the darkness I couldn't see. He said there were a lot of bad people around that I needed to be careful of, that I shouldn't ever stray far from him. It made me feel safe to be protected, to be cared for, to know that I was good enough to be concerned about. I was afraid of these lower levels. I blocked out a lot of the world I didn't want any part of. Friends said I always saw the best in people. Cash said I was naive.

"Cities are dead," Cash said and I believed him. But I still kept tabs on the charade. The decline fascinated me.

I spent my days lounging around waiting for the words I needed to write to come, doing work tasks for Americorps here and there to maintain illusions. The dream, though the dream got pretty wild. He changed me. I was awakened, elevated, vibing, writing constant poetry. I ritualized my writing with candles, sage, and tobacco. I started smoking cigarettes on my own. I read my Balzac, my Twain, my Cormac, my Lispector, my Bataille, my Barthes, and the Civilization newspaper of the avant-garde in New York.

I had been floating on air for a while, manifesting the world I was entering. The dreaming was done. It was time to implement and build. We were in a war for souls.

What was he? Not the part I covered with my own limitations – I wanted to know the entire world map of Cash: the crying, cumming, ecstatic, suffering, vibing, conquering power.

Why had my manifestations brought Cash, the cult leader to me? I was about to find out. I'd studied systematic power for years and now I'd found raw power in a man.

Part of me thought I might be going crazy. So I consulted a few people: an old friend, my sister, and the tarot.

The old friend was my college ex, an accountant. He was the exact same as I last spoke to him, and the exact same as I left him. Worked the same job, lived in the same city, hung around the same friends, watched the same news and had the same views.

He had just binge watched *Wild Wild West* on Netflix for the second time. This time he decided he was in favor of the cult. How pertinent. It was exactly what I wanted to talk to him about. How my new boyfriend wanted to be a cult leader. How he wanted two wives.

"But can you date other people?" My ex twice removed asked.

"No."

He was repulsed.

"Why is it so disgusting to be one of many? Isn't that the truest, most devoted love- one that knows no bounds, no rules? Where did the concept of monogamy even come from?"

"I don't know. It just seems wrong," he said.

"If I want to have a baby, wouldn't I want to have one with the strongest, most powerful person I could find?"

But I had lost him. He was so revolted by the two-wife thing, he couldn't consider anything else. It reminded me of how annoyed he got about people who didn't wear masks or who were anti-vax. Even before covid he had always been extremely anti about anti-vaxxers. It was always the people without a sense of adventure who got riled up the most by basic questioning of social norms.

"...but why monogamy? Why only one other person?" I asked.

"I don't know," he said.

His life consisted of moving about in an upbeat and positive manner, paying attention to little else besides the subtle palpitations in his subtle heart which told him how to entertain himself.

I told him that instead of watching a Netflix series I wanted to live a Netflix series.

My sister knew right away what was going on, though I told her very little. "He sounds like *50 Shades of Grey*." My sister still lived in our hometown and would probably stay there forever. But she was practically psychic sometimes by default. She did nothing to cultivate it.

Consistently tarot told me not to let the events and fears of my past affect my future. If I stuck with Cash, I would eventually be the queen of swords; sad but strong and powerful.

When I tried to describe it to myself, all I could think was how dangerous it all was, how risky. But what did I have to lose? The success and intellectual power were impossible to ignore. If I lost him it'd be a mountain of recovery to lose so much magic. So I just needed to keep him entertained as well as myself. It was role playing. It was trad. It was revolutionary.

And it was fun. I liked to be his little girl. "Daddy's girl or good girl," he purred when I sucked his cock.

I knew the odds. That he was going to hurt me again, more likely than not. I would have to be incredibly strong once the inevitable came. He would say things like, "I want you to be so committed to me that even if you find me in bed with another woman you will stay by my side." Dating him was like doing shadow work. Briefly I wondered if I was dating the devil himself.

I could feel when Cash was about to text me and I stopped feeling surprised when he did.

Cash wanted me to go with him to St. Pete's the next weekend. He had a photo shoot for his company. He was going to take Mary but now he wanted to take me. He said he was finished with Mary. She wasn't willing to share him after all. I didn't hold my breath though.

I was supposed to work that weekend, go to an event with my friends, and go to an estate sale with my neighbor. Cash said I should always put my boyfriend first. I should cancel all my obligations so I could be with him.

In college, I was invariably obsessed with my boyfriend, the future accountant. By default I did everything he said, went everywhere he wanted to go, and did anything he wanted to do. But he wasn't trad, wasn't a real man, and he didn't know what to do with me. I was perfect, malleable, soft, childlike, devoted. He loved me, sure, but he was just a silly boy who loved to watch sports and would only become an accountant one day. He couldn't lead me.

And so, with a broken heart I left him and went off to see the world on my own. I built up my independence, my self-reliance, my desires, my dreams, my identity. Cash said it wasn't natural for a woman to travel alone like that. He called me out for using my sexuality to travel. It was true- my sexuality came in handy all throughout my escapades. People wanted to help and protect me. I was an extremely privileged traveler.

My most recent ex had at least attempted to domesticate me, make me more obedient, submissive. He wanted me to live with his mom for a year to study her cooking. But he didn't pay the bills and he wasn't man enough, didn't command me right. However, he planted the seeds for Cash to nurture.

My Mormon upbringing helped- my own mother a housewife, and my father, the breadwinner. But my parents also told me I could be anything and do anything I wanted. No designated duty, role, or responsibility in terms of my relation to neither men nor the world.

Cash believed that modern women ran after careers because men were emasculated by society. I hated being a career woman. I had always thought the word, "career" to be a dirty word, unnatural. I didn't have the motivation or drive to work hard at facades; I preferred to be myself. Cash preached a return to the Bronze Age. He said he had books for me to study. The greatest foes against masculinity were pornography, passivity, and pussy power.

Cash had all the answers to the questions my liberation as a woman left me with. What was my purpose? As a modern woman I felt rotten. I was like one of those stray dogs in third world countries, domesticated from wolves only to roam the streets, starving, without purpose, belonging nowhere and to no one. Maybe I belonged in someone's home. Maybe I was meant to have a master. Better to follow a powerful man than a decaying ideological empire.

I was playing a role and the rules were clear, the formula written by thousands of years. Tradition may be the only functional structure in a dark chaotic world. There was relief in devotion. I was developing a taste for this relief, exhausted with the lonely concept of myself, drowning in wicked intellect. I didn't have to worry anymore about who or what was right or what I was supposed to do. I could just love him, follow him, serve him. Devotion was simple, ancient, and sweet.

When I finally told my girlfriends about the two-girlfriend thing, they were fascinated.

A bunch of us from the permaculture club were at Leslie's house for a girls' night. We made a picnic inside her apartment with candles and incense and crystals. Leslie made us vegetable stew.

I tried to explain to them how Cash believed in the past.

"Like Ancient Greece?" They asked.

"No, like Bronze Age," I said.

I talked about the falling empire. Floridians were on board with this depiction of America, especially since Biden became the first dead president, so I didn't have to worry about shocking or offending them. Once I had them following, I explained how a cult could be used to convert people to break away from the empire to join and build the new world and usher in a new age of freedom and peace. I didn't use the word "cult" though. I think I used the word "community."

The girls said I was really cool and powerful. When I told them he was hung they understood why he'd try to get two girlfriends. They understood how he was evil maybe but not for certain yet. He could just be a boy with a big heart, big enough for two.

They said they knew something had been up with me. It felt good to tell them what was really happening, to be honest.

"Live the adventure," they said. "Ride the ride, he's rich!"

Cash said I dreamed him up. We had conversations even when we weren't together.

"Did you also dream me up?"

"You certainly are dreamy."

Every conversation I had with him was the best conversation of my life. He had awoken a not-giving-a-fuck part of me. It had always been there, dormant, waiting. He deepened it, brought it above the subconscious surface and into the conscious so I could apply it to all my actions, all my values.

When people asked Cash how old he was, I never heard him answer in any way other than "timeless." Because of him, I finally figured out my age and where I came from. I didn't have to be modern, I was timeless. I couldn't conform to modern standards of living, even if I wanted to. I no longer wanted that- the greatest relief. Like the ultimate way to revolt now was to be trad, lounging around being a housewife, cooking, cleaning, reading, and writing to my heart's content.

I was at Neenie's House drinking coffee, working on my laptop, and waiting for the next yoga class to start when Cash texted me, "Come over." I skipped out on yoga and went over to his house, excited to be with him, to follow his orders. And that's how the next adventure started.

We met up with his friend, Lucci, along with Dez, Dash, and JT at the kava bar. Dez was Cash's other assistant. When I asked him what happened to the other one, he said he had to fire her for misbehaving. I didn't ask questions because I didn't care.

Dez had been his assistant for years. They shared the same birthday. She was as bubbly and charming as a typical Libra. We got along easily. Cash told me his other girlfriends got jealous of her so I decided to give no power to those kinds of thoughts. I saw him spank her that night but I let it fall right out of my head and didn't let it stick.

I wasn't intimidated by Dez. She was definitely beautiful; apple cheeks and white blonde hair that gave her an old Hollywood toots look. She certainly didn't look 36. Her eyes were wide-eyed innocent and blue. But she had a fucked up life. Her daughter, Rose, age 16, was born with a father long gone. She ate like shit and almost always wore sweats. But I liked her crassness. And she was a good mother. Even though she was definitely in love with Cash I didn't blame her.

Lucci was back from Dubai where he had flown to impress a woman. He sent Cash videos of himself in the hotel he got. Then he found out the woman was already dating someone else. Poor guy. But he wasn't the type to feel sorry for himself. He was clever and quick-witted. He liked to cross the line.

After that first night, Lucci started hanging out with us on the reg. I think Cash had been searching for a new right hand man. Nothing was more important to him than genuine comradery.

His previous right hand man, Spark Twain, wasn't a very bright guy. I ran into him at the kava bar once. He was a wet blanket and rather rude but in a low brain function way and not on purpose. Cash cut him off when he attempted to cheat Cash out of money somehow. I'm not sure exactly of the details but when I told Cash I ran into him, he told me, "You have no business speaking to him."

But now Cash had Lucci. And even from his right hand man, he demanded total devotion. His values came from a different era. Cash didn't have friendships, he had pacts.

We were all standing in the parking lot outside the kava bar. Cash and I told stories about our time in Key West. We glittered as our own entity.

"Shall we take a jump off Duval Street?" I asked Cash.

"You want to join our cult?" Cash asked the others.

"Blood pact?" Cash or I asked. The craziest ideas can never be sourced. Probably because they come from above.

Cash asked JT if he had a knife and he happened to have a pocket knife.

"My man! I knew you'd have one!"

Cash took the knife and tried to cut his own palm. His first cut didn't draw blood so he had to cut himself a second time. I laughed the whole time.

Next, he took my palm and cut me. I couldn't stop laughing. Then he cut Dash, Dez, Lucci, and, after a while, JT. JT was the only one who resisted at first.

"He's the only one who's acting normal!" We all laughed.

Dez took me into the bathroom to wash the blood off. She was paranoid that people were watching us.

First we took pictures of the blood on our arms. My blood dripped down my arm and into the sink. I pretended to lick the blood on my arm in the photo. We were on drugs.

We went to a bar where there was a dart board. Cash announced we would play darts. I grabbed my colors and got ready to throw. Dez stopped me and said Cash always went first.   Cash threw a dart but then he didn't want to play anymore. Dez pulled me away from the dart board.

We went to the Golden Buddha. We got kicked out for some reason but everyone was too drunk to know why. Maybe we were smoking cigars or doing cocaine. I'm not sure. But I do remember Cash and JT going on stage and singing. They always sang the same song together, "Little Talks" by Of Monsters and Men.

I didn't think Cash had very good stage presence. His voice was so soft you couldn't hear what he was singing. But then I felt ashamed by my thoughts. This man exuded confidence; was totally in his power. He set an example. And he wanted the same for all of us.

"Don't tell anyone about the main thing," he said. He was talking about the cult, of course, but secretly, I considered the main thing to be my writing.

Everyone except Dez crashed at Cash's that night. Cash always had a bunch of mattresses lying around his house.

In the morning I went out to Cash's truck to get my purse where I had an extra swisher for a blunt. I threw on his pink polo before I went outside. Rummaging around in the truck, I heard, "Who the fuck are you?"

I turned around to face Stacey, the baby mama.

"I'm Maria. Hi."

"Why are you wearing Cassius's shirt?!"

I didn't say anything.

She stomped into the house. I waited a minute and followed after her.

"What is going on here? Why is some random girl wearing your shirt, Cassius?"

Cash was serving coffee to Lucci. He asked Lucci if he wanted cream and sugar. After Lucci replied in the affirmative, Cash turned his eyes to Stacy. "Yes? Can I help you?"

"Why is there a random girl wearing your shirt?" She screamed at Cash then turned to look at Dash, who averted his eyes.

Dash looked like he was on edge, prepared for the worst. He was sensitive to emotions, like me. He told me that Stacey sometimes attacked Cash.

"Why are there all these people here? What are all these mattresses lying around? What is this? A frat house?" she screamed.

She caught my eye as I sat down on one of the mattresses.

"Yes. Yes it is." I said, nodding solemnly.

We all held our breath but not Cash, who was as calm and cool as always.

"You are not allowed to be in my house," he said softly. "You have no right to be here, woman."

After a lot of screaming and repeating, "in Cassius's shirt?!" Stacey finally left.

For the next few days we reenacted her screaming, "In Cassius's shirt?! In Cassius's shirt?!" and riffed off our own reactions. We reminisced on the night before.

"Last night Lucci lost his keys at the bars!"

"We all made a pact!"

"A blood pact!"

"And JT was the only one who acted normal!"

I guess it was a bonding experience. It was also the first time I realized his ex still worked next door to his house.

Cash and I decided to go for a float.

After floating and showering, I found him in the waiting room, already sitting in a lounge chair, writing notes.

When I sat down, he told me he had a vision of walking in a forest. He saw the Great Creator who turned him into a tree. He spent 100 years as that tree, seeing all kinds of things.

"I could feel you floating around with me," he said.

"I felt you too!" I said and it was true.

Like all the conversations we had when we were apart, we were always connected. The past lives we'd experienced were unraveling in real time, all the memories, all the time we'd spent together, thousands of years catching up to us now that we were together again.

In my float there were times I thought I could see Cash but it was my own reflection. I was always looking for him like a little lamb.

We went to meet his friend, Penny Lane, on the tide at the beach. We went for Pina Coladas and a toke on the swings. Then we went to the boardwalk. That was when Cash started hustling Penny Lane's flower crowns. She made crowns and sold them to the tourists walking around the boardwalk and beaches. And that's how she made a living.

She asked strangers in a sickeningly sweet, high pitched voice, "Have you ever met a fairy before?" And then, "Well guess what? Now you have!"

She had big buggy eyes and white blonde hair. She certainly looked like a fairy.

"Make that money, man," a guy said to Cash, passing by.

"This is harder than I thought," said Cash, the sun GOD.

Penny Lane just smiled. I laughed.

Next thing you know we made a friend, a potential new follower. He had an ancient name and lived in ancient ways. He bought one of Penny Lane's man bands she brought all the way from Guatemala.

"The quickest way to align your chakras is to stare at the sunset," Cash said into my ear.   We both turned and stared down the sun as it sunk across the water. After the last of the red disappeared we realized we had acquired a following.

Somehow we learned it was Greek Independence Day. We all sat down for a meal and had some opa cheese lit on fire by our newest friend, a Norwegian captain.

When we were sitting at the table eating our feast, the ancient man had something to say about the blood pact we told him we had made. When he saw two cuts for Cash, he said that made him the leader. Cash told people about the cult anyways, he was too excited.

We made promises as presents to meet again so that the present would be more precious and I let all my obligations go to shreds. Was it Thursday I went over to Cash's – no it was Wednesday because the day was Friday. I lived in the moment nonstop for 48 hours with him.

Penny Lane asked Cash for business advice. He gave it to her but she was too distracted to absorb anything. She just demanded more even as he was giving it to her right then and there. It's like she knew of his greatness but it was too much for her to fathom, to grasp.

The three of us went to a kava bar and talked to some

young kids and did yoga with them outside. One kid was going to become a soldier after high school. I wanted to tell him not to but I didn't.

Cash offered Penny Lane one of his mattresses to crash on that night which she accepted. She was a true hippie.

Mary, Cash's ex-girlfriend, showed up unannounced at the house that night. She ran around the house angry and clamoring around, shocked to find Penny Lane and me there.

I went to hide in his room, squeezing an emerald. She yelled at him. I wasn't sure whether she would hurt me. I moved her stuff she put in his bedroom into the hallway. She banged on the door before she left.

Cash just laughed at her and played the guitar on the porch.

"Never a dull moment," he said, after she left. I was a little scared by his lack of empathy.   He comforted me, told me these other girls didn't compare to "people like us."

We were born leaders – it was true. So I let it all fall out of my head.

I told him it was a good thing we floated since that day got even more dramatic; first Stacey, then Mary.

In the morning, as we were getting ready to go our separate ways, Cash pulled me aside and said he didn't trust Penny Lane. I didn't understand why. She put cacao in our coffee. But when his workers came over, he didn't want her around them or near the factory. He told me to make her stay away from them. I think she had an alliance with Stacey. He told me she was simple and that I should look closely at her.

"She's 30-something and she just runs around hustling stupid flower crowns to people? She doesn't know what she's doing," he said.

Cash left for St. Petersburg on his own. I almost went with him, even changed my mind and offered to cancel all my plans but he said he'd go alone.

It was finally over between him and Mary. Now he was really just mine. But it couldn't last long. He was looking for another wife. And maybe he would get back together with

Mary again. They had broken up before.

Penny Lane and I decided to do yoga in the park. She led me in a chakra-cleansing routine. I shared my food with her. Then we went our separate ways, promising to meet up at a Grateful Dead concert that night.

I was looking forward to putting my finger on that pulse.

I went to do some work and then I met up with Ashley and Leslie at the kava bar.

I told them all about the cult. Ashley broke off my explanation a few times to talk about her own experience in a cult when she was a little girl but she was fucked up off little sleep so her mind wasn't all there. I told them about the blood pact.

"It was more of a playful teenage-hearted pact and less a serious ritual. As is the whole project really."

They were fascinated. And then the conversation moved on.

Leslie had gotten the exact same dread extensions in her hair that Ashley had. They were both practicing talking to men more. We practiced talking to some men at the bar and then we left to go watch a movie at Ashley's house.

She talked the movie up, saying it was all about our lives and how we were manifesting magic. It was a terrible movie. I watched Ashley laugh at all the stupid parts. But I was patient and told her it was good. I was used to masking my true feelings around friends. If I didn't I might not have any.

CHAPTER EIGHT: UNCONDITIONAL SURRENDER, ROAD TRIPS, AND STREET DRUGS

I was hanging with Penny Lane at the Grateful Dead concert, talking with everyone about how good it was to be in Florida when Cash called and told me I needed to get to St. Pete's immediately. It was 10:30 PM and I was two hours out.

I had agreed to be submissive and totally devoted; concepts that weren't entirely new to my nature, but concepts that had been lost, misplaced.

Cash wanted unconditional surrender. He picked up the phrase from that famous black and white photo of the sailor kissing a nurse on the streets of New York after the announcement of the end of World War Two. There used to be a giant statue of the kissing couple in Key West but it was moved to Sarasota before we got there.

I asked deadheads what I should do. They told me to give the relationship time, make him miss me, and not to go. I ignored them all and left for St. Pete's at 11 PM. I picked up his assistant, Dez, and we raced up the freeway going 100 miles per hour.

Cash never grew up. And he never asked anyone else to. He only asked for devotion to the cause: undermining the dominator culture that pushed you to grow up and give up. If you gave him your whole devotion, he gave you everything. But you were indebted to his control. You had to do whatever he said. Though you might not agree with his behavior, he'd never lead you astray. He only led you deeper into yourself, deeper into your own power. But you had to use that power to serve him, and for nothing else.

As I drove I thought more about how lucky I was to be in Florida: no lockdowns, no masks, no pandemic. At the concert everyone was talking about the rumors from outside; extended lockdowns, depression, suicides, hysterics, small businesses shut down forever, livelihoods lost, diminished IQs, lost learning, immune systems weakened, alienation, psychosis; all deepened through the loss of community and socialization. Every day I said it, thank GOD Florida is free.

The data wasn't showing a story the epidemiologists could tell us but they still convinced most of the world to obey the government rules and lock downs. But then again, there were rumors that the data was being mishandled, corrupted, tainted, skewed. Which data? Hell if I knew. I stopped reading the news a long time ago and I never liked data. Data was another form of industrialization; another form of modern propaganda that I didn't care to pay any attention to. I didn't believe you could quantify human behavior.

I'd mingled in hippie circles long before moving to Florida. I had always preferred the people practicing alternative lifestyles that went against the system, who cultivated holistic practices and studied ancient rituals, anti-Big Pharma, Big Meat, Big Media, Big Everything, who dove into alternative histories and theories that went against the colonial paradigm of Big Business.

At the dead show, there were hippies vending art and handmade clothes so they could live and keep traveling with the band; true festival people. It was a return to the simple life. Everything was getting increasingly complicated and convoluted in the age of information. The hippies wanted to turn away from all that to establish a new age of intuition, community love, and self-reliance.

From Orlando to Key West, Florida was all back-country small-town spots in between four big cities, the heaving crazy roaring 20s. People were out getting down and wild enough for everyone else in the country. We watched people celebrate Saint Patrick's Day for an entire week in Key West. I kept hearing that Tulum was where it was really at.

Real estate and businesses were booming; our little southwest corner of Florida had turned into a goldmine. People were moving here in droves, bringing with them their lockdown stories from the outside.

Before the pandemic, Florida was already the land of outcasts, getaways, and eccentrics. Snowbirds flocked to escape the Northern and Eastern winters. Others used it as a middle ground like the DJ I met who moved back and forth between Milwaukee, Fort Myers, and Tulum, working as a tornado chaser part-time. He told me how Milwaukee, his hometown, had changed since George Floyd was murdered, how car robberies had become rampant, what the city looked like after half of it was burned to ashes.

I thought about my roommate, Dexter, watching MSBNC, bumping NPR, and what he saw as the memorial instead of the illusion. He didn't know how to interpret the data for himself. He didn't think about who controlled the narrative he chose to consume and be consumed by. He parroted their propaganda with big blinking eyes and a condescendingly matter of fact professional managerial class tone he copied off the newscasters and "reporters."

Dez was stressed, chain smoking cigarettes in the passenger seat. Cash's baby mama, Stacey, was at the house. Dez was freaked out about what Stacey might do when she finds out I'm there. But what Cash demanded, I supplied and Dez did too. We had to believe in him. We couldn't question him. That was the game. I wanted to play my role for my cult leader perfectly.

People are always fascinated by the cult leader but forget the woman behind the man. The trance she enters devours all doubt. Her strength comes from her devotion. I wanted to be in that power; to fully embody the cult leader's most devoted and do a really good job. It takes a great woman to have a mind of that kind. I would have made a great executive assistant.

We finally got to the Airbnb in Tampa a little after midnight. Cash said it was St. Pete's but it was really Tampa – that's Florida for you. Someone invited you to Miami and you ended up in Fort Lauderdale.

We met the boys at the kava bar down the street, the usual crew minus Lucci. Cash hated the excuses Lucci made to not hang out, like working, being tired, that sort of thing. Cash lived in the present moment and demanded it from everyone.

He'd call up his friends, "Where the fuck are you? Get your ass to the beach!" And it wasn't always the actual beach, though it often was. Usually it was a metaphorical beach. In Cash's world, one should spend most of his time at the beach. Any attempt to make excuses was absurd and he would joke, "What are you talking about? Your friends are at the beach!"

But that didn't mean we weren't preparing our escape. We still spent time in the rat race to make it big before the big one came, scrambling for all the biggest pieces: real estate, gemstones, precious metals, stocks, crypto. Before we joined forces as a cult, it was every man for himself. That sucked. This was better.

Cash wanted to buy an ark ASAP so we looked at yachts a lot. He often talked about alien invasions, whether they were real or government-led conspiracy, and a single sun flare that would destroy all technological communications and bring a whole world into survival mode. I liked picturing upper and middle class Americans struggling. Maybe they'd feel something. Maybe they'd start listening to their thoughts.

Sometimes, when my phone didn't work I began to panic: the beginning of the end. Then I would laugh at myself. I didn't want to be surrounded by people who would panic so why would I panic? I wanted to be around those that expected the end; those who were awaiting the upheaval and would welcome it with a good sense of humor. And no matter what, I wanted to be with Cash.

Cash also talked of a future where he'd have a school for boys to teach them about the traditions and rituals of masculinity. He believed in and lived in multiple realities at once, just like me. We aimed to be multidimensional beings. Shoot for the moon sort of people.

At the kava bar, Cash said, "There's a time machine back at the house, we're going back to 1998!" Another one of his magic metaphors. It was a Jacuzzi. They were definitely on drugs.

Cash's mom and a friend of hers were also at the kava bar but I didn't know until his mom introduced herself to me. Cash stayed true to his poor introduction skills.

"I'm Stephanie," she said coyly. She had a bright and playful energy.

Ashley had warned me that Cash's mom used to be an addict. I didn't know why it should matter that his mom was, at one point, an addict. She was sweet and jolly, making jokes and laughing a lot. No one was tethered to their past. She had a raspy, cheap cigarette sort of voice and she waddled like someone who spent too much time at the TV but she had a sparkle of mischief in her eye that I liked.

Walking along, JT whispered something to Dash and Dash went, "Oh, I didn't know she was the one!" They were talking about me. I was Cash's "one." I was the one, I was Maria, and Cash and I were forever, had always been and always would be.

We all went back to the house and got into the Jacuzzi except Dez who went to sleep.

Stacey came outside with the children.

Their elfin two-year-old, called Helena, slid into the Jacuzzi and sat on Cash's lap, looking around at everyone in shy curiosity.

Stacey tried to argue with Cash. But Cash wasn't fighting, just playing. We were all shrooming.

Cash held Helena close, told her to get a good look at me, and asked her what kind of animal I was.

"Rabbit," she said, after looking at me for a good thirty seconds.

Ashley had also said their children were light workers. I didn't really know what that meant, another one of her spiritual buzzwords but it made me think they had magic powers.

After getting nowhere with Cash, Stacey turned to me and demanded,

"So you're interested in Cassius?"

"I'm very interested in him," I said.

"You want to have a relationship with him?"

"Of course."

"Do you know he wants multiple wives?"

"So what? I'm Mormon," I shrugged.

She looked at Cash who grinned.

"Do you know about the White Salamander letters?"

"Sure."

"Well, what do you think about them?"

"I think that sort of shit happens all of the time," I said coolly.

"Now it's Maria's turn to ask a question," Dash said.

"Okay, what's your favorite color?" I asked.

She ignored me.

"So you want to be totally submissive to Cassius? You're going to do everything he says?"

"You're not going to get to know me by grilling me," I said. "Why don't you join us in the jacuzzi?"

"Yeah, come inside! It's a time machine!" Cash said.

"No! I should be sleeping right now. We have a photo shoot tomorrow."

We all just looked at her as she stood there with a baby on her hip.

"Here, you should probably get used to this," she said, handing me the baby.

I held the baby, who had huge eyes and looked like a Buddha.

"So what do you do?"

"I'm working for a nonprofit as their specialist in anti-human trafficking," I said.

She turned and tried to argue with Cash again.

"I can't believe you're ruining my vacation. You were supposed to watch them but you're partying with your friends instead."

Cash ignored her, transfixed with his daughters.

"This is my Airbnb. You can't just bring anyone over."

"No it isn't, little girl. I paid for it," Cash said.

Stacey went back inside and took the children with her.

The next morning, Cash and I had some quiet time in the lovely old Florida historic home before the photo shoot. Everyone else had already left. Maybe it was a house of ours in another lifetime.

"See you must always obey me this way and we should never be apart!" Cash said, cuddling me in bed.

Dez and Stacey used my car to get to the photo shoot. I felt bad for them since the air conditioning was broken and it was hot outside.

At the photo shoot, the employees scampered around

dressed as forest creatures and fairytale characters, fixing each other up, adding to one another's look. There were professional makeup artists and photographers scattered around. It was like seeing Cash's mind come to life.

Cash was a king. Stacey was a queen. Dez was a sun goddess. Dash was an underworld wolf prince. I helped Dash pick out his makeup: a Bowie-inspired scar across his face.

I tried to avoid Stacey. She stayed busy and kept her cool in front of her employees. I took photos with my phone as Cash commanded, made friends, floated around, stayed calm and secure.

It took all day. When it was finally over, Dez, JT, Dash, Cash, and I went back to the Airbnb. After chewing Dez out like Dez was afraid of, Stacey left with the kids. Dez's job was to take the heat, at least she got paid. Cash was supposed to watch the kids. But he just wanted to party.

And party we did.

First, Cash took a long nap after we had sex and I slipped out of the bedroom once he was asleep, did some yoga and crunches, drank rum with Dez and the boys, and listened to hushed hurried exchanges between Dez and Dash diagnosing Cash's behavior. Their worry implanted something in me that I didn't want to ascribe a name to, like Cash said, "I don't want to cast judgment." I didn't want to worry about him. I only wanted to believe in him.

When Cash woke up, Dez was pretty drunk and the boys were ready to get out. We ordered sushi and Dez slipped inside Cash's room to get him out of bed. I tried not to think about their tension as sexual, to drop it, to let it slide like I let any noise slide that might disrupt our music, our magic, our perfect movie. Then we ate and all piled into an Uber to go to the middle of Tampa to visit the Castle.

We started at a kava bar where there was some grimy music. Then we went to another bar that had a bunch of cool dance rooms. Dez pulled Cash into one, crowded with strange blue lights and I followed them in. That's when my ex called. I answered and left the room.

"Hey, I'm out at a club," I said.

"Oh. It's my birthday," he said.

"Oh yeah, happy birthday!" I said.

"Yeah, so have you still been thinking about getting back together?" He asked.

"Well, actually I have a new boyfriend. I'm with him now, sorry. I should go."

"You have another boyfriend now?" He asked, surprised.

It had only been a week since I told him I wanted to get back together.

"Yeah, I'm sorry. It's hard to hear you. I have to go."

I hung up the phone. Cash stood behind me, fuming silently. He grabbed my phone.

"Who was that?" He asked, scrolling through my texts and my call log.

"My ex-boyfriend. It's his birthday," I said

"You have no business talking with him. Did you tell him to not call you again?"

"Yes. I'll even block him right now."

Cash gave me my phone back and I blocked him, eager and willing to do his bidding, to show my allegiance. I had no room for any other concerns, anyone else's feelings.

Cash's rage quickly evaporated and he gathered us around and asked if we wanted drugs.

"If there's anything I'm good at, it's finding drugs," he said.

We took sacrament with the divine candy Cash both blessed and bought off the street.

"You are absolved of your sins!" I said, like the man said on the streets of Key West into the starkness of night time and like we repeated when Jacob and Lilith jumped off the dock into the starkness of the Atlantic Ocean and like we repeated to our cult when Cash cut our palms and the starkness bled out of our own blood.

"These taste like the bones of Christ!" Cash bellowed.

On drugs, on the streets, Cash and I talked about the son I was to have. Dez told us to slow down just like the lady at the bar had said one night at Fort Myers Beach. Everyone told us to slow down but we only wanted to speed up.

We crossed a bridge over Peace River.

"Take care of your own," it whispered. "And be free."

There were men with biblical names: David, Matthew, and Patrick who followed us around. Cash was enamored with King David and his own inner reflection of him. They were annoying but they still made me feel like GOD had to be with us.

Cash told me he and his brother decided I was a truth teller, that I revealed the truth. They glanced at each other, making me think they had discussed it earlier. Though Cash made all his actions seem contrived that way.

Cash was still trying to get us to the Castle. At one point we were very lost but having a blast just sitting on a corner on the sidewalk, talking and giggling together; me, JT, Cash, Dez, and Dash. Eventually we made it to the castle. There were four stories and eight different clubs inside. There was grunge, fetish, house, trance. Many people dressed like goths with chains like they worshiped demons. The castle was perfect for the end of the world. Grimy club scene, fun sounds, Cash, the best dancer knowing how to move just when the beat dropped, knew to smile at me like I was another beat he was dancing to, everyone trailing us, the boys wandering, Dez following, not really dancing, I never saw her live in the present moment.

Eventually we got back to the house and got into the time machine again. Dash was rolling hard and licking his lips, making funny noises.

Cash asked him if he wanted a girl. He nodded his head. Cash had me text and call different escort services but it was too late and no one came. Later I found out that Dash had a girlfriend.

The next morning, I woke up to Dash grabbing all my stuff, shouting, "Let's go, princess!" Cash, Dash, JT, and I headed north in Cash's big meaningless blue truck.

Dez took my car back to Fort Myers. Cash told her to get the air conditioner fixed on his dime. It would cost one thousand dollars.

Dash was excited I was coming along to the Ocala house. I was too. It'd been awhile since I'd been a part of a boys club. No matter how old you were it always felt like you were kids again playing in the neighborhood with your imaginations.

We planned to stop in Ocala for a night, drop JT somewhere in Georgia the next day, and finally, the main goal, drop Dash in Southern Tennessee with their dad.

We drove north to a new ecosystem where palm trees didn't grow. The trees that did grow grew taller. The air and the forests got cooler and lusher.

It got more southern the more North we went. We were driving through the Ocala National Forest: cleaner air, brighter greens, nicer people. Cash said there were too many people from New Jersey in Fort Myers. He said he had a theory about why people from cities are unhappy, that it's unnatural for strangers to live so close together.

I told him about the time I stopped a New Jersey woman from verbally abusing the grocery store checkout clerk.

"Excuse me," I had said, standing in line behind her with my grocery cart. "Is something the matter?"

She sneered at me, asked me how old I was, and called out to the ceiling, "Oh dear GOD! How much longer do I have to deal with this generation?"

We got to the Ocala house. It was like a cabin but modern with the smell of fresh cut wood renovations and big glass windows where forests peeked in on us.

"You shoulda seen this place when I bought it. Total crap."

Dash and JT knocked out on the couch while Cash and I went next door to visit his neighbor, Jean, to "see how he's living" a Southern phrase Cash's grandpa taught him by showing up to Cash's house without calling to check on him.

When I told Jean I was from California he rolled his eyes. "Oh, jeez," he said.

"That's what I said," said Cash.

"From the land of fruits and nuts. You like your

governor?"

"Gruesome?" I asked.

I knew how to talk to Florida people because my red family in California talked the same way. I picked up the things I'd heard them say. I knew who the enemies were and why. I knew what things made them feel what kind of way.

"Everyone is leaving California because of him," I said.

It was partially true. Lots of people were leaving California, New York, and other locked down states and going to Florida, Texas, and Tennessee where people could be free without Covid restrictions. The media called it a mass exodus.

Southerners hated the Californians. They thought they fucked everything up. I couldn't blame them. That's where Hollywood and Silicon Valley came from. The Californians would have to give up on their dreams eventually. The earthquakes, the mudslides, and the fires; they're only absolved if they leave.

I told Jean I experienced my first hurricane in Florida. He told us how tornadoes spawn off of hurricanes that come from the gulf and run rampant on the land.

Florida was wild. Everything was up for sale. We were sitting on a goldmine. Cash bought his house in the middle of the Ocala forest at 80k: a steal.

"We're out in the country," Cash told me. "We can do as we please."

I got to see real country ways with real country men.

Another thing his grandpa used to say: "All you need is a pistol and a thousand dollars." Cash showed me how to get his gun out of the glove box with the little key from his key chain. He showed me how to shoot it into the woods in his backyard. It didn't have a safety.

"Mean it! Mean it!" He snapped before I pulled the trigger.

"Now you know what to do if anything gets sketchy."

We all went to a local swimming spot called Rainbow River. The water was clear as a blue crystal.

JT sat smoking his vape on the river bed. Cash, Dash, and I swam across to the other side where there was a tree we climbed and jumped from. Cash went first and I knew I had no choice but to go next. Halfway up, I wanted to get down. I was afraid of heights. But I simply gave myself up to Cash as he coached me up. He was the light I now walked in.

When I swam to him, I told him that he could make me do anything.

"I know," he said and kissed me. He lassoed GOD's light for all of us to walk under.

If I were to lose him – there'd be darkness. I'd have to figure out how to create my own light again because I was giving it all to him. It would be possible but painful, pitiful. I didn't think I'd ever be as whole again without Cash. But I suppose there would be a sense of freedom in it.

I hypothesized a life without him to depict a confidence I wish I had. The thought of losing him appeared merely because I hadn't had him for very long, just a little over a month. I was still seducing him.

Back at the house, Cash cooked for us. "A king serves his followers," he said. After we ate, he told me to clean everything up.

Cash had anarchist texts I'd never heard of littered all over his life – at both his houses and in his truck. He was tapped into an alternative scene that I had no experience with. I opened a book randomly where the author wrote that there was no consciousness in media consumption. I liked that.

Cash let me take a historical account of squatting in Europe. I had always wanted to squat and be free of a lease. Make my good money off poetry and performance art. Or maybe find someone who could keep me in a room for cheap or sleep on some couches. That was my back up plan if Cash left me, as I feared he'd one day do.

Cash told me I didn't know real anarchy and that I spoke of libertarianism. I disagreed but I didn't say so because labels meant increasingly less anyways. You either thought for yourself or didn't. Every day I understood deeper how many of us had already chosen fascism over freedom, how it'd been that way since nearly forever. People chose their own enslavement.

We were sad for those locked up but we handled them with care and we didn't share that we were having the time of our lives because we knew they couldn't hear the music. What would Mark Twain say and Hemingway and all the masters? They'd say just as the talking sun did in Cash's vision, "Be cool." But so many people were listening to the noise, and the numbers. We sought out the unbroken and the strong.

Take care of your own. I began to cultivate this message – sent it around like I was blowing on a wish weed – spreading it around to grow. The more we were together, the more our power grew and the closer we got to GOD. Fuck the system, take care of your own, lead by example. Live the life you dream.

"I don't know about that," I said to Cash a lot. His ideas could be faulty, unfounded. I blamed them on the south. He liked to tease me about my critical race theories.

"Oh I'm sure it's all about access," he would say, whenever a ghetto black person did something stupid like bump bad music or whatever. His racism was like a spider I didn't want to squash but had to keep in check to watch where it was headed.

His southern homophobia was less unattractive. I found the whole pride movement to be obnoxious and humiliating.

"Why don't you come out with a pride candle and then release the next six deadly sins after that? Envy, greed, sloth, wrath, lust, and gluttony? Lust could come out on Valentine's Day. Gluttony on Thanksgiving. Greed on Christmas. Envy on Saint Patty's Day. Sloth on Labor Day. Wrath on Veteran's Day. You could totally troll your customers."

Cash's company was zoomer trendy. He regularly received complaints about his spirit animal line and sage candles from hypocritical white zoomers with little else to do aside from displace their feelings of inadequacy on outrage of what they deemed to be cultural appropriation of indigenous people.

I thought a seven deadly sins line would better reflect Cash's mischievous play and wit.

We hit the road again and not long into the drive, Stacey called. Cash answered and after a few minutes of listening to her yelling, bellowed, "Well, when I meet my second girlfriend, I'll be sure to introduce you," then he hung up.

We decided to keep me at mine for the next few weeks. Stacey was looking through my records and talking to my friends. Good thing I had a squeaky clean record on the internet. Cash said she used to work for the CIA.

"Keep the wolves away," played on the radio. And then, "I Will Wait" played. I looked at Cash, wondering if he was thinking about his second wife. Or maybe he saw the three of us together: a trinity; anti-societal, transcendental; and maybe, in the next global society, universal. Did it have to become a global society? Maybe. Of course. *Claro*. Of course we were on course. Of course we would take to the sea. First a dream but soon to be.

"I need you to be quiet for a while," he said, driving. "I am working. I work by thinking."

I could almost hear his mind working. It never stopped.

We drove past the most beautiful and brightest greens I had ever seen.

"Those are silos over there," he said, gesturing towards the large, round structures.

"Silos? What are they for?" I asked.

"They're used for food storage."

Back in Silicon Valley, the word silos was used to express a lack of productive connection between teams or employees at a business; corporate speak. But in the South, silos was a word for the container of life's necessities.

California was competitive; a managerial headquarters of sorts. It was easy to stay afloat in Florida. You could even drown from time to time and still survive. You didn't have much room to fuck up in California. A panic attack hovered nearby, pushing you to do more, be more: compete, create, produce. Florida was more about basic necessities, easy living, the simple life.

When it was my turn to drive, I tried to drive like a man through the state of Georgia. I told Cash I had always wanted to go mudding. I told him I loved Southern vegetables like okra. I manifested that mud and okra mere minutes later when we stopped at a market and landed in mud and found okra. Cash was mystified.

We picked up some Mayhaw jam at the market to take to his dad. The Mayhaw flower grew out of the Florida swamps just like the lotus flower.

"Maybe the Mayhaw will be on our cult crest," Cash said.

We first started noticing crests back in Key West. Then we saw them everywhere as we started coming up with our own.

JT called the police for his arrival home. When we got there, they were parked on his land where a small tin house sat. We stood by and said our goodbyes with a police car there the whole time. I didn't even bother asking about it. Cash would tell me if there was something to know.

We spent the full Libra moon on our Libra love, driving through America's heartland, filling up our hearts with miles under the moon. I thought about the dozens of moons I had seen when I was in love with someone else and before I knew about the manifestation mechanism or how true love was falling in love without boundaries, borders, obstructions; a free fall kind of love. Unconditional surrender.

Cash told me I could name the ark.

"Our ark will be called *True Love*," I declared.

"And as for our Treatise, we must always speak to the gods. We must have rituals – like the ones Cash leads all of us on, rituals that go outside time and bring people into the present moment."

When we finally got to Cash's dad's house Cash used the word reckon more, talked slower, took longer. His dad looked just like him: a full head of hair, a big grin, and sparkly eyes.

His dad shed big happy tears about how happy Cash was, how good I was to Cash and how we were going to have a beautiful life together.

"You're a fixer." he said to me. "You fix things. I'm so happy you found each other"

His dad was a jolly, funny, story-telling man who studied the bible and drank too much at the bar. Talked about GOD like he was his buddy, shared his drinking stories between winks of mischief. Cash told me he spent ten years in prison. I thought Cash's dad and mom would have burnt down any room they entered with their huge mystic energy. They must have been too much together.

We booked it on our way back down to the southern tip of Florida real quick, smoking cigarettes the whole way.

We stopped for another night at the Ocala house and he took me out on his fishing boat in the morning. When he let me drive I almost drove the boat straight into a tree but Cash saved us just in time.

"You were just writing poetry in your head." He didn't panic at all. Just did what needed to be done.

The south was manatees, alligators, turtles, and cypress trees; ghost orchid hunting, and invites to frog leg dinners.

I first started to count the hours we'd been together before realizing it'd been a whole week. We'd been together nonstop for seven days. The time passed quickly and we lived moment to moment.

Mary called him incessantly. She used an app that changed her phone number each time she called so he never knew who was calling. Random numbers flashed across his console. She was a biblical lady – texted him lots of bible quotes when he wouldn't pick up her phone calls. I read them over his shoulder when we stopped to eat meals.

"I need you to protect me," Cash said.

"Okay," I said. Inside I felt irritated but I hid it. "So then it's really over between you two?"

"I don't know," he said. "She surrendered to me. I'm

responsible for her."

His concern for her made me feel safe since I had also surrendered to him. Even when I had visions of crucifixion, when I started to wonder whether every soul would be crucified one day during my paranoiac spirals, I believed he'd still protect me.

We thought up ways to slay Stacey, the dragon. We still had hours to go driving down the state of Florida.

I read Balzac's *The Wrong Side of Paris* to him while he drove. The novel just so happened to be about a beneficent cult. I had picked it up just because I was into Balzac. Stories from the end of Napoleon's reign of the French Empire especially appealed to me as the American one dissolved. I figured it could give me an edge for the end. I'd see the signs and know when to move.

What do you do when the culture is dying? You join a cult. The people who leave cults talk about them like they didn't mean to be in them as if it was all an accident. As if they were tricked somehow. But they knew from the beginning that the whole thing was a magic trick, an experiment. It was an attempt at true love, true romance, true life. And eventually, something in them screamed, rebelled, reverted. But the sickness wasn't in the cult. The sickness was in them. The cult couldn't free them. They didn't want freedom from themselves after all. They wanted slavery to themselves, to a society drenched in cults. You break out of one and you're in another. Choose your own, transcend yourself and be free.

Aliens, devils, angels. We chose the fairy tale world to survive, to break out of the matrix.

A cult is how a new culture starts. In order to live I had to be guided by Cash and by GOD. Our connection was divine. Our cult was divine.

We scribbled out our treatise on the road. First draft, a list: rituals, sacred dance, singing, rites of passage, meditation, tai chi, yoga, archery, prayers, chanting, blessing our food and drink, mindfulness, initiation, final breaking point, gray area, liminal space, the borderlands, being sustainable and self-sufficient, studying pirates, studying icons, nurturing iconic behavior, inner eyecon, divine destruction, main thing is to keep the main thing the main thing, remembering whose show it was (it was Cash's), knowing which part of the show you were in, knowing your role in the show, traditional ideas from the golden age. We wanted to make it clear: we didn't just gain you – you gained us.

"Which tier of oppression do we try to reach?" I asked.

Cash paused for a moment. And then he picked up on my subtle notion and expanded it into an entire philosophy.

"The way I see it, there are two tiers of oppression, maybe more but we'll focus on two for now, for the sake of exploration. Each tier has its own vibration. The lower tier is concerned with the material. They are stuck in the tier of oppression chasing primal desires: security and instant gratification are at opposite ends of the same spectrum of primal desires. Shock them and you might reach them. Once you transcend the primal problems, you encounter the psychic, the second tier of oppression. There, higher forms must be wary of who they are reaching for, who they are contacting. It's an ego death but it is easy to get stuck there as the ego can also kill. Very hall of mirrors, surrealist, speaks to the subconscious. Instead of shock, these people must be reached through mythic proportions."

"And we want people on the higher tier?" I asked.

"No, little girl. We want both."

Cash showed me how to have fun with people again. I pushed people away constantly with my reading and writing and analyzing. I always felt like I had better things to do than hang out with people. He was down to hang out with whoever whenever. Every time we went out it felt like the last night on earth. We attracted a posse if we weren't already rolling with one. We made friends everywhere we went.

It was about the little things. It was about every single second. It was a different pace of life that I adored. It was one that didn't stop. It was one that kept going even when you didn't want it to. It was like he deeply understood not to take life for granted.

"You're in *my* story now," he would say. He pointed

145

out when other people tried to pull me into their story, their drama, laying it on thick so they could pull you in. I hadn't seen it that way before but now I couldn't see any other way. I felt lucky to get to be in Cash's story. It was magical, mystical. Others tried to pull you into their anxieties, their insecurities, their banal dramas, mundane depressions. But Cash lived in a castle where there was a moat of mystic music.

He claimed he was a handful but I didn't care. I was ready. I'd never been in such close proximity to greatness, to this pure of a power source; to the sun himself.

It was so alluring to live in someone else's life. I had been over everything for such a long time. If I could just participate in someone else's life story, I wouldn't have to think about my own. Cash was exactly what I had asked for. I had settled for mediocrity for so long.

And now I was protected by a holy man.

CHAPTER NINE: TWO GIRLFRIENDS, SIGILS, AND WITCHCRAFT

I got home and someone was repainting our house yellow. I hadn't been home for a week. And I wouldn't be living there much longer.

Going back to Bonita Springs after Cash's magic was, in a way, like going back to who I was before Cash, before his blessings and his untethered drive.

But every time I went back into the normal world without him, I knew I was changed. People saw my light, could feel my aura. I felt precious, protected, holy.

On a beautiful day, we looked at a yacht for sale in the Fort Myers yacht basin.

Cash told me that Mary thought he had two new girlfriends instead of just me. I asked him why she thought that.

"Because I told her so," he said.

The sun was bright, the wind was light, and my beautiful boyfriend, the cult leader, was lying again. But instead of caring, I tuned out my fears and continued living in the beautiful moment as Cash had taught. Plus we were on a yacht.

Mary wasn't out of the picture after all. Cash was priming her and had been priming me. I knew I could never believe him though I believed *in* him. I believed in him more than any dream I'd ever had. And that made up for all his guile. I didn't trust him. But I aligned to him.

"What are you envisioning for *True Love*?" Cash asked me.

"Well, I see you running around running the boat."

"That's from an ant's perspective."

"Okay, so I'm an ant then?"

"Well, what would the wisest wife say?"

I took a deep breath, concentrated, and said, "The ark is searching for true love and in doing so, brings true love to people through the freedom of the seas and pushing the limits of the self."

"Good. I like that."

He told me it was a difficult day yesterday, that he had wanted me there by his side, at his house with him. With the baby in her arms, Stacey had stormed in on the Cosmic Candles employee meeting and demanded he keep all relationships away from the business. He told her that they can discuss personal matters in private but she kept going. He excused the employees. She continued ranting and raving with the baby in her arms. Cash tried to hold the baby but Stacey screamed, saying he was breaking her arm. He stepped back. She sat down. He placed his hand on her head and fired her.

After yacht shopping, we went to my house and had sex. He said it was the first time he objectified my body. I couldn't tell the difference. The sex was as mind rocking as usual. Got put in a void. He said he summoned the gods when we made love. That really, I was making love to a GOD.

I still had the bleeding problem that started way back in Key West. Cash tried to pray it away, spoke into my womb and called her a peridot. The blood went away for a few days but then it came back again, with an orange-red spluttering, splattering vengeance.

"Something is healing inside of you," Cash said.

But he could still make me cum. We decided no more sex. Then we made love on his freshly made bed, another bloodbath.

"The come down is tomorrow," I said on the last night it was just us, the night before dinner with Mary.

"Why does there have to be a comedown?" He asked, shredding my negativity with truth. And the next day I radiated luminous energy all day just to prove him right.

When Cash critiqued me, as an acute and brilliant man must, I turned myself into the ocean. His Midheaven in Cancer and Pluto in Scorpio were his only water placements so I liked to take to the sea when he criticized me.

I was glad to be girlfriend number two and not one.

We all met at Cash's house and then drove to the restaurant together.

She wore a black cotton dress to my blue velvet. Her eyes were beady, colored a warm brown to my big ocean blue ones. Her hair was huge with curls that went all the way down her spine. Mine was cut short to my shoulders with blonde highlights, straightened and glossy with chemicals. She wore heels because she was so short. I was too close to Cash's height to be allowed to wear heels.

Mary was uncomfortable at the little restaurant we went to.

"People are looking at us," she kept saying in her raspy Southern drawl.

Cash and I smirked. We thrived in the attention, or at least Cash did so I flowed off his glow. We commanded the limelight, showed them right up front what we were all about: everything that they weren't but wanted to see. Maybe we made someone think a little more. Question something deep inside.

Cash took out gifts he got for each of us: ruby earrings for Mary, peridot for me. Mary was a Leo, fiery, sultry; the dark red ruby. I was Libran light, peaceful, creative energy: the lime yellow peridot.

"Let's go to Puerto Rico," Cash said.

"Yes!" I said.

"When?" Mary asked.

"Monday."

Monday was in three days.

"Monday? I can't go then. I have a work training," Mary said.

"Quit," Cash said.

"Quit!" I said.

"I can't do that," she said.

"Sure you can," Cash said. "You must."

"Say you're sick," I said.

"I said I was sick just the other week."

Mary dragged this on for nearly the whole dinner before she agreed to go. She could do her work training there.

After dinner, we landed on Mango Street at Lucci's. Cash's first date with both his girlfriends- of course he wanted to continue celebrating and take a victory lap at Lucci's. Cash wanted us to have a three way kiss in the truck before going inside but I jumped out, scared of the performative element, as Lucci was standing outside in front of the truck to welcome us.

Later he told me Lucci couldn't even see us in the truck and that I should always obey him.

Dez was already there sitting on the floor in Lucci's living room. She had us put Easter egg baskets together for the Easter party Cash's company was throwing the next day. All three of us had become overwhelmed with each other so we delved into the task eager to focus on something to do with our hands.

On Mango Street, everyone was excited. We all drank wine on Lucci's boat that sat in his yard. I was fiending for weed – displacing all my anxieties on the perfect high. We all chain-smoked cigarettes except Lucci who kept reminding us how much we were smoking. We chain-smoked trying to grasp the sensation, trying to meld, to burn into one another.

Cash hinted to Mary about the initiation she would have to undertake. She kept her cool and didn't ask much, knowing to wait and stay calm and cool, just like I always did. For both of us, it was a constant exercise of keeping the heart at a good beat, a good pace, so that we could keep sparkling, unbothered. Like the Thais say, *jai yen*. Cool heart.

It's trippy to see the one you love with someone else he loves. It's like seeing the past or future – like you're not even there in those in-between moments, when you disappear in their gazes at each other, their glances, their smiles, their kisses. And you want for the next time he looks over at you so that you can be alive again, you can be real, you can exist. So you're living and dying, reborn over and over; a transcendental ego end. We transmuted ourselves into the will of Cash. And he picked it all up.

Mary and Cash got into a fight and went into the other room. In the living room, drunk and stoned, I convinced Dez to drive me to Cash's house so I could sleep. It took about 20 minutes to convince her to take me and Lucci to let me go. Cash and Mary were still fighting.

As we pulled up to the house, Cash called Dez, yelled

at her, and made her take me back to Lucci's.

"I told you he would get mad at me."

"I'll tell him it was my fault," I said.

"Doesn't matter. You're gonna get me fired."

When we got back to Lucci's, I told him in the front yard how I hated conflict and that I would run away when it got tense like that.

"Just like a rabbit," he said, shaking his head but he wasn't mad. "That's just how we communicate," he added.

"Are we going to have a threesome tonight?" I asked.

"No, no, not tonight," he said and I felt so relieved.

I ran away again that night.

The three of us got back to Cash's house and got into bed. But Mary started crying in bed. Cash was cuddling me more. As he turned and comforted her, I slipped out and went to sleep in one of the guest beds, now empty since the boys had left.

In the morning, I went back into the bedroom. Mary and Cash looked stunned.

"Where'd you go?" They asked. Cash put his arms around me.

"Cash looked for you all night," Mary said, staring at me.

"I just went to sleep in the other bed."

"Don't do that again!" Cash said. "You never leave my side!"

"Okay," I shrugged, thinking that it would probably happen again.

I'd been commanded to fall in love with another my lover loved. Was I up to the task?

Cash, Stephanie, and Dez each told me they liked me more than Mary. I was pleased and suspicious.

Mary was going to be my girlfriend too. I was supposed to love her, not compete with her. Or maybe they said the same thing to her too. Cash had a lot of people working for him at all times. We all were.

What were these pages were leading up to? It was ours. It was for us – Cash corrected me when I said things were mine or if I talked about anything having only to do with me. I thought it was sweet. I was writing his story.

He said he could hear me inside his head, transcribing everything. Falling deeper into the greatest love I'd ever known. But I also needed my space. I needed my space or someone would get knives. But Cash didn't want me to need space.

Independence was a muscle I had to learn to rest. His plans and ideas seemed impossible but he had accomplished the impossible already, my gangster priest. I was in a whole new sphere of reality. We'd been looking for each other our whole lives – the philosopher's stone. And now we had a whole new world to make.

I tried to help Cash sort out his social affairs. Stacey filed a restraining order against him claiming he pushed her. She was keeping his kids from him. I could only trust my compass and let him push back if I was too forward in trying to help but I found he only ever wanted more help. He knew I was an asset.

"Oh, this is weird," he said, on a morning we were lounging on the beach.

"What?" I asked him as he looked at something on his phone.

"My mom just texted me that she really likes you. She said you're the best match she's seen for me out of all my girlfriends."

"Well, of course. We're soul mates."

"Yeah but my mom never says things like that."

His mom, Stephanie, had been living with him since she went through a break up with a man named Remmy a month ago. Cash paid her to take care of the house: the cleaning, the dishes, errands, dry cleaning, yard work, and laundry. And when he had the kids, she took care of the kids too.

Cash was rough and tough to the little boy of a friend she looked after who looked just like a little surfer angel strewn onto the beach. The young boy's father had left, and Cash said he lacked virile strength in his life. Cash said it was crucial to his development that he was exposed to a real man. He said his own nephew was timid because his father wasn't in his life either, was shy and timid. Cash never wasted an opportunity to heal masculinity.

We went to Wub night with the cult, sans Mary. Cash was taking turns with us before Puerto Rico. Everyone wanted more time with him, even Dez. But I was getting the most time. I knew it was because I was sparkly and new. So I sparkled like the fucking moon.

"Are you swooning over me?" He asked as his eyes scanned the room as usual. He was grinning. He was right, I was swooning. He left me to talk to another woman and I danced to the grungy dubstep, dancing with my shadow side, my jealousy.

We were sitting at the bar when a man started talking to me. I turned to introduce him to Cash but when I turned back the man had quickly turned away.

"How rude," I said to Cash. "He only had interest in me until he found out I had a boyfriend."

"No, he's being respectful," Cash said.

Cash thought women shouldn't have guy friends. Every time a guy texted me I would have to say goodbye to him once Cash saw. He looked through my phone at intervals. I didn't mind. I understood his reasoning. I knew they all wanted to fuck me anyways. All my ex-boyfriends had only pretended they didn't care about my guy friends. Cash took no shit and I respected him for that. He knew how to lay down the law.

"We need a front for the cult," Cash said. We talked about opening a rock climbing gym, a coffee truck, or a kava bar.

We talked about the potential of Fort Myers. Cash's house was right next to downtown but still in the hood. In a few years it would be prime real estate once the neighborhood gentrified. His house had already tripled in price from when he bought it a couple years ago.

"We're sitting on a goldmine."

Herds of people were moving to Florida from all

across the country.

Cash took me to Green Lizard Kombucha. We met and spoke to one of the owners about sharing the space with his candle company. Afterwards, he told me she had been trying to have an affair with him even though she ran the business with her husband.

There were a bunch of little businesses booming in Southwest Florida. And everyone was helping each other along on their small business journeys. They all considered themselves quite incredible and capable. Everybody knew it was a gold mine situation. But they made sure to keep up with their soap opera drama.

We'd been seeing a lot of Chinese people around – Cash said he'd never seen so many in all of the eight years he'd been living in Fort Myers. We figured they came for the real estate boom. We were in the midst of massive change. We counted the shortages like stars in the sky: chicken wings, toothpaste, wax, wood, napkins.

And yet so much stayed the same: like the people in power.

"Look into Big Sugar. Then you'll see who really owns this state," Cash said.

For Puerto Rico, on the morning of the day before our flight, Mary's sister, a nurse, took all three of our Covid tests for us. We all tested negative. Cash had to pay $700 to the government so that we could use the tests for our flight.

"I'd like to follow that money," Cash said.

After the swabs, the three of us went our separate ways. Cash went to the Easter event for his company, Mary went to a hair appointment, and I went to my permaculture club.

My friends, Ashley and Leslie, ended up abandoning me that afternoon. They said I was messing with darkness in the cult. They couldn't associate with me anymore, not with that energy.

"Be careful out there. Not everyone is good." They both bit their lips, trying not to cry.

We were outside of the house we had just been

gardening at in our permaculture club. I had just invited them to go to lunch with Cash and I.

I laughed at them. I told them I'd make it up to them, figured they were just upset I had blown them off the weekend before when I went to St. Pete with Cash. I thought they were being dramatic and stupid. I told them they didn't have to break up with me if they didn't want to.

But they both looked at me with whirlpool eyes and I knew the friendship was over. I knew I wouldn't be able to take them seriously anymore. They had whirlpool heads, so concerned with their own emotions that their whole world was underwater, unclear. Fucking Cancers.

I went to meet Cash for lunch on my own. Dez was there. They had just come from the Cosmic Candles Easter event. Stacey didn't show up at all and Cash still didn't get to see his kids.

When I told Cash that my friends broke up with me, he immediately comforted me. He was good at that. He said when he looked into Ashley's eyes during the eye gazing ceremony there was nothing there but emptiness. He thought she didn't have a soul.

Ashley was spacey and easily affected by external circumstances. She certainly didn't have a strong soul. But I had found her friendship deep and meaningful. She gave me lots of presents and made me laugh.

"Maybe you shouldn't tell people about our cult," Dez said.

"They're just jealous," Cash said.

Cash and I went back to his house. Dez went to run some errands for Cash.

Cash took a call and I asked him what it was for.

"It's our fun things," he sang-songed. "Pure grade MDMA."

In bed, I fell asleep with my mouth on his opal ring.

We woke up from our nap and it was time to go shopping for Puerto Rico with Dez on Cash's credit card. Mary's hair appointment was taking too long so she wasn't joining us. She was going to stay with Cash that night. I was going to sleep at Dez's. But I wanted to be with Cash that night.

"You've had a lot of time with Cash," Dez said when she came into the room to get us out of bed.

"Let me talk with her," Cash said to her.

Dez went to smoke a cigarette on the porch.

Still sitting together on his bed, Cash told me a story about wanting a puppy.

"You want a puppy so bad. You even come up with a name. You know where you're going to have it sleep, you know what you're going to feed it. You worked an extra paper route so that you could buy it and take care of it. You've told everyone about this puppy you are going to get, what it will look like, what you're going to name it. But when you get the puppy, you realize it's not what you thought it would be like. You aren't as happy as you thought."

"What does that mean?" I asked.

"Your subconscious understands," he said.

Cash was always telling stories like that. Another time he told me how he wanted a man in his neighborhood to stop speeding. Obviously, it bothered him because he had his young daughter running around and it made him nervous for her safety. But instead of telling the man to slow down, which could possibly provoke him or make him defensive or even make him drive faster, Cash bought a carton of eggs. He drew faces on the eggs with a black sharpie. Then, in the middle of the night, he dropped each egg on the dashboard of the man's car, letting them crack and splatter yoke all over the place. He never caught the man speeding again. And Cash never had to say a single word to him.

I felt sick, sort of queasy. I was sitting on Cash's porch, smoking a cigarette with Dez. Cash handed me a smoking stick of Palo Santo and an emerald.

"Hold onto these," he said. Then he drew large symbols on the driveway with the burnt black part of another stick of Palo Santo.

"What is that?" I asked.

"Sigils," he said. "To ward off bad spirits. You can hold

159

onto the emerald for now."

I got into Dez's car still feeling terrible. I thought maybe it was all the drama with my friends.

"Put your feelings into my hand," Dez said.

Then she acted like she was tossing them out the window.

"All gone!"

Then we were in Express and she had me try on a bunch of clothes she thought Cash would like. As we were checking out, I had to run outside to throw up. I threw up all over a Jeep. Dez ran across the street and got me some water. I sat there on the sidewalk for a while, feeling better than I did before but exhausted because it was more throw up than I'd ever thrown up in my life.

At Dez's house, I threw up three more times. I was worried I wasn't going to make it to Puerto Rico. Dez took care of me, brought me coconut water and a smoothie.

That was when I first experienced Mary's witch powers.

Cash told me she was a witch, back when she was the "ex-girlfriend" not the "other girlfriend." That she killed her last two boyfriends and was attacked by spirits when they went to visit the Indian burial grounds. But he said that back when Mary was just an idea and I had never met her and didn't think I ever would.

So I figured it was food poisoning from the jambalaya soup I had at lunch. I forgot he told me she was a witch. He told me so long ago, or at least it felt that way. So much was always happening.

CHAPTER TEN:
PUERTO RICO, LSD,
AND SATURN

But I got better. And I made it on the flight.

In the air, I realized I had no idea where Puerto Rico even was. I thought it was near Mexico. I looked at it on GoogleMaps. It was in between the Dominican Republic and the US Virgin Islands.

The vibes were off in Puerto Rico. We were spoiled in Florida. In Puerto Rico, we had to wear masks everywhere. And most of the businesses were shut down, including the salsa clubs. But we made our own vibe. And what a vibe, dressed to the nines, polished footwear, heavily adorned with jewelry, anointed with oil. Our hair was undone, wild, free.

Dez booked an incredible Airbnb for us. It was an estate with ocean views and a pool. It looked like a castle. There was a labyrinthine of rooms filled with statues, handmade fabrics, relics, and antiques.

When we first got to our room, the three of us made love together and I thought it sweet to see the happiness, like sunlight on Cash's face. He beamed, energized, whole. He had been waiting for this moment for so long. I was happy for him.

In bed, Mary and Cash were rough together. She would moan, "Harder, harder!" and he'd slap her face. He told her to eat me out while he fucked her. Later he said I wasn't as freaky as Mary, and no, I definitely wasn't, I agreed. There was no pain in that though, even when I heard them fucking. It was just a whole new world. It was a practice in selflessness. I felt myself getting stronger, more powerful as I said no to jealous thoughts.

Sometimes he surprised her with his dick in her ass. Sometimes she surprised him with her tongue in his. I wanted no part.

Between the three of us, I was so docile. Maybe that was because Cash told me things and did things, like cum inside me to make my mind right. He didn't ever cum inside Mary and it made her upset, amping up their weird kinks.

I sent a mirror selfie to my lesbian friend in California.

"You look like you're getting fucked good," she said.

"I am. I just had my first threesome with our

girlfriend."

"You had sex with a woman?" She asked.

"I guess you could call it that but it didn't really feel like sex with a woman."

"Are you devaluing the LGBTQ experience?"

"No, I'm just speaking of my own experience."

We went to the pool which was small and surrounded by busts and the heads of statues. It felt antiquated, like we were traveling backwards to a more elegant, sophisticated time.

I started snapping photos of Cash and Mary with my DSLR. Cash took the camera after a while and began directing us into different positions. He was particular with his direction, intensely focused. He had a vision for everything and knew how to orchestrate it, how to make it happen.

There was a little window leading into an untended underground bar next to the pool.

"Go get us some drinks," Mary said to me, giggling. I accepted her dare and crawled through the window from the pool and took out a bottle of cava from a mini fridge. We all took swigs out of the bottle, using it as a prop in our photo shoot.

Cash and I went into the underground bar from a different entrance as Mary stayed in the pool smoking a cigarette. I was looking for more cava and he wanted to see the room.

There was a beautiful mirror that told me to take my clothes off so I did and Cash took pictures of me from behind. No one had ever taken photos of me naked before. Looking back at those photos, I look beautiful, timeless. For no one's eyes but Cash's.

Cash took his clothes off and I snapped shots of him sitting at a dining table with a cigarette under a chandelier. It was our own moment, just for us.

He commanded me sternly as I took his photo.

"Don't yell at me," I said.

"I'm not yelling, I'm passionate!" He yelled.

I did not want him to speak to me the way he spoke

to Mary or Dez. I never wanted to be disrespected the way he disrespected them. He could be short with them, irritated, impatient. He insulted them when he was most frustrated. I didn't blame him so much as they were pretty batty but his irritation made them even less competent.

Cash said that in ancient times, the ways of the warrior were two modes: leisure and preparing for war. So we plotted for war poolside: the battle for the children and the battle for the business. He wanted to make a documentary in the middle of all this shit, to reveal the truth behind alleged narcissist claims and the ugly side of feminism.

"If there is one thing I'm good at, it's making money," Cash said.

He talked about starting a new business in Puerto Rico somewhere, a hostel perhaps, or a kava bar, something Mary and I could run while he went back and forth on the mainland between his kids and us.

Cash's got tanks of angels, a hotline to GOD, and a mind so pretty it'd make a war criminal cry. We were going through spiritual warfare but we knew we'd be alright. I felt like crying a lot but I stayed strong and centered, all for Cash. I stayed focused on the prize: Cash's heart forever.

I looked up their birth charts. All three of us had our Venus in Virgo, quite a feat as we were all born years apart: aged 29, 32, and 36.

In a threesome there are times when you want to run away, but that was how I had always felt about everything anyways. I tended to scamper off like the rabbit I was from time to time no matter what the circumstance.

My Berkeley-brained ex and his circle of friends taught me how to argue, dispassionately and detached in a sophisticated manner. I used to argue aggressively like Cash, throwing insults to weaken my opponent, sneering, excited and passionate. The ways my corporate BLM ex reformed me were elaborate and elegant. All that time I was being prepared to handle and be handled by Cash. We couldn't both be so passionate.

But when he wasn't arguing or delegating, Cash

spoke softly. I heard that was what the powerful did, so that everyone listened carefully. Nothing was more powerful than being listened to.

Cash referred to himself as, "our humble narrator," or "your dear narrator." Sometimes he called himself "papa," like "papa's tired."

I think we weirded people the fuck out in San Juan. They weren't receptive to our magic. We waited everywhere for hours, the Puerto Rican pace for white people.

On Wednesday, our usual cult meeting day, we facetimed the cult: Dez, Matt, JT, and Lucci. Everyone's faces lit up on the screen. I loved them all so much. Cash took care of his circle and didn't worry about anyone else.

"Love people like you're getting paid to do it. It's the easiest job in the world," was his mantra.

One morning we woke up and took LSD before going to the Spanish fort.

I put on denim cutoffs and a white crop top.

Mary looked at Cash for his reaction to my outfit, "Really?" she asked him.

"What?" I said.

"Cash never lets me dress like that," she said.

"It's fine just this once. For Puerto Rico," he said.

Mary put on her own denim cutoffs and a white crop top. Sister wives vibes.

"But for your birthday, I'm buying you tons of prairie dresses," Cash said. "I want you to start dressing like a lady. Look through womens' fashion from the 1950s. That's how you should dress."

Cash hated slutty dressing on girls and women. He thought it made men weak, as they had to fight their lustful thoughts and waste energy.

Cash was teaching me to be more cognizant of the effect I had on men as a woman. Since twelve, I had fought for my right to dress as a slut only to realize, nearing thirty, I had been conned. The media conditioned women and girls to seek attention through provocative clothing resulting in compromised feminine values.

Cash said he had to be the father in his love which was different from the maternal love.

"Like Saturn?" I asked, thinking of Goya.

"Yes. I don't know how you would understand people without astrology."

I started to notice all the mannequins at the mall dressed like hookers. Fashion ripped off and commodified the most vulnerable populations. Today's trends ripped off gold chains, booty shorts, halter tops, crop tops, and ripped denim. If you knew how to look, women under the spell of these trends suddenly all looked like cheap hookers. It was bleak.

At the fort, Cash bought us a kite and three Pina Coladas.

A truck full of people drove by and yelled at us, "Welcome to Puerto Rico!"

Mary yelled back, "We're from here!"

She could be quick and fun. I was happy that Cash fell in love with her. She deserved it.

Mary took the kite and ran it and I took the handle and flew it up. It took us two tries to get it up. I flew it high, high, high until someone else drove their kite into it. It fell near a cliff, a good quarter of a mile away. I ran to it, picked it up and held it over my head running back. It all felt victorious and virtuous.

Cash told us that he was going to marry us in every country but the next day he told me she wasn't the one. He said he was done with her. He said I was the one.

When I gave him a look, he just said, "What?! I'm giving you a story!" And he was right about that. The main thing is to keep the main thing the main thing. I didn't believe a word he said.

I still loved him though. I couldn't believe how obsessed I was with him. Even just looking at his stupid backpack lying on the floor that night, I felt deep things.

It was all kind of dumb but I was intrigued, stimulated. I would wonder - was any of this actually going to happen? His mind moved so fast.

I picked up on Mary's language. She was certainly redneck. I wanted to be the cultured one. I let my start up corporate show off talk come out. She would sing along to a hip hop song, saying something slutty and I'd catch Cash's eye and we'd exchange looks. She was trashy but cute and entertaining. I climbed higher in value on my emphasis of intelligence, coolness, and class.

"Well aren't you so sophisticated," Cash teased me, or, "Oh hey, cool kid." He knew exactly what I was doing.

I never allowed Mary's nervous energy to get to me. I always looked at her through glass. She got into lots of little moods, little fits. Cash had to go collect her at times. I just chilled. I knew it was worse for her, being the first one.

Cash struggled with us. "Maybe it's because you're trying to fit together two different realities," I told him. He laughed at me, called me, "little girl."

Through Mary, I saw Cash's shadow side. I wondered if he would ever treat me the way he treated her. He told me she was the reason he started smoking cigarettes, which he said he had never smoked before, though I saw he held a cigarette in an older photo on social media. But whatever. I knew he lied to everyone else, why wouldn't he lie to me?

We were all on cocaine, waiting for hours at a restaurant for someone to serve us. Cash and I went outside to have a cigarette.

Cash told me Mary was annoying him. She kept leaving, upset, making Cash follow her and bring her back. He complained about her a lot. I found it exhaustingly annoying but it also gave me hope that he would leave her and I would finally have him all to myself. I just had to stay patient.

We strategized about how to enter the mythos in Puerto Rico with Mary.

"We're in the ethos," he groaned.

He told me he felt like he was still chasing me, that I didn't belong to him yet. It reminded me of when my ex told me I wasn't ever going to be satisfied- that he could tell I would always be searching for something.

I didn't know what to tell Cash but mostly I was just glad to be in Puerto Rico practicing my Spanish and surfing.

On our last morning in San Juan before we set off for the West Coast, Cash and Mary went looking for food and dropped me off in an alley for coffee. Mary was constantly hungry and ate lots of snacks and candy. I ate like a bird but I needed coffee every morning.

Since Covid happened, everything was possible and everything was up for interpretation, even eating. Three meals a day was just part of the consumerist conditioning. I needed much less food than I once thought. Especially since living in Florida – I rarely ate more than one meal a day as if the warm weather was more nourishing than food. I always liked humidity, the way the air was thick and warm.

In the alley, while waiting for my coffee I met a drunkard who told me he was a Kung Fu master and he showed me some moves. I told him we were on our way to surf at Rincón. He told me that the word *rincón* meant a boxer's strategy for cornering another.

When Cash and Mary came back with their food, I introduced them and told them what the man had said and that he taught me a Kung Fu move. Cash started fucking with him.

"*Lleno de chistosos, siempre chistosos*," I told the poor man, "Full of jokes, always joking."

"He is very wise," the drunken Kung Fu master said in Spanish, "like an owl."

It was true. Cash was an owl. That was his spirit animal.

When I first moved to Bonita Springs, I set about looking for owls. I saw one in Koreshan Park, where the Koreshan cult used to live. I was running through the bamboo forest when I stopped and looked straight into the eyes of an owl sitting on a branch. And then a month later I met Cash, the owl cult leader.

We ate some edibles for the road and drove to the west side of the island. Mary and I traveled in long, bohemian dresses. Cash wore bright floral button downs, gold chains, pastel pants and a black hat. We looked just like a cult.

On the way we stopped at an overlook. Cash took a photo of Mary and I. We looked at it on his phone.

"See, there's my adorable, loving Mary looking at me and smiling. And there's Maria looking GOD knows where at GOD knows what."

I was looking out at the ocean as Mary posed for the shot. I didn't know Cash was taking a photo.

I figured he was projecting back at the restaurant when he said I was always searching for something. He was the one who couldn't enjoy our time alone and wanted to have Mary too.

Cash played a lot of 90s music. It added to his timelessness. Or maybe it was a Florida thing because my roommate, Karen, did the same thing. We listened to 90s love songs driving through the island.

Before we went surfing, Cash and I did some yoga on the beach. We tried to get Mary to join us but she was in a mood. Then Cash had to take a phone call.

Mary and I went to get drinks at a beach bar. Mary always ordered things obnoxiously with lots of specifics and preferences. I could either be embarrassed or laugh at her. I chose the latter and made fun of her in Spanish with the staff.

We took tabs of acid and got into the ocean with our rented surfboards. We surfed for hours. Mary got out and it was just Cash and me for a while. I saw turtles but Cash didn't believe me. Walking out of the ocean, I looked at him and remembered the acid we took when I saw that he was the same color as a rainbow. Cash said we didn't trip while we were surfing because surfing is tripping. We laughed and laughed. And then we had to go find Mary.

We collected Mary, who got yelled at by Cash for wandering, and then we bought some coconuts off the side of the road and maybe it was the LSD, but each coconut had different water flavors. Mary was frustrated. She didn't like any of the coconut flavors after trying all three and that made Cash and I crack up. I was laughing so hard I started to choke.

Cash snapped at Mary, "*Stop it.*" My choking stopped. We got to the Airbnb and Mary went inside.

"She's mad," Cash said.

"Is she? I didn't think so," I said.

"I love how naïve you are," he said.

Cash set up doses of MDMA for us and then, as the sun went down, we sat in the Jacuzzi in the mountains looking out at an impossible sky and for the first time in my life, I didn't want to die like I usually did taking LSD, didn't have the same ego death war, the same back and forth of whether to stay on this planet, didn't need the coercion to fall back in love instead of taking this grand play for granted, this place, this planet, these people.

Instead, I was just happy to be alive – so simply divine, with so much beauty. I didn't have to struggle with myself to whip up a desire to be there. I simply wanted it. I didn't feel tired or bored or frustrated. I felt complete and completely enamored, like royalty, like the great kings and queens who had once lived in honor to proclaim beautiful, reverent truths. I felt every cell shining and glittering like the peridot I wore in my ears that he gave me.

I was in Cash's light. I'd given it all to Cash's plan, Cash's world.

For so long I had been ready to die but then Cash came along and offered me a better ride.

I sang Lana songs to the two of them in the Jacuzzi. Cash liked them all except for the song "High by the Beach."

You can be a bad motherfucker, but that don't make you a man.
Now you're just another one of my problems. 'Cause you got out of hand.
We won't survive. We're sinking into the sand.
All I wanna do is get high by the beach, get high by the beach, get high.
All I wanna do is get high by the beach get high baby baby bye bye.
The truth is I never bought into your bullshit
when you would be too good to me 'cause I knew that,
all I wanted to do was get high by the beach get high baby baby bye bye.

He told me never to sing it again.

"Yeah, that wasn't a very nice one," I agreed.

Cash put on an electric song with his speaker that sounded like cinnamon smells.

Mary got out because she was so cold and went to put clothes on while Cash and I stayed in the water.

I went over to Cash and wrapped my arms around him, squeezing him tight. And then it felt like GOD's arms were around the two of us, squeezing us even tighter. I felt so clean and pure and holy like we were bathing in the light from GOD's smile. I felt Him beaming at me, angling the sun to shine directly at me. The ocean looked impossibly silky underneath a velvet sky.

"Can I trust you?" Cash asked me.

"Yes," I said, beaming.

"It's impossible for you to understand how much I have to lose," he said.

Though I was boggled by my smallness to him, my uprootedness, I had more freedom. I could hear him arguing with my interpretation of freedom inside my own head, that without ties I wasn't free, I was lost, and therefore, enslaved. Or perhaps it was my own voice. As we became one it became harder to tell the difference of what was me and what was him inside my own head.

I saw Cash's face in the sun – smiling, laughing, joking, grinning, teasing. I saw Cash's face in the dark – smirking, smoldering, mean, disgusted, turned on.

"You can trust me," I said.

"Okay," he said.

I said something silly and laughed at myself, splashed around, getting lost in the MDMA feelings.

"But you can tell what she is, right?" Cash's voice was suddenly stern and he was looking at me intently.

"No. What is she?" I asked.

"I can't say," he said.

"Faerie? Elf? Gremlin? Pixie?"

"I can't believe you don't see it. Especially how she looks right now."

Mary came back outside with a towel hooded around her. She looked like a witch. And then I remembered. He

173

told me before that she was a witch, that she had killed her last two boyfriends.

She made me sick the day before Puerto Rico and she choked me earlier in the car.

I was now in Cash's mythos more than ever before, really believing.

My eyes went wide. He grinned.

I knew he was engineering me with lies and illusions. But I needed his engineering so that I could break away from societal engineering. Every lie he embroidered was threaded with truth that led me out of the lies I had grown up on. But it was getting harder to know where the engineering stopped and reality started.

And then I found out he didn't take any MDMA.

"He does that sometimes," Mary said.

We all went out to find some fun. Cash quickly learned how to navigate the maze of a route that took us from our Airbnb atop a mountain to the main road along the valley, sans GPS.

Mary and I giggled in the car when Cash asked us for the cigarettes, the lighter, the weed, the CBD, the water, more petting, more kisses. Because we both had the same thought: we were starting to see why two girlfriends for a man like Cash was such a good idea. He was a handful.

Standing in line for smoothies and milkshakes, we met a couple who asked us if we were sisters.

"That's our boyfriend," we said, pointing at Cash who was in a chocolate store.

"See babe? We should be a thrupple," the girl said immediately.

I hated the word, "thrupple." It sounded like a cheap millennial commodification of our beautiful and elegant world.

"But then I'd get too jealous," she said.

Yeah, no shit, I thought.

Now look at me: a single week of being one of three and I was a changed woman. Cash was right about the power of a trip to Puerto Rico.

The couple invited us out to a bar with them but Cash wanted to go back to the Airbnb so that Mary and I could give him a massage. He flipped a coin to decide. The coin said we go back to home base.

"Next time," he told the couple.

When we got to our room he told me to get more pillows out of one of the other bedrooms. We had rented the entire house out and slept in a different one of the four bedrooms each night.

I grabbed my face moisturizer to use for impromptu massage oil: Egyptian Magic.

When I came back to the room, Cash had a movie playing. I was immediately pulled in. It was quick, witty, dark, and brutal. It was called *Swordfish*. Cash said it was his favorite movie.

In Swordfish, Gabriel Shear is a powerful titan of organized crime. But what the layman might deem as narcissistic, sociopathic behavior, the mythos suggests Gabriel works towards a higher calling, a true purpose, a hero's journey. Gabriel transcends normal and mundane morality and walks the path of the true icon, above good and evil, above systemic justice. He answers to no one but himself and fulfills no other mission but his own.

It was about the fight for America's freedom through being as rich as possible. Maybe the elites were the good ones. Nobody really knows who's actually fighting who. So we have to make up our own concepts of good and evil.

And from the crux of *Swordfish*, "We are at war... with anyone who infringes on America's freedom: terrorist states. Someone must take their war to them. They bomb a church, we bomb ten. They hijack a plane, we take out an airport. They execute American tourists, we tactically nuke an entire city. We must make terrorism so horrific that it becomes unthinkable to attack Americans."

We were all in it together. We felt insidious forces at play, making up the world, constructing the illusion. We reacted in extremes, lived in extremes. The only fight there ever was had always been about freedom. Now I recognized that the only fight I needed to fight was the one for my self, for my soul.

For us, Cash's voice inside my head adds.

Cash said all his passwords contained the word *swordfish*. He said it was a statement.

You can see a lot of people in their favorite movies. I saw Cash in Travolta's Gabriel easily. He was Swordfish and so was his life. So then it was also my life.

We were leaving the logos to live in the mythos as icons. I'd been on the path for a long time - I just didn't know what it was until I met Cash. But as everything crumbled and as more people lost the plot and fell into mass psychosis the more I could see that it had been spiritual warfare all along.

"He exists in a world beyond your world. What we only fantasize about, he does. He lives a life where nothing is beyond him. But it is all an act. For all his charm and charisma, for all his wealth and expensive toys, beneath it all he is a driven, unflinching, calculating machine, who takes what he wants when he wants, then disappears."

Cash saw how quickly I gravitated towards the message of the movie. I told him I wish I had seen *Swordfish* years ago.

"You need to read Nietzsche's *Thus Spoke Zarathustra* and Plato's *The Republic* again," he said.

During his massage, with me on his back and Mary on his feet and legs, Cash checked our departure flight and said we were leaving tomorrow "at high noon."

I had no idea how that happened as it felt like we just got there. I guessed it was all the drugs. Cash decided to extend our trip one more night.

"We should always have a day of rest before we end our trips," he said. "You're going to love the next hotel."

On the drive back to San Juan, we stopped at a cave. Cash was thrilled to go inside; said he hadn't been inside a cave for years.

"Maybe I'm the only one excited about this," he said. He always wanted his enthusiasm to be matched.

"Yes! I'm so excited!" I said to make him happy. I was

excited but not as excited as him.

We took more edibles and I got super high. I was giggling and laughing and joking as the cave guide spun her spiel. Cash laughed and laughed at me, the sweetest sound.

Before we got inside the cave, Cash got a phone call. I had a sense of foreboding. I worried something happened to his children. As he listened, I prepared myself to comfort him, to stay grounded, to find a sense of calm before disaster struck.

But it was a call from one of his employees.

Somehow Stacey found out that Cash was in Puerto Rico. She was flipping out. She was starting a new crystal pyramid candle company and was trying to get other employees from Cosmic Candles to go with her.

The social media manager quit and gave Stacey the password and username for the Cosmic Candles Instagram. That was where their hundreds of thousands of followers were and a big piece of what made their company so profitable.

She took a photo off Cash's personal Instagram of Mary, Cash, and I and reposted it with her own caption: Abusive Narcissist wants Two Wives. And then she quoted his caption, "'*We are aesthetic fascists and we are not on your side.*' Hey, you posted this, not me."

The guide and the group were waiting for him to get off the phone. He finally got off and the little crowd continued on into the cave.

The three of us held hands as Cash said a prayer before we followed the group. When we came out of the cave, Cash said he was a new man. Said he was prepared for battle.

He got another phone call and this time it was Stacey's step dad, Greg. He was yelling at Cash. Cash went into a southern accent and spoke calmly to him, mob boss style. Greg wanted him to give Stacey money for Cosmic Candles.

"There are three sides to every story, Greg. Hers, mine, and the truth."

When we got back to San Juan, in the bougie boutique hotel Cash got for us on the water of the bay, we took more drugs.

On the balcony at the hotel, with the setting sun, I told Cash and Mary about the time I woke up in a hotel room on a family vacation in the middle of the night, in a cot, with my mom and dad sleeping in one bed and my sister in the other.

That night I had felt GOD speaking to me, telling me that the seven deadly sins were real and that I should take them seriously. I remember being afraid for the world, for all the people who thought backwards. I felt saved since I knew the truth.

I also told them about the time I closed myself off to GOD, to the universe. I was so depressed and at such a low point, I couldn't handle what the universe said to me when it wanted to talk to me.

At a bookstore, someone asked if I wanted to guess the password to get into the secret room of books. I said I wasn't ready. I said I could barely even eat breakfast that morning.

Cash asked me about the Zoloft he found in my bag. I was scared and told them everything about it, the mental health startup, the effects, and the way I hadn't been taking it consistently for weeks.

We poured my Zoloft out into the bay. I didn't know Zoloft was psychotropic until Cash told me it was. I didn't believe him until I googled it. I used to give psychotropics to all the traumatized, abused foster kids I worked with.

"You're a taker," Cash said to me as the three of us sat by the water.

I thought it was a test but I started to cry anyways.

"And tomorrow, we're going our separate ways," he announced.

Was he dropping a coin into the well of our womanly abyss in order to hear the watery sound of compassion?

Mary looked at me with big, confused eyes. It all felt despicable and cruel. It turned out he was just testing us. He just wanted to see where we were at.

Again, he hadn't taken any drugs.

My crying turned to sobbing. I couldn't stop. It was all so cruel.

"You're on a loop," Cash said.

He made us get up and go walking into the baby blue evening.

He tried comforting me. He made jokes. Mary was especially sweet to me. It took time to crawl out of the pain. We walked around downtown and I slowly came out of it.

It was April 2021 and San Juan was mostly shut down because of the pandemic, the bars, the restaurants, the shops. But people still roamed the streets drinking, smoking, playing music and partying as police cars drove around surveilling, stopping sometimes to tell people to disperse if a group got too big or too concentrated.

We sat down in a grassy area to observe, smoking cigarettes and drinking wine. Mary and I sang "King of the Road."

Trailer for sale or rent.
Rooms to let for fifty cents.
No phone, no pool, no pets.
I ain't got no cigarettes.

It was a song my dad used to sing to me and Mary was the first person I met who knew it too.

I went to buy more cigarettes. When I got back to them on the grass, they were both looking at me intently.

"When you go off on your little adventures, when you go around doing your little tasks, socializing or whatever, Mary is going to start going with you."

Mary and I looked at each other.

"You're kind of…naïve. You shouldn't be alone."

"Okay," I said.

I had traveled on my own to over a dozen countries but I didn't mind. I liked the idea of being innocent and sweet, though I didn't believe I was either of those things. I knew how to act that way though and I guess that's how Cash and Mary saw me. I liked being babied too. My life had been a long show of keeping peoples' expectations low.

In my journal he wrote: *I didn't want to write in your book. I couldn't stop reading and the only way to stop is to write.*

I'm sitting on the rooftop of this bougie-ass hotel contemplating how cold the water is. People on vacation all look the same from up here: their new sunglasses and sandals.

Anyway, I love you. Every day I fall in deeper.

I'm a wee bit afraid you might break this humble narrator's heart. I feel like you are always searching for something. It's like you haven't stopped to celebrate finding what may be the greatest something we get to find. I just want to take a moment and be there.

I can't believe how much I love you. I see your soul. I think we're perfect for one another. There are times when our eyes (souls) meet and I swear I can perceive 50 lifetimes together. All around us I see us meeting, loving, fighting, and dying, a gazillion frames per second, 50 lives, one story. I trust you. I haven't trusted a woman since the 80s. Please never lie to me or ignore me. It's really all I ask.

As you may now know I'm a master manifester and so are you! As GOD reveals my future, I want you at my side through war.

Cash kept using me for a vacation but I needed to be used for war. His Mars was in Aries. Mary and mine: Scorpio. Scorpio and Aries, the two most battle-ready signs of all, holding the planet of war, we had battle instincts. It was time to take Stacey down. She was using the Cosmic Candles logos and content for her new company, had stolen the million dollar Instagram account, was trying to steal employees, and she was using their children to try to get his money.

Mary wanted to kill Stacey but I told her we couldn't if we wanted to get into heaven.

Cash and I read Jung on the plane back to Florida, learning how to balance our shadow sides, and preparing for battle – for the kids, for the business, for our family, for our new way of living. Piece by piece, we were creating a new world. Mary slept.

My parents bought plane tickets soon after I told them I had met "the one," and that he had children from a former relationship. They argued with me, sent me articles about why you shouldn't date people with children, and then they bought plane tickets to Florida.

We plotted out my parents' visit, their entire week. He cared so much, wanted everything to be perfect for them. We plotted out the days hour by hour. He gave 100% to everything, from commanding me to pleasing me.

Cash had been right about Mary, about the three of us. He was a lot to handle but split between the two of us, we could manage. I loved Mary and she loved me. We even had the same soles: size six. We shared our clothes and shoes like sister wives.

When we got back to Florida, we stopped at a bar near the Fort Lauderdale airport before driving back to Fort Myers. We all got White Rascals beers to celebrate our return. The logo read, "mischief, authentic, zesty." Cash said I was mischief, Mary was zesty, and he was authentic.

We got back to the house and made love with our third, our firework, our louder love, our sunbeam. The three of us devoted to falling deeper into love: Mary was fire, Cash was air, and I was water and earth.

Cash decided Mary and I were going to work for him at the factory since he lost his social media manager and Mary got fired for missing the work training to go to Puerto Rico and I was going to quit Americorps. Cash said he liked for his girlfriends to be unemployed.

We went to the factory the day after we got back. Mary and I sat on the bean bag giggling about something until he told us what to do. We felt like a novelty with our sister wives vibes.

We worked on emails for hours until it was time to leave. I felt close to her and loved being around her. But I still would have preferred Cash to myself, isn't that funny?

At night after working at the factory, we watched old movies.

"See watch how the girl takes care of her man? That's a good girl. That's a good wife. Nothing's more important to her than her man. That's how I want you to be."

I wanted to be a good wife. I was finally learning how. I was never told that was my role. I hadn't been told what my role was. All I knew was that I loved him and that I didn't care about anything anymore. Just him.

When we first dated, he was more boyish, charming, playful, flirty. Now he was becoming more fatherly, mature, and controlling. I'd noticed he was falling more and more into a gentleman's southern accent. He had a love for Saturn the father.

Mary told me there were different sides to Cash that I would have to get used to.

"You'll see. He likes to be a lot of different people," she'd say when we drove the long way to the factory in her car so we could talk about him and smoke as many cigarettes as we pleased.

When we drove around in the truck, Cash made Mary switch seats with me so that I'd be up front with him sometimes. She always tried to milk it and stay up front with him longer though we were supposed to share the time equally. I didn't really care. Sitting in the back I could look at my phone and write. Cash hated whenever I used my phone.

But then the following week, Cash spent almost all his free time with me and my visiting parents.

Out of spite, Mary went to hang out with Lucci alone. Cash broke up with her after that.

CHAPTER ELEVEN:
PUBLIC LOVE,
AND ADAM CURTIS

Cash texted me and told me he broke up with Mary again and then she walked into the restaurant I was at with my parents. Cash wove thick interdimensional webs around all of us. We were all deeply connected.

I hugged her. She was shaking like she needed alcohol or drugs. But she always vibrated like that when she was nervous, which was most of the time.

Her skin was ashy and dry. Her coveted lion's mane was sad, wilting. She had her sunglasses on indoors. It was lunch time but she was going to the bar. Lots of people had these issues in Florida but I never really knew what was going on because I'd never been around alcoholics or users. Just looking at her made me feel like I was on a bad acid trip.

I got a ruby red pedicure in her honor.

"Are you happy to have me all to yourself?" Cash asked me.

I smiled and said, "Well of course... but no... not really. I'm an angel and would never entertain thoughts like that."

Later, Mary called and I told her that it was going to be okay. That Cash would forgive her. That he knows she loves him. That he loves her. She just needed to stay calm and do the work. Be patient and take care of herself.

"He demands a lot, he expects a lot, and it's only going to make us better, make us level up," I said. She kept trying to justify her actions.

"There is no justification to be done," I said. "You know what he wants. Just be sorry and don't do it again."

Cash's court date regarding the restraining order Stacey filed happened the week after he broke up with Mary and my parents left.

The police had become a recurring theme in my life since Cash. They kept showing up at his house for something. But Cash never got in any trouble. He just made friends and gave them candles. The people were more useful than the courts.

"Justice is public love," Cash said, even though legal action was so slow and we hadn't seen his kids in two months.

Sometimes I understood the details of Cash's vision better than he did. On the night before the court date, he tried to make love to me but he couldn't get it up for the first and only time. He made me cum and blamed his impotence on the Adderall he took. I reminded him what he once said, that before battle, warriors wouldn't cum so they could use their virility for power. GOD preserved his virility so that he would be strong for court. Sometimes I understood the details of his vision better than he did.

"There is one thing we have to do each day. And that is connect with GOD," Cash said in the morning. He spritzed himself with the same cologne worn by Stacey's late father.

Written lightly in pencil on the inside of his bedroom door, I read, "Crowns are made on battlefields."

I told him that I read it when we were waiting in the hallway outside the courtroom.

"No one is supposed to see that," he said, but he looked pleased that I had found it, like it was a good sign.

Stacey claimed Cash was a narcissist, the word of the year. The fuel the elites use to fire up the masses, everyone's favorite scapegoat, and the easiest to blame for general dysfunction. She had been posting these claims on social media, claiming that he abused her physically and psychologically, that he stole the company from her, that he wouldn't give her any money to take care of the children with. But if relationships are reflections, wouldn't that make Stacey the narcissist?

"I know how to poke the bear," Cash said.

"For the next six months, I'm GOD," Cash's shitty lawyer told him.

We waited in the courthouse for over an hour. I tried to ask questions but his lawyer cut me off. The lawyer was an idiot but even when things went wrong, Cash put a positive spin on it. Cash said the lawyer served his purpose.

The court threw away the claim once they realized Stacey had no reason to restrain Cash. But Cash's lawyer forgot to ask for relief and we went two more months without seeing his children. But we didn't realize it then.

Mary came over afterwards. She had some paperwork to give Cash.

The next thing I knew we were having another threesome. This time he had me eat her out while he fucked me.

The first pussy I ever tasted was my boyfriend's ex-girlfriend's. It tasted like skin.

After he came, Cash made sounds like he finished a really good dessert.

"That was fantastic! Superb! Muah!"

He and Mary started arguing so I left the room.

Cash's mom came home and I smoked a cigarette with her outside on the back porch.

"Where's Cash? Is he fucking with Mary?" she asked. Leave it to a mother to point out the ghastly truth.

Mary had a way of slithering back into Cash's life shamelessly. I felt embarrassed for her but it didn't matter, it still worked.

"She serves me," Cash said, shrugging.

And it was true. She was a lot better at remembering to take his shoes off when we got home to massage his feet, never forgetting to put honey in his morning tea and lemon juice in his water bottle. And she didn't have any outside interests aside from drinking alcohol at bars with her friends so he faced no obstructions to being the center of her world.

I had other things going for me, other worlds I was interested in, other angels, passions.

Cash said she was on "borrowed time."

Mary and I talked about how we would introduce each other to our parents. I said I would keep everything a secret from mine: the cult, the two wives, the mythos.

Mary said, "Well, my mom wants me to settle down because I'm older and I want that too. Plus, my mom was in a threesome relationship too, so it wouldn't be so out of the ordinary for her. I could introduce you eventually."

She was trying to slink her way into the New Orleans trip my family was going on in a month.

I knew I didn't really have any say. It was all up to

Cash. But I said anyway, "My parents only just met Cash. They might notice something. Who knows? Moms are psychics."

Like at the karaoke bar when my parents were in town and my mom caught on that something was up when Cash's mood suddenly went sour. I covered it up by laughing at her, saying, "There's nothing the matter," when really, I was deeply concerned by his mood change, having never seen it before.

Outside the karaoke bar, with my parents inside, Cash and I stood smoking cigarettes.

I tried to figure out what was going on, why Cash had ditched me and my family to hang out with a bleach blonde forty-something-year-old in denim cut-offs.

A guy approached us and introduced himself as our therapist and told Cash to stop being a bitch, to which Cash replied, in a deep dark voice, "I wouldn't let the warden speak to me that way."

I didn't need any sort of apology from Cash after that but eventually he gave it to me anyway.

But not until after we had rough sex, so rough it made me cry. It felt good to cry, to have the psychic hurt matched by the physical hurt so I could purge the pain- so that we could purge the pain. I had to recalibrate all over again. I didn't mind. I liked feeling my brain work and contort through different spheres.

Afterwards, he explained everything lucidly, handsomely, suavely, owning up to it all, teaching me lessons and values in between in a deep rusted voice that made me think of the brown tobacco leaves of the cigars he smoked, the wood in the workshops where he developed his ideas, the straw in the chicken coops he built, and the leather of the bibles worn and torn by his ancestors.

"Nothing good happens after midnight," he said. We had been out that night with my parents past 2AM. He felt the bad vibes, and saw other men looking at me. It made him upset.

The next morning, he said "When you're not kissing me I'm unsatisfied." So I was all over him from then on, touching him, stroking him, kissing him. I wanted to do whatever it took to serve him.

That night after he sent Mary home, as we were watching the end of the fourth part of Adam Curtis's docuseries, *Can't Get You Out of My Head,* I was thinking about the crazy day we had just had. Between the spazzy-ass, screwball lawyer, Jorge, who was inappropriate, unprofessional, and very unfunny, asking if Cash if he could date his assistant, and Greg, the money-grubbing, low brain-functioning troll, who kept calling Cash to yell at him, and the threesome with Mary, we had ourselves a day.

"You know this stuff is all horseshit?" Cash said, out of nowhere.

"I thought you liked Adam Curtis," I said, a little hurt.

Gently and calmly he began to explain to me the different species of aliens living on our planet that had embedded themselves into our DNA. Between the Lamurians, the Pleidians, and the Reptilians, I couldn't get straight which were the bad ones and which were the good ones.

Cash told me he was going to ask my dad to marry me in New Orleans. We were also going to bring Mary. Cash liked to be surrounded by women.

Cash's back tattoo had 29 marks on it. He told me it was about marriage. He got it from the monks when he was studying Muay Thai in Thailand. I was 29 years old- yet another physical manifestation of our destiny.

Cash decided we should just fix the girlfriend we had. There was too much risk involved in finding a new one. We were going to send her to Thailand on a yoga retreat to heal but then we decided we should all go to Sri Lanka.

Secretly I thought he should break up with her because she irritated him so much but I couldn't say that. It wasn't my place. He wouldn't listen anyways. He always did what he wanted to do at the end of the day no matter what anyone else said.

As Cash's follower, you got jealous as hell and then you moved on. You acted like a complete idiot, made a mess, and then you picked up the pieces, examined them, and decided what went back in and what got thrown out. And when you broke, you tried to avoid not taking anyone else out, especially the one you were freaking out about because if you hurt him, you were only hurting yourself, and everyone around you, especially when he was the cult leader, especially when his mind moved faster than you'd ever seen anyone else's mind move, when he only meant what he said in the moment and there was nothing unconditional about your love but instead it was your own unconditional surrender that you depended on, that you had to perform each day. When you started to dramatize, stir up your sorrows, whine in your head, victimize yourself, what were you doing? Writing a tragedy, a drama? Why would you want to live like that? Why should he only get you? Why do you think you're so special to be his one and only? Why not be special enough to be one of two?

I cared increasingly less about Americorps and the mundanity, the dishonesty. I didn't want to save people anymore. My mind had shifted. I didn't want to fix the old world. I wanted to make a new one.

Survival had become key. I was ready to prepare for the worst in the most beautiful of ways. I didn't have time to fuck around with human trafficking, a symptom of a diseased society. It was probably just another front to subordinate American privacy anyways.

On the phone, my sister asked me if I was still miserable at work.

"Did I say that?" I asked.

"Yeah. You're so dramatic," she said.

"Well I'm quitting soon anyways."

"Oh! That was fast," she said.

"I lasted six months. That's solid enough. I just gotta call T up and see how she's living."

T was a young woman who came to the homeless resource center where I was distributing human trafficking materials. She had been abused by her boyfriend who had thrown tea all over her and beat her up.

I called around looking for shelter. It took about an hour to discover that there was no space for her. But even when I was inquiring, there would be all this bureaucratic nonsense about getting information about her first instead of just figuring out if they even had shelter in the first place.

I asked her a fifth time if she had another place to stay and she finally admitted she could ask to stay at a friend's house who had offered her space a long time ago. She hadn't wanted to ask for help because it made her feel uncomfortable.

"You have to ask for help. You are young. You are at a place in life where people will want to help you. Get the help while you can."

I told her that I'd check up on her soon.

A month later, I wanted to find out if she went back to her abusive boyfriend or not because I didn't believe I could make a real difference since most of the time, women in abusive relationships return to their abuser. Either way I was going to quit my job but I still wanted to know.

It had been a month. She hadn't gone back to him yet.

Dear Americorps, My sincerest apologies – I have been deliberating over how to best phrase and compose myself but for now I think writing is best.

When I finally went to the doctor they said my bleeding was a bacterial infection, normally caused by a new sex partner, especially another woman. It was Mary.

They gave me antibiotics and the problem cleared up in a few days. No more blood.

Cash said things to me as the jockey to my horse, brandishing and using his whip on me so that I moved the way he wanted me to move: master and mare. He revealed my inadequacy, prodding lightly at times, careful, gentle, and at others, striking and harsh. I was determined to race on, to move in increasing agility, increasing strength, so that we could win the race and change the world.

Sometimes he said I was intimidating. Sometimes he said I wasn't intimidating enough. He said my laugh was too flamboyant, that he loved my classic body and feminine walk.

Cash liked to remind me I was a people pleaser but I knew he was projecting. I saw him do it all the time, a Libra thing.

I knew he was trying to break me down to be more subservient by revealing my insecurities and pointing out my weaknesses.

But I always had something ready. I peddled my wares shamelessly, gregariously.

"I'm surprised I'm not married yet," I would say, insinuating I had a notion of my own worth.

"I'm not your typical catch."

"There are millions of pretty girls," he said whenever I talked about my life before him and the men I used to entertain and be entertained by. His mini aggressions were cute, harmless. Like he was throwing pebbles at my window late at night. I knew he was just an insecure, traumatized mess underneath all that power, all that talk. Cash was just a boy and we could have everything we ever wanted if I just played my cards right and kept our ship in check. He was just afraid of what modernity had done to my femininity. We all were.

When my parents were visiting, I explained to them how I would be Cash's housewife and that I would raise his children and our own. I told them about his philosophy that children needed to be with their mother for their first six years. These were the years they needed to be nurtured and coddled, nourished and loved. My mom was shocked and slightly disconcerted about my change in philosophy. My dad was pleased.

When my parents left, after Cash had won them over, he got invited to the New Orleans trip and I moved into his house. My parents were happy about this arrangement only because they didn't like my roommates; thought they were lower class because they were alcoholics. But that was just Florida. That's what they didn't realize. Something made everyone lower class down here.

The extended invite to the New Orleans trip was all Cash. Cash was a master manipulator. He repeated phrases and words back at people that they used so that he could condition them to like him and think he had their number. I watched him do it to my roommate, Karen, and her boyfriend and then to my parents. I knew he was doing it to me too.

JT came back into town on his motorcycle. He had been away for weeks. As usual he pulled up at the exact same time Cash and I arrived, the brotherhood bond.

We had just finished having dinner with Cash's family from his second half-brother's side. Driving back to the house, Cash pointed out how happy his family had been to spend time with us, how much power there was in making people happy with our presence. His family was surprised how much Cash and I had in common, how many similarities we shared, how alike our minds.

Cash told JT that we were getting married.

"Take care of each other," JT said somberly.

Cash told me to make some tea. I tried to make a cappuccino for Cash since the restaurant we were at had forgotten his. I wanted it to be a surprise but then he complained about how long I took.

He usually acted that way in front of his friends and followers, like I was his dumb little maid. I didn't mind. It was clearly an act. Playing a tale as old as time.

Cash told JT about the summer plan for the men in the cult to ride motorcycles through the Appalachians to find Bigfoot.

"Or we can use Captain Ahab," Cash said, in a boyish rush of enthusiasm as he remembered his trusty camper sitting on the side of his house.

"Yeah brah!" JT said, always down with the plan. "Let's go!"

"I want to go fuck with normies," Cash said next, with a sneer on his face after he downed his cappuccino.

"Okay," we said, always agreeing to whatever he wanted to do.

We went out to play pool and met Dez at the bar. Cash started talking to some girls and JT hovered around in the corner.

I chatted with Dez about nonsense by the pool table while we watched Cash out of the corner of our eyes.

"He's changed so much over the past few years. He's a completely different man than the one I met." Dez said about

Cash.

"How?" I asked.

She babbled on, "Mary helped him a ton in getting away from Stacey. A ton. Stacey controlled him with her emotions. She thought they were still together for the longest time even though he broke up with her. She was totally delusional. Mary helped him kick her out of the house after he asked her to leave but she wouldn't go for a whole year."

I didn't know what to say.

"He still doesn't know the effect he has on people. On Stacey."

It sounded like she was hinting at something or giving me a warning but I couldn't tell or I didn't want to hear it. Dez babbled a lot.

Dez had to wake up early to take her kid to school so she said her goodbyes and whispered to me, "Don't ignore JT."

"Obviously," I said, rolling my eyes.

We both annoyed each other when we tried to help the other behave well but we both did it to each other all the time anyways.

I chatted with JT at the bar. Cash said he talked to girls to try to show JT how to interact but JT was incredibly shy and never talked much at all. Sometimes he had moments of extroversion and he would monologue about his life. He was a pretty interesting person actually though he always dressed in skateboard shoes and shorts and had terrible teeth. He built his own guns, fought in Brazil as a soldier, spoke Portuguese, and remodeled houses.

I tried pulling JT into the conversation Cash was having with the girls who turned out to be in their early 20s. Cash was clearly enjoying himself, turned on and flirting heavily. That's what Libras are all about anyways so I didn't blame him. I could always see a little bit of myself in those conversations and knew they didn't mean anything.

Libras love to charm. It gives us a sort of high to be delicate, dazzling, and deviously sweet. That's why Libras are so hard to meet. People fall in love with them and then they lock them away.

We all took shots, paid for by Cash of course, another one of his dazzling charms, and I got into conversation with one of the girls about line dancing. She said she would teach me.

When a country song came on, we went to dance and I pulled JT along with us. But the line dancing girl was really good and knew a lot of complicated moves. I didn't even know line dancing could be so complicated. JT escaped after a few seconds but I kept up with her.

Later, in bed, I asked Cash if saw me dance at all.

"No, I didn't," he said honestly.

I was always surprised by his bouts of honesty. He couldn't cultivate his persona consistently and when I saw him reveal his inadequacy I was disappointed.

"Wow, I thought you would at least be watching out for me," I said. He was always talking about the darkness around all of us and how I needed protection, especially at bars.

"Well, it's something I can work on," he said.

I was disappointed he was so enthralled by such young, boring, normie girls. I thought I had pulled aside the most interesting one, who actually had something to offer.

But Cash liked attention and didn't care who was giving it, as long as it was complete. I set these thoughts aside so they didn't taint my vision of Cash.

A few nights later when I got up to sing karaoke at the kava bar, he gave me his smiling, beaming, undivided attention, his hands clasped in his lap, his body directed at me the entire song. It felt like the sun was looking at me.

We had a bonfire to celebrate JT's return that weekend. That night JT told his best jokes and we saw the best side of him yet. Cash had been worried about him. He thought demons had gotten to him.

I thought it was all the shrooms. Cash gave him these chocolate shroom bars. We'd all be going to bed and JT would ask for one after we finished a jam sesh at four in the morning.

"JT is always fucked up on something," Cash said. He didn't seem to notice it was mostly thanks to him. But JT could get worse things from worse people in worse places if it weren't for Cash. Cash had pulled JT out of abusive relationships, employment scams, and drug addictions before.

JT said we should swim in the morning and I remembered yet again the power of our cult, the power of syncing up to each other. He knew I needed a baptism. I'd been craving water.

I thought we released all the demons at the bonfire but they hung around the whole next day.

Cash wrote in my journal, *Every day I am so excited to spend with you. I swear every time our eyes meet the entire world disappears. For you I would do anything, except eat anchovies. We will get this ark and I will take us to Shambhala. I will marry you in every country.*

Cash decided we'd live in the apartment above his old factory. He wanted a fresh space that wasn't tainted by Stacey. He had his mom and JT clean it out for us.

It was just like a nest. I loved it. He ordered fresh appliances for us.

Mary slithered her way into moving day. She started bringing her clothes over and Cash never stopped her. I was sad and disappointed. I thought it was going to be just us in the little nest. But when I complained, Cash told me it was his house and I had no right to make any demands.

We learned that hibiscuses symbolized good wives. Cash bought 20 hibiscus bushes to plant in front of the house. He paid JT to do all the work. The flowers were white.

It was like he had me so in the moment I forgot I was in Florida. Florida was so surreal. Especially when I moved in with Cash and my life became more cemented there. There was something magical about Florida and how I ended up there. As a kid, in the divination game little girls played called MASH OUT, I used to write Florida in the list of places I might live someday. You had to pick one dream, one bad, and one mediocre. Florida was always my dream.

Every day in Florida, a new animal to meet, a new

flower to know, a new body of water to pray to, a new kind of tree to see.

And the way the people spoke. I liked when Cash's mom called herself a Florida cracker. People greeted women with, "Hello, beautiful!" They were kind but sometimes they let their whole life story slip out in a brazen sentence.

There was Fort Myers beach, Cash's favorite place to go, where all the tourists went to get wild and then there was downtown, where the locals went. Those were our regular hangouts.

My favorite building in the world was the downtown art museum made out of coral and fossils from the ocean. You could see dinosaur bones embedded in the pillars. A man handed me a twenty dollar bill out of his pocket for telling him about it.

"Thank you for being a true American," he said.

In Fort Myers, everyone thought they were the real Americans. There were the winter homes of Thomas Edison and President Ford, sitting side by side next to a whole museum created about their friendship of business and science. You could explore Edison's workshop.

Cash said he usually had a workshop set aside like that, that he considered Edison to be one of his heroes. Now he just had a factory. He loved Edison. I loved Lana. We both loved Hemingway.

I loved Cash's southern ways, his southern family. How sweet he was when he told veterans, "Thank you for your service." He was a real, traditional American, just like his truck: strong and deadly.

His mom cooked us grits, dumplings, pot roast, biscuits and gravy, collard greens, and other southern things. I loved how he jumped out of his truck to help someone push their car into the gas station or carry something heavy. He never considered his kindness, he just was kindness.

"A king must serve his followers even more than the followers serve the king," he would say.

After Chinese takeout one night, Cash's mother pulled her fortune out of her cookie and read, "The future is the ultimate luxury." She made a funny face and I laughed.

"Well that's something I could think about for a few days," I said and then I did.

Being rich felt normal fast. It was a mentality I knew I had to struggle against – or, not necessarily struggle but remain aware of. I didn't want to forget how much easier I had it now that someone took care of all my bills.

Cash left half eaten dinners behind at fancy restaurants or half-drunk drinks at bars. *We have to finish this!* I used to protest. Soon I left things unfinished too. Wasting- the most luxurious luxury of all?

The dry cleaning and laundry costs were outrageous. He spent hundreds of dollars every time we went clothes shopping, which was often. Usually I only shopped at thrift stores but Cash insisted on changing my look to be more sophisticated.

Which was a more human condition – wealth or poverty? Lack or abundance? I got grumpy at the grocery store because instinctively I thought I shouldn't be there ordering food, I should be cooking at home. But alas we went to Ada's Market frequently, eating expensive, organic, fresh juices and smoothies and sushi rolls.

I didn't like talking to the workers there because I felt alienated from them already. I didn't understand them at all. They were working for a wage I no longer had any connection to. Perhaps I would have to return to their lifestyle one day. I suppose I stayed open to that because I didn't want to be closed-minded about anything ever. But part of me thought I was being silly. I would never live that life again.

The precarious aspect still lingered. There is an advantage of privilege but is fate not equally distributed? Does fate not hover backstage for everyone's plays, everyone's myths? Is not all precariousness then equally distributed?

Cash told me about his old life at the bar. He spent $35,000 in one year at a single bar in Cape Coral, the one he met Stacey at when she was bartending.

"You know how many friends I have left over from that era?" He asked. "None."

While Cash was drinking his money away at the bar, I was traveling around the world, collecting tools of transformation: studying improv, literature, poetry, philosophy, history, systems of power, physical training, yoga, meditation, and travel. Now I could see it had all been leading towards spiritual warfare, towards preparing me for battle. I was no longer participating in societal decay. I was choosing to forge my own way, to lead by example. My career had become loving those around me, putting my inner circle first above everything, being Cash's milk and honey.

Cash was my Gabriel, my angel of revelation, the strongest of all angels. He was my antihero. It was dark but we illuminated the path. It was cold but I'd never felt a love for the world that so warmed my soul.

I looked at Cash and saw an extension of me. We scorned normalcy, loved to question everything, lived spiritually, intentionally. It was painfully rare to find others like us.

Cash hated the scene I wanted to paint that we saw at the Lani Kai one day. Two young women in bikinis leaned seductively against the wall of the tunnel between the Lani Kai entrance and the beach, talking to two police officers in full uniform.

Something about the way I was engaged disgusted him. I thought the painting could be a demystification of our generational trauma, our cultural failure to rear strong men and women, our retardation of sexuality. I thought it aligned with all of Cash's teachings on masculinity and femininity.

"There is enough darkness in the world," he said.

He didn't want me to paint the darkness.

He got irritated whenever I used the adjective *crazy*. As in, that's *crazy*! Or, this is *crazy*. And, how *crazy*!

"You're a poet, Maria," he would say. "Why don't you talk like one?"

He also didn't like when I called him dude.

He wanted me to clean, do the dishes and keep track of his things.

He coached me, "I need you to get me to bed," and

then he would take out his guitar and sing songs for his friends.

He was preparing me to be his wife.

"I don't want to dampen your light."

"I'm a lot to handle."

"I'm needy."

I told Cash that I loved him so much I could put up with his shit.

"All of your shit!" I repeated.

We were sitting in his truck on the road on our way downtown or mid-city or to the beach or driving across the bridge between Fort Myers and Cape Coral or the bridge between downtown and North Fort Myers. All the places we always went. Cash liked to be on the constant move.

"What shit?" He asked, his mouth crooked trying not to smile, peeking at me from the corner of his eye while he drived.

"Your shit!"

"What, with Stacey? With Cosmic Candles? With Mary? With what?"

"We don't ever go to the islands around here," I pointed out, changing the subject, and Cash immediately booked us tickets for sailing classes on Sanibel Island at the end of June. But we were always living on our own island anyways, our own show.

"You know, you remind me of the first house I remodeled. It was a Cape Coral modern beach bungalow but I wanted to make it into a Spanish home. My mentor said, 'Cash, why are you trying to turn a bungalow into a Spanish house? Keep it what it is and go buy a Spanish house later.' You should be wearing respectable, pretty prairie dresses. Not this liberal hooch shit."

"So I am the house?" I asked.

Every night he fed me ashwaganda, glycine, and various cell regeneration pills that he got from his elite inner circle.

We wrote a song together about his baby mama and called it, "I Never Married That Bitch."

We talked to his lawyer.

"Does the TikTok still have her name?" The lawyer asked.

"No. She only got the Instagram," Cash explained. Every time we visited he had to repeat his whole story to the lawyer.

"A few years ago, she stole all the money from our business account and went to go live with the "frog people," as I call them. It was a commune that used frogs to induce some sort of ancient healing process. But after a few months she returned and we got back together because my dog died and I was sad. Another time, she left and went to go be a yachty. But again she returned and that's when we got pregnant."

After we met with the lawyer, we went to go float.

In my float, GOD told me I was worshiping at some dark altars. This was the most I'd ever talked directly to GOD. I asked him for the one thing I wanted and then I cried in fear of not getting it. But he dissolved my fear that I wouldn't get it. It was having Cash's children and being with Cash forever.

And then Cash stared down at me from above for some time. He was serious, severe and unsmiling. As dark as the dark altar GOD had shown me. And here and there I saw a few angels. The angels were rainbow and smiling, lighthearted. And I could see on my phone that a couple angels even texted me while I was floating.

No more phone in the mornings, I told myself. I needed a better routine – one of my own. And I knew I needed to keep my mind holy. No more stupid Twitter research about leftist politics.

I reflected on some stupid shit I said, like the bit about me not wanting to come off as the bad guy around Mary. Cash used me as a correspondent between the two of them at times. Who cares what she thought? I was Cash's queen.

Cash had another one of his intense visions in his float, entire worlds he went to inhabit for years at times. As usual he was waiting for me in the lounge chair taking notes. When I told him about my float, he said he didn't like the idea of my own routine. He didn't like when I meditated at home, when

I went into my own world.

"You need to stay in mine," he said.

Cash was a shark. I could also be a shark. If he was a shark, I was a shark. His love was conditional on how obedient and submissive I could be. He wanted unconditional surrender.

And my love? I had to make it up as I went, each day a whole new castle to build, a whole new scene. I had to laugh and pretend I felt normal. I touched myself knowing I was just an illusion, a character, an archetype. I knew I wasn't real so no one could hurt me.

I knew I should never consider him as mine completely. He would always have a space carved out for Other Women, his muses.

I once inhabited that shadowy realm but he had placed me on a pedestal, in an empty open temple. I beamed awkwardly, glowing, no one else knowing, revealing nothing of my true disposition, accustomed to walking around all casual with a sword through my heart. Part of me was the happiest I'd ever been and part of me would never be happy again.

Cash knew I was judging him in my writing when I got back into bed with him and Mary that night. I looked back on my writing in my journal to see if he had read something but there was nothing. Maybe it was in my phone. But when I checked it wasn't there either. He must have felt it coming from my thoughts. Before I knew him, I didn't know a person could be so perceptive.

"Don't go writing just to detach yourself."

"I don't, it's to do the opposite, to feel everything deeper and examine it, pick it apart – it's to get more intimate with my meaning."

"With our meaning," he corrected me.

The full moon was in Scorpio. I asked Cash what he thought that meant and he said sex. I laughed and said try again.

"Fucking," he said.

"Vulnerability," I said.

As Jung said, one must be full to cast a shadow. And there we were in Scorpio, the darkest of all shadows.

Cash was up and down because he was going through hell. He still hadn't seen his girls. I had to pull him out. I could with my love but sometimes I had a bad connection to my light.

We had a long weekend and I was so exhausted, unclean. Naturally I wanted to go cold and be calculating, wanted to put my emotions away for some time but he hated my cold side and that was not what he needed. He needed love, that milk and honey. I needed a fucking swim, a baptism.

I knew that when I got into some water GOD would baptize me, like he always did. I looked at the trees in the yard, the forest. I saw myself. I was wild, I was free. Even in unconditional surrender I could still be wild and free.

I had seen something dark about him. He wanted me to see him only in light. When I saw his darkness, I knew it was my own.

He tried to be sweet but I put up a screen. Damn that screen. No more screens, only unconditional surrender. I was determined. What did I need? His love. He didn't need anything from me. Or that's how he wanted it to seem.

To define what I felt as compared to all other points in my life – impossible? All I could do was manifest my future and what I wanted: Cash – us – our time.

But when I meditated I saw another woman who could never work for someone else again. I think it was me but I told Cash it was someone else when he asked. He wouldn't like that I was thinking of myself as independent from him. He didn't like when I meditated. But I insisted it was one thing I needed.

Time was moving incredibly fast. Thanks to the internet, then the Pandemic. Maybe it was the natural acceleration of space and time or maybe it was just the nature of the culture. Who knows what was holding it all together.

Adam Curtis' *Hypernormalisation* documentary and Mark Fisher's capitalism critiques left me with the uncanny feeling that escape was futile. I aimed to do anything but participate. I didn't have to participate. I went from feeling guilty to wanting to help the world to a complete reversal with the sole aim to save myself.

In wanting to save the world I only hurt myself. But in saving myself I saved the world.

I used to try so hard to make space for others, to make myself meet the differences in their ways, their inadequacies. Cash was teaching me to lift them up instead, not meet them down where they were. And for a while that's what he tried to do with Mary.

That Scorpio full moon, Mary's 11th house was activated – her relationships, goals, and dreams were transforming, morphing. We helped her along and sent her to yoga. We showered her with love- our fire starter, our flame.

On the drive home from the factory one day, JT said, "Hey Cash, I'm kinda into Mallory. Can you make that happen?"

Mallory was one of the employees at Cash's factory. She was also good friends with Cash's mom. She came with us when Cash went to court to defend him as his employee. He had fired her but then he rehired her after that.

She was a nervous sort of woman, never staying still. She used to be a drug addict. She had a lot of tattoos and piercings.

"Oo oo!" Cash said, looking back at JT through his rearview mirror and smiling.

"I got you, dog," he said.

"Aw yeah. Make it happen."

Cash invited Mallory to the cult meeting that night. She was the first person invited to attend who wasn't a member. Mary was also allowed to come that night as the second person who wasn't a member. Mallory became a regular. Mary only attended that once.

At the cult meeting, Cash and I made salmon and broccolini with an avocado dill sauce for dinner.

Cash put a sprig of dill on each person's plate and pulled a candle out to place in the middle of the table, making everything more elegant. That was his way – adding elegance and intention to everything.

After dinner, we all went around and said something we were struggling with and each person gave a piece of advice.

Each meeting Cash gave us something to reflect on and share. Like the last cult meeting, we all had to say a person's name that we hadn't forgiven and choose to forgive them right then and there.

When it was my turn, I said I was afraid of losing myself and, from the phone, Dash told me to look to Cash.

I remembered I had an improv show that night. Cash said they were going to a kava bar and I should flip a coin whether I would stay for improv or go with them to kava.

I decided I didn't want to go to improv but Cash still made me flip the coin and when it said I had to stay for improv, he made me stay at the house.

In my journal, I wrote:

I am sad and it seems wrong because I know that nothing is normal anymore. And yet we scorn normality. That is the inner essence of everything we do, everything we are.

No one to talk to about it.

Multiple people in my new family set me off, the true nature of family anyways. They set you off so that you can know how much you care.

I have to confront Mary. Because I have learnt how to confront. Because I have already set out to confront all things familiar. I know that Mary is me. I know that all the ways she has hurt me are ways that I've hurt her.

And now he leaves me to confront these things.

We all miss Dash. And so he has the most power right now. There is so much power in a lack of self. In a lack of who we are, in placing everything onto one man.

I tell Cash I just want to make him happy.

I want to throw myself on the ground with the three black cats, because I cannot stand the cruelty, the meanness of both him and Mary. I don't fucking care about my fucking improv show. I guess that's what I'm supposed to confront.

I wanted this loneliness – this alone time anyways. I wanted to have my moment, my shiny, golden, glistening, blistering moment.

I keep looking at Cash – waiting for him to fall like Icarus, though I'm starting to get the hint that I've been Icarus this whole time, flying too close to the sun GOD.

Even improv was always about the writing. And so here I am with these fucking words, my holy grail, my opium. The click of the pen, the slick feeling of ink on paper, these are my heartbeats, how I feel alive. My real heartbeat has always been hard to find.

I keep picturing them coming home, the family. I think about the food I gorged on, the dishes I've been washing: the mess of the family.

I crave exercise. I crave a good run, and if that's too obscene, which it probably is at this hour, and with this much wine, then perhaps a Pamela Reif workout on YouTube, the Barbie saint who leads the pointless warriors to sweat, fitness with a sad and beautiful face and songs that renounce former failed lovers that make you wonder how beauty could ever end up so broken.

This ground is so alive; the concrete warmth heats me from beneath me. I've set myself down on the ground like a sacrifice. The coin decided my fate even though it was written so long ago.

"We're progressive," Lucci says.

"No, we're trad!" I protest, gleeful to make a wicked argument soaked in accuracy.

"We are ancient," Cash says, climbing up, once again on top of me, always on top of me, farther ahead, always righter than me.

And so I let myself get used to the feel of the ground, searching for a disaster, a good cry, something to know that I'm still alive and that time will still pass, though for now it has stopped.

This old dark house haunts me – the spot we met haunts me because it reminds me of death because this was where I died. Both these places are my reckoning, where I lost myself, gave myself away. I still yearn, still look as if I forgot something, as if I could ever get it back.

Freaking out and suspension of belief, looking back at my old identity, trying to hold onto a semblance from the previous world I inhabited. My previous life has become a relic.

Sometimes I see a memory of me. From outside, the three black cats trade places in their company. People constantly bike by even at nighttime.

I'm always looking to hover in the gray parts, the borderlands, the liminal, because in those spaces I can be all alone. I'm in control.

What is the family thinking? Probably wondering why I'm so dramatic. I started to cry when they left, begged Cash to let me go with him. Why am I so dramatic? Why are my emotions so strong and turbulent? Why am I always wanting to hold the paintbrush, the microphone, the rules of the game? It's a deficiency, a delay, a malnourishment, a game.

I see a black woman walk by with a grocery cart snickering and babbling in the middle of the wicked world. No – I'm the wicked world.

The cat attacks something, meows wistfully and eats it. It's all a game anyways, that's why people like sports. That's why men like sports, Cash writes on top of my writing later, correcting me.

Where's GOD tonight? Oh he's around. Though I wonder who tried to scoop him up. The truth is I'm grateful for this solitude, something I haven't had in weeks. I finally feel like me.

It turns out that this whole time GOD was in the tree.

Cash came home and asked me if I missed him. I was doing the dishes.

"Yes!" I said, turning around and running into him with wet hands, meaning it deeply for once.

He said Mary was annoying him. At the kava bar, she followed him around like a puppy, waiting for his every beck and call, clinging for affection and attention.

I never wanted to be like Mary.

He read my writing. He didn't like the bit about him being Icarus so I told him I read somewhere that Icarus was fine when he landed in the ocean. That some GOD or goddess took pity on him and turned him into a dolphin or something. Or maybe a dolphin saved him – I wasn't sure but I had a different feeling of that story than most other people had. Other people saw the fall as the end but I saw it as the beginning. Every ending was a beginning.

But then he flipped to the beginning of my journal when I hadn't met him yet. He read my dream I had of hooking up with a platonic friend, the one I was supposed to visit so long ago in Arizona, when I had to postpone our first date.

He got angry and stomped out of the room. I finished the dishes slowly, singing. I thought he just needed to cool off.

I joined him and Mary in bed. I tried to cuddle him but he was unresponsive. I turned over and away from him to sleep. I was tired. I figured he needed to emotionally regulate and that he would be over it in the morning.

Mary touched my arm. "Hey, we don't go to sleep mad," she said, speaking to me over Cash. So I turned over and tried to take Cash's anger seriously.

He was still furious, still fuming. He told me to leave. I went over to the closet and stood there trying to decide what to take, trying to figure out if he was serious.

"What are you doing?" he shouted. "Get back over here!"

So I went back to the bed. He told Mary to leave the room. He yelled at me and asked me if his soulmate wouldn't show any emotion when he was upset. I had already shut down my emotions. I handled his temper clinically and coldly.

Mary was eavesdropping on our conversation outside the door. She stormed off after a while. She always stormed off whenever she went anywhere.

Cash and I made up after some time.

"I hate when you go cold!" He said.

"It's a defense mechanism. I do it when I don't feel safe."

"We need to find Mary."

So we left the apartment to go looking for her.

Outside we found JT and Mallory coming home from the bars. They were all over each other. I was pissed that I missed the courtship happen.

Back at family dinner, Lucci had been making all these gross moves on her, while JT sat silent and shy as usual. I wondered how the switch had been made, how JT had achieved his goal, how much Cash played a part.

Cash sat in a chair outside to play guitar for JT and Mallory as they swooned over each other, shrouded in blooming azaleas in the warm spring air. I sat down in another chair and admired the scene until I remembered Mary. I went inside the other house to look for her.

She was sitting in the backyard reeking like alcohol. I didn't blame her. I had been taking secret swigs of wine throughout the afternoon, ever since I knew I'd be around her all day and night. It made dealing with her energy and the humiliating dynamic between her and Cash easier.

She was upset. I tried talking with her and listening to calm her down. She talked about how hard it was to hear Cash say the things he used to say to her to me. She gave me some secret drags off her cigarette.

I wasn't supposed to be smoking because I had snapped at Cash last week. He said it would be a lesson in not putting myself first. He said I got selfish when I smoked cigarettes. But Mary and his mom slipped me drags when he wasn't looking.

"I know it's just because you're new," Mary drawled.

She was so whiny for being 36. I had no idea what was coming but I hoped he would always treat me better than her. But even more I hoped she would just leave.

Cash was furious when he came outside and saw us talking. He said I was undermining him.

I told him I was serving him. I only told her sweet things, I never told her how I really felt. Maybe I should have.

Back in bed, she questioned him, "Do you even love me anymore?"

I didn't think he did, not how he spoke about her, how he dealt with her, how he treated her. That wasn't love; that was contempt. But he said he did.

"And one day you will both be mothers," he said.

"The mother of your children?" I asked

Mary didn't say anything.

"Yes," he said, snuggling into me.

We had sex that night.

As I was sucking Cash's dick, Cash was whispering directions into Mary's ear. Mary crawled over to me and whispered, "You're doing a great job."

I started laughing and then Cash started kissing me, laughing too and Mary started sucking. He rammed his dick into her mouth and she ran into the bathroom and threw up. I couldn't stop laughing.

In the morning, I woke up to full moon leftovers in the sky. Cash and Mary were still asleep. I felt like the moon and I were spies.

In my journal I wrote, *Manifest a man, who knows his land, and knows that everything good in life is by the sand. A golden man who knows good things such as nothing good happens after midnight or that no plans are the best plans. One who makes you feel royal, whose aspirations for you are astronomical, alchemical; who coaches you up trees, and talks you down mountains.*

Cash showed Mallory a lot of care and invited her to more cult meetings after that.

He had us all go with her to an AA meeting one night. I had never been to one before. We all had to introduce ourselves. I got shy in front of everyone. I always had a tough time talking to crowds. My cheeks flushed pink.

"You're so shy!" Lucci said to me after. "You're like an old soul but you're still a little kid."

"That's what I love about her," Cash said.

But Cash also said I was immature. He knew I was stuck, in a sense, at three years old, when I lost my baby brother and that a part of me would never grow up. He knew I was like a child. He was the first person to have seen that, or at least, to tell me he saw it.

Cash was obsessed with getting people dialed into the present. The first time he played "Spirit in the Sky," we all lost it dancing in the car after the acro yoga class he took us to for our cult meeting.

"Everyone was so into it," he said later, beaming, transfixed, in awe of himself.

And everyone was in awe of Cash. When people came to the house for various tasks and it was just me and Mary there to assist them, they always asked after him. Everyone wanted to be around him, just to be in his presence was enough. And no one ever wanted to say goodbye for good.

CHAPTER TWELVE: BORROWED TIME, ATLANTIS, AND NEW AGE BULLSHIT

Cash finally broke up with Mary for real. "She's already on borrowed time," he kept saying until one day there wasn't any more time left for her to borrow.

It was the day after we all went to the beach together. Cash and I were already there with Mallory and JT. Cash paid Mallory to make a picnic for all of us.

I chatted with Mallory and JT about religion and they both swooned when they realized they were both raised as Jehovah's Witness.

Mary showed up and changed the vibe as usual. The words to describe her had been growing in my mouth but I held my tongue for days. The words became even more accurate.

Cash played that song again, "Spirit in the Sky." Or maybe it just came up on Spotify.

Mary slithered around provocatively on a beach blanket with her huge, size E tits bumbling around. She made rude comments about my hair. She clawed desperately at me, at Cash, at anything.

Cash told us the story of their first date and how she was carrying a bottle of alcohol around at a party.

He was disgusted by her. I didn't like to watch. We all three went for a swim in the water and they started arguing so I left and went back to read on the sand.

Mary came back and told me that Cash threw her on the sand and made her scrape her knee. She waited for my reaction but I gave her nothing. I turned back to my book.

She said she had to get something from her car and left. She was probably taking a swig of something.

Cash came back to the beach. We went over to the grass to sit in the shade and smoke a cigarette. We watched Mary walk over to where we had been on the beach, looking for us. She couldn't see us, though she could have if she looked around better. Cash ignored her phone calls.

"She never sees," Cash said.

That's when I revealed the words to Cash. I said she was always fiending for something.

"Yeah," Cash said. "You're totally right."

Her biggest mistake was when she hung out with Lucci that one night without Cash's permission. He could never get over that. That was what did her in. Not her desperation, sleaziness, anxiety, or their incompatibility. Because when it came down to it, Cash would put up with anything if you were subservient enough.

Our apartment finally felt like a castle. Our romance was finally real. Trees bordered us through every window and it felt like we were in a treehouse. They flowered through multiple cycles in a matter of a couple months. We watched over the neighborhood from up there like royalty.

I didn't feel like I ever needed to leave that little house, I was so happy. Sitting around at Dez's pool, eating and sharing barbeque food and laughing, Cash and I performing improv for everyone, putting on a show. He picked up on improv immediately, just from the little tips I gave to him and the scenes he saw me do at the computer for my online course.

I picked out furniture on Craigslist and Cash and Lucci picked it up in the truck. He surprised me with a beautiful clock that read, "With You 'Till the End of Time."

I bought beautiful rugs and placemats and curtains and silverware on Etsy with Cash's credit card.

We started doing normal couple things, like going to the movies. But we did it in a slew. We went every single night for a while which wasn't really that normal.

Our first: *Nobody*.

Cash thought I wanted to see *Nomadland* because I identified with the main character.

"No," I told him, "she's a good actress. I admire her acting."

Her character lives in a van somewhere out in the cold Midwest.

"I'd never live somewhere so cold," I told him, weeks after we left the movie fifteen minutes in, it was so boring. I was still perturbed that he thought I could ever desire to be so slovenly and sad.

"Or at least so cold and flat." I added as I remembered

I could live in places like Utah and Scandinavia since I loved mountains and snowboarding.

Again I tried to explain that I was most curious about the neoliberal propaganda of living life in a van and working at Amazon. He and I tended to take turns scorning the mainstream culture while the other found it curious. When one found the decay amusing, the other scorned it. We were both in survival mode and knew that one only had so much time to waste on exploring bullshit agendas.

It was getting harder to tell what was supposed to be interpreted as positive or negative anymore. I'd spent so much time saving face at other peoples' hysterical personas, it was harder to understand their demented thought process.

Was *Nomadland* poised to influence people towards alienation disguised as independence, towards slavery disguised as convenience, towards humiliation, completely undisguised but no longer recognizable as people chose to humiliate themselves over social media in increasing frequency?

I couldn't argue with Cash about how stupid *Nomadland* was. I walked out of the movie with him and into another movie that we also left after twenty minutes.

The movies were all complete trash. We got a good soundtrack out of *Nobody* though. We even got some wedding songs.

I never wanted to forget those silly days that were dotted with pain all because Cash couldn't see his kids and there were so many women at his back; both his baby mama and Mary kept asking him for money. But we still fell deeper into love. He drew my portrait every day on a notepad. We worshiped one another.

Our nights were so pretty. Cash never stopped giving. And I just wanted to sit there basking in it, gobbling it all up. I wrote these moments down like the sweetest grocery list of all time. He was finally just mine. Without Mary and with Cash all to myself we were on a constant honeymoon.

We went to church one Sunday and the pastor just happened to be talking about Cash's company, Cosmic

Candles.

"Now I met with the owners who had no idea what they were getting themselves into with their spiritual bypassing. They reminded me of a movie, *Mosquito Coast*, where a man takes his family out on a ship to flee the evils of society."

We decided to watch the movie as soon as we could. It was like everything was all up in the ether, hovering there for anyone to grasp, our whole life laid out on an accessible plane.

The day before Mother's Day weekend, Cash's mom, Stephanie, and I went shopping for new swimsuits. Cash wanted me to get one pieces.

"Hi beautiful," she always greeted me.

Stephanie liked to pull me along on errands whenever she could. I enjoyed her company when she was in a good mood. But sometimes she let a shadow take over and she was nasty. Though never directly towards me, the shadow cast itself upon everything in her vicinity so that the world became grim and murky.

"How do y'all know each other?" our cashier asked.

"She's my soon to be daughter-in-law," Stephanie said, giving me a squeeze.

"Y'all have the cutest relationship," she said. "You're very lucky."

We sat in the car smoking cigarettes and Stephanie told me all about how she and Cash's dad were addicts from before Cash was born. One night when they were on drugs and fighting, Cash's dad beat her to a pulp and left her to die in a ditch on the side of the road when Cash was about three. She lied there for two days with a broken jaw until she gathered the strength to crawl out and get help from a passerby.

And then we walked into a 7/11 for juice and more cigarettes. I was in a daze. So that was why Cash's dad went to prison for ten years.

She survived but still struggled with addiction for the rest of her life. Her most recent stint to rehab last summer was paid for by Cash.

We drove home, and then she said simply, "I better call the roofer before he gets too drunk. I've known him for a while and he has a drinking problem. If I don't call him before noon he'll be too drunk to work."

As if she hadn't just taken me back to what made Cash who he was, that she hadn't just jolted me back in time and then forward again, leaving me disjointed.

Cash talked a lot about how he wanted to kill Stacey, the mother of his children, how if it were the Bronze Age, murder would be permitted, even expected. He hated the modern age and how pathetic men had become. He wanted to get his kids, beat her, and leave her for dead. He thought demons controlled her.

After learning about his dad, I wondered if he really was capable of that kind of violence. I had considered it hyperbole.

I learned that Cash's sun and mercury lived in the 12th house, the transcendental, the criminal, the psychic. Maybe he had psychically transcended his criminal past. Maybe it was a ticking time bomb.

Cash was renting an Airbnb for his mom that Mother's Day weekend right on Fort Myers Beach. Dez, Mallory, JT, Cash, and I got there first. Stephanie would show up the next day.

Cash was on fire that trip. I took the first and only video I have of him. He was so alive, I had to capture it.

Nothing left to do but be happy and enjoy him. I could wonder and hypothesize all I wanted about his past. But that wasn't real. All we had was now.

I had the most beautiful acid trip of my life. It started on the beach.

Cash gave tabs to me, Dez, Mallory, and JT. As the effects started to kick in, the sun was setting.

Cash left Dez and I to stop JT and Mallory from fighting.

Dez asked me how I felt anything on the acid. I told her it simply magnified what was already there. She could never trip on acid, never had any hallucinogenic experiences.

Cash said it was because she was an alien. I never knew why she kept taking psychedelics when they didn't affect her.

I told Cash after the most decadent sunset that he was the first thing I'd ever trusted and that even as the sun went down and I began to think about how badly I'd miss it, I knew I'd be okay with having Cash – he'd always be my source of sunlight. I revolved around him. I was his moon. It was the freest I'd ever felt; the unconditional surrender, the relief in devotion.

We joked about going under the pier and hiding from everyone. All these people neither of us had ever wanted anything to do with though without them we'd be less powerful and so would they without us.

Being in a cult was like taking off in a spaceship. You went completely out of your comfort zone. But it was exactly what you felt like you'd been searching for. We served each other and put the cult first, before everything else.

Cash told the followers that I write everything and then it happens. And they believed him.

When we got back to the Airbnb, I saw ancient patterns all over my body in the kitchen. Cash told me to meet him in the shower. Both Mallory and Dez tried to stop me from taking a shower with him like the demon and alien they were. The LSD sliced through masks.

In the shower, under the sparkling droplets of water, Cash transformed into what he really was. He looked part mermaid and part lion. Through the water, he took me halfway to Atlantis.

We stood on a threshold between the world we were living in and the world we came from, the one in the water. We had a purpose to fulfill in this world and that's why we couldn't go back to Atlantis yet, as rightful king and queen.

There were terrible forces all around us. I wanted to talk about them but we had to keep the sacred a secret. Cash wanted me to be quiet. He kept shushing me every time I tried to talk. I felt the others wanting to get in with us but they were dark, tainted. We had to keep the portal protected.

"Take all the magic out of it, why don't you?" Cash

said, outside the shower in the bedroom, when he put his cock in my mouth as I was freaking out about the dark energies. I felt that everyone could see us, that everyone was watching. We were all there, there in the room somehow, but they were different creatures, kept shifting forms.

I knew that Cash and I came from the same place but the darkness prevented me from seeing what he saw so clearly mapped out. I had darkness inside of me, blinding me, a part of me, as a woman. I had a connection to the darkness that he didn't; I could talk with Satan. And he could marvel at that wickedness, but he would never descend to my depths. I was cursed to embody the wholeness of everything. While I attempted enlightenment I had to carry temptation like it was my own suckling.

In Eden, I worked with the snake as an accomplice. I was Satan's mistress forever. He would always be my first lover, soulmates from a previous world. Maybe we broke out of heaven together to destroy the world. But that was my previous life. I was now living Cash's story. I was a secondary character now, a supporting actor in redemption.

I kept thinking Cash's mom was there already but she wasn't. Thoughts strapped up into my head like Velcro and became realities. It was the first time I admitted to myself the darkness of the others. Before, I only wanted to see them as beneficent, kind, innocent creatures. But the acid awakened me to their dark intentions that lay not so dormant at the bottom. Was it their lack of awareness of their own darkness that made it so dangerous or had they given themselves up to this dark power long ago?

I was starting to understand how people could be so closed off; to themselves, to each other, to love and to light. I was different from other people, and it wasn't a bad thing. I was a being of light. It was actually really good. I was finally learning who I could trust – only Cash and my own family.

I felt anxious writing any of it down. Dark energies surrounded us. Everything suddenly felt critical and perilous, like we couldn't make a single wrong move.

We went out on the town and followed Cash around.

I hovered close to him like a shadow. The others looked at me with suspicion or curiosity. I couldn't tell. My world was reprogramming again. I held onto him like an anchor. He walked around the streets, yelling and whistling at people a la provocateur.

Who was willing to spread true love? The true music? Cash was electric while I came down from the acid; his curly, wiry hair, with wide-open eyes and shirt like he was on constant vacation.

The next day, Stephanie arrived, "Hi beautiful!" and we had a beach barbeque for her and Dez. Dez's daughter, Rose, came too, along with Cash's half-brother and girlfriend and son.

I told Mallory we'd have a picnic on the beach next time, for father's day.

"Just the four of us, without all the extras," she said roundly, as if making room in her mouth to slip curses inside of the words, dipped in her Key West accent which she said sounded like a Puerto Rican New Jersey accent but, "…is all keys, baby."

She was talking about the people in our crew she didn't like or didn't trust or didn't understand; one of those three or maybe all of them. But mostly she was talking about Dez. No one ever trusted Dez.

"The toppings?" I asked.

"Cute," she said.

Later, Rose, refused to eat her burger without ketchup. She even walked to the grocery store to get ketchup packets as if toppings were essential.

It can be frightening how simply one can tune in to the orchestration, to accidentally sit in the director's chair, to rewrite the script.

Cash's brother's girlfriend said she hadn't been to the beach in five years, though we all lived a mile or five away. I guess not everyone had that same interest or call to water. People got stuck in monotonous patterns somehow and missed the point.

Cash was mean and cruel to me at the beach during

the day and at the barbecue during the night. It was a cold slap in the face after experiencing the Atlantean magic with him the night before. He was angry I had taken so long to get to the beach that morning, wrapping presents and making popsicles at the Airbnb before I biked there.

I moved slowly on purpose. I reveled in the alone time. Cash picked up on that, he picked up on everything. He was hurt so he lashed out. Dez and Stephanie were sympathetic to me. Stephanie mouthed at me, *just be patient.*

Cash and I joined Stephanie and his half-brother in the ocean. Clouds cast metallic shadows on the water. We were standing in the middle of one of the shadows.

We played her favorite word game, categories through the ABCs, laughing and cheering at each other. I tried to manifest Cash not being angry at me anymore. But when we got to the beach, he hit on every woman that walked by.

That night I let some words slip out to the crew, without meaning them. Cash and I were getting ready for bed. But the words came from what I could hear in their heads. I wanted to give to them. Cash called it people pleasing. He said I could read their minds. I just wanted to make them happy. I didn't trust the others to express what was going on in their own heads, whether they even knew what was going on inside.

And so, because of what I said, we found ourselves going out with the crew instead. That's what they all wanted. It was a lovely night anyways. They just didn't know what was good for them.

But I couldn't blame them. It was Florida after all. Everyone was constantly seething, hungry for the next high, the next fix under the fluorescent lights and palm trees.

Lying in the sand on the beach under the stars after ditching the others and making love, I asked Cash if Dez was the second wife. I didn't want her to be, didn't think she would be a good one, but I wanted to know. She was so loyal. She did everything Cash asked. He toyed with the idea of her as his second wife but she didn't think she'd ever be able to submit how he wanted.

It was the first slab of two weeks we'd stayed in the vicinity of one place.

We stopped at an antique store coming back from Fort Myers Beach. Being around all the old stuff made our love feel even truer, like it came from a different time period, was just as timeless. I picked up a book about sea adventures. This time I was just as excited as Cash.

We flipped it open to read about a real life account of a Viking funeral back in 922. All the dead Viking's girls were asked who would die with him. The girl that offered herself was given spirits to drink and then was taken to different tents where she had sex with the friends of the Viking. Then an old woman called the angel of death killed her. Her body was burnt alongside the Viking's body.

When we went to buy it, the woman working the cashier commented on how well we got along. Said she didn't see many people our age getting along that way.

Nearly three months of love, we counted the synchronicities like fisherman, astronomers, sufis.

Later that week Dez had to take Rose to the ER and then again that weekend. Dez worried to us on the phone that something was lurking in Rose.

"Watch your words," Cash said. "They have powers."

"I know," Dez said in her flat Wisconsin accent. "I'm stayin' pahsitive. I'm bein' pahsitive."

Maybe it was in her Lithuanian blood. Maybe it was the way of her people from the cold preferring to simmer in cold, dark thoughts because that's just what was familiar to them.

In the fourth grade I used to tell people I didn't believe I would die. That was when I was considered "ditsy" and then later, "outspoken". But Cash taught me I was just a poet and inaccessible to many people. That was how GOD made me.

I told Cash it was because I was educated well, in private school for 13 years but he shot that down without hesitation. I accepted his rebuttal without blinking. He easily destroyed my argument with a quick flick of the tongue. I was so malleable by him.

We disagreed rarely. I'd start to argue with him or explain my position on something but then I'd realize I had recently changed positions as I was speaking to him. He was simply on another level than people I was used to talking to, questioning my every intellectual move and, therefore, I had to question myself, leading me to transform my stance. My logical fallacies were easily revealed and then Cash erased them.

And it was the same thing with the way I acted. I started to notice how I'd demand attention from men, almost expect it. I was able to see from Cash's eyes how I was acting, how I was attention-seeking.

When we did disagree, it was a matter of principle. We both scoffed at each other – the truest Libran love, keeping each other on our toes.

We disagreed on how to read, whether one should finish every book they start. I saw his desire to finish every book, his pride of completion, of accomplishment, to be a point that I was once at but now I knew I'd never finish half the books I started and I didn't care anymore.

I never believed in endings anyways because nothing ever ended. My hunger could never be satiated – I was constantly seeking new worlds and sometimes, I didn't have the time to finish a whole world up as you encounter more spheres of being. Progress isn't anything more than just a stupid push forwards.

Like the 1000 books before kindergarten campaign that was being advertised all over the libraries. I didn't know if it was just in Florida or if it was a nationwide campaign in all public schools but it was a horrific way to attempt to control children's relationships to books. It was terrible pressure. How intimidating: 1000 books before kindergarten. Quantity of books means nothing when you're little. It's all about quality and effort and connection and falling in love and repetition. Of course it depends on the individual child how much they should read, which is why one size fits all governmental education is insidiously ludicrous.

Cash and I would never put our kids in school. That was just the kind of people we were.

I was getting antsier by the day to get our yacht and get the fuck out of the USA – the decaying country, the berserk population. My anger at injustice was waning, but I still had a lot more anger than Cash. He used to be mad like me, inclined towards red pilling the world in the hope of spreading salvation.

Now he was more sophisticated in propaganda, focused on exposure therapy; the exposure being to himself and leading others by example; healing the world by being. I was still hung up on trying to get people to think.

It turned out it took a soulmate to figure out what everything was about. That new moon I started thanking my lucky stars each day for bringing me my treasure. I didn't have to look around anymore. He was my North Star. His house brought me closer to my source, to our source. All he had was his Pluto in Scorpio though he had Key West eyes with a mood just like the tides. And a wavy way about him that was just right.

Cash didn't like when I wrote in the truck instead of paying attention to him so I stopped. I felt the sensation of having something to write pass through me over and over again without acting upon it until it didn't come so often anymore and I wasn't jolted to write.

He didn't like when I wanted to go for a run. He said he needed me around whenever I tried to go. So I let the urge to run pass through me until it didn't come up anymore and the habit was gone.

He didn't like when I went into the bedroom to do yoga or workout when he was playing guitar; he wanted me close to him, listening or singing along.

"Stop talking about the CIA so much on your Instagram," he told me one morning before he left for work.

Cash talked about the autonomous zones that we could go to, places where people like us went when the culture was rotten. They were always in flux, just like us; living our lives as experiments, in constant movement, never cementing in thought or identity.

We moved in on the full moon but I finished moving all my stuff in on the new moon. From Scorpio to Taurus and on to the final frontier: a wedding at the Hemingway House.

As I was redecorating the apartment, I found a painting that Cash and Stacey had made together on acid. It was Stacey's first time doing acid and she had written a letter to him on the back. I asked him if I could destroy it.

"No, it's a good memory," he said.

But later, after a day of so much drama and Stacey still keeping his kids from him, I broke it into pieces and threw it away.

"Let me see my girls and you give me back the Instagram account so I can make the money 'cause I'm not making any money. Our agreement is 2% of the weekly sales. How do you want me to make money if you're not going to give me the Instagram account?"

"Oh so you can just do whatever you want?"

"NO! I'm trying to make money! So. We. Can. Keep. Making. Money- HELLO?! We haven't made any money in weeks!"

"Are you able to put gas in your car? Are you able to eat wherever you want?"

"No! I'm living off credit cards. I'm living off credit cards."

"Well I think you know what you need to do."

"Yeah. You need to give me the Instagram and you need to let me see my girls on the weekend and we can just settle this."

"No. I need money."

"I just said I'm going to give you money. You've got to give to get."

"You've taken everything from me! You kept everything in your name. You've taken everything."

Their arguments circled around and around the same like a game.

We went to the attorney to see about all the paperwork Cash had to fill out. He was concerned about his privacy, giving up information about his income, his business, his assets, his stocks.

"You two are so in love. I want you to tell me if you ever go to Costa Rica. I'll tell you all about it, get you guys all set up" the joke of an attorney said, his blue eyes blinking, right below the red scrapes he had on his forehead.

He told us about his women: a 23-year-old, a 28-year-old, and another, Michelle, with a name instead of an age. Though out of all of them, he told us he still couldn't feel anything. He'd been in America with no vacation for five years.

I told him he'd find himself once the plane got into the sky. That's how everyone felt about America, whether they knew it or not. Once you were up in the air, it all fell down, all its gravity, all its weight, all its pull, all its power.

We finally realized the attorney did not file the correct paperwork so that Cash could see his children. The attorney had completely forgotten.

"Where did you get this attorney?" I asked.

"Mary's friend."

"Mary? That's what you get for working with someone she recommended. Of course he's trash," I said.

I started shit-talking Mary only after Cash repeatedly asked me for help in keeping her at bay. I didn't like being mean and I didn't like how naturally it came out of me. I liked to think the spite in my heart came from protection, from wanting to keep Cash safe from Mary's low vibrations.

At times we both admitted to missing her, but as a person, not as a lover. She wasn't good enough for us. She hadn't done the work like we had and she wasn't a genius.

I wrote my morning chores down to keep track of them: make tea, oatmeal, and lemon water, water plants, make bed, fill Berkey, make sure Cash's sketchbook is in his truck, make prompts for his writing at lunch, make lunch. I wrote all of Cash's to-dos down. I was responsible for half and the other half I had to make sure he accomplished.

At first, Cash wanted me to go with him to work every day but we quickly figured out it wouldn't work. He snapped

227

at me once and I snapped back.

"I work quickly," he said.

"I know you are brilliant and it is hard to be among others not as brilliant. But I hate when you talk to me like that."

It was the voice he used for Dez, Stephanie, Stacey, Mary- who knows what other women.

I spent a lot of time at the patio table in the backyard smoking cigarettes with Stephanie and her friends. I hit the splif when I got Cash's permission beforehand.

They liked to talk shit. I tried to steer them in holier directions but it was an uphill battle.

"Stacey is addicted to weed, kava, and kratom. She uses them while breastfeeding! She's not supposed to do that! We'll get full custody if we can prove she's an addict!"

For a while I was convinced that Cash should get full custody but I soon learned it took a lot more for that to happen. But I had visions of us getting out on the boat, just us and his kids, free to roam and go anywhere. But I was learning slowly that was never going to happen. We would never be free from Stacey.

"I don't trust Dez," Stephanie said, when I tried to change the subject away from Stacey. Nobody trusted Dez. If it wasn't one person they were shit-talking, it was another. And I knew they must have shit-talked me.

Stephanie even told me one time, "A friend of mine said she could see y'all dating but she didn't see a marriage happening."

On the beach one morning, Cash wrote in my journal, "*Mother, mother ocean, I have heard your call. I've wanted to sail upon your waters since I was 3 feet tall. These prisons exist only in my mind. There is but one task: connect to GOD. The problem with detaching is you leave drawbridges down across your moats. Spirit calls me to solitude, so my mind goes in lieu of body.*

I love Maria so much. I hate that she sees me like this. Enthusiasm in others irritates me. I want to matchstick everything and feel the heat upon my naked self. Forgiving others is easy – it's forgiving myself I find most difficult.

I'm already living on the water inside, care-free, making love to my two wives, making and raising babies, telling them stories. The second I see that teal water I'm jumping in. I'll bring my spear gun and catch a grouper, the aroma of blackened filet will tickle my nose while I move my bishop to E5, challenging her queen. Then I'll smile as I think back to these days and see all along that I was just playing a silly game. Much like the one we play now. The fish is done. Dinner is ready. The seat across from me appears empty but the sun is setting and GOD dines with us every evening."

When Cash talked about his second wife my insides turned into a furnace.

He asked me what I was thinking about after he read his daydream aloud and I said, "not really thoughts."

"What should I do?" I asked Cash when my emotions got the better of me, when he talked about the other wife he wanted and I felt surges of nausea, fear, jealousy.

"Worship me," he said.

With a task, I felt better immediately. We did some yoga on the beach, read a book together, swam. Cash made sure to tan his thighs.

Cash told his friends what he loved most about me was my unconditional surrender to him. But he also said I was rootless. He was afraid I wasn't going to put him first, that I still had other dreams. He said I needed to stay in his story.

I loved being in his story – I wanted to be there forever. I thought about the cliché of the dream of being a performer, of being in an international touring improv troupe versus being a mother and having a family. I saw the higher power in the latter.

Cash brought me more inspiration than I had ever received from one source. He was like an entire country – no – he was his own universe. And here he was muddling around in the normal world.

Living with him, I saw his masculinity and power multiply. Before he left the house, he would grab my twat with his fingers and rub me a few times and groan. He was the first man I had been with who was divinely inspired to please me. He ate tons of eggs.

"My favorite part of a woman is her stomach," he once said, taking a hit of the joint he got from a visiting friend. "That nice, beautiful belly fat." He made my unsexiest parts feel sexy.

We began to only eat bison for meat. Cash said the animals you consume end up a part of you.

"That's why they have people eating so much cow and chicken. Herd mentality."

He was scorned about the way people drank water. "You don't need that much," he said.

"Eight glasses a day is bullshit. You just need to swirl it around in your mouth."

He made us put the toilet cover down every time we used it or else he said it was like someone didn't finish. He despised overhead lighting, only used candles and lamps. He made me rinse my mouth out whenever we went into the ocean. He never locked anything because he said he was protected. He hated the sound of someone locking their car. *Beep!* He would grimace and yell, "That's a five hundred dollar fine!" He only liked white sheets.

One morning I woke up with a short story in my head about a black boy who gets put into jail for marijuana possession. It really was racist in Florida, like everyone said, and in a blatant kind of way instead of a hidden way like other states. And then I watched a black man swinging an ax walking down the street as if he was going to cut down a tree, one of the red flower trees.

I tried to hold the story in my mind but I think Cash fucked it out of me. He fucked a lot of fucked up things out of me.

Cash wrote in my journal before he went to work: *I prayed today for a son. I spoke into her womb – into the infinite. Come forth our angel, let us fill the ark with royal kin. Mormon Family Swanson.*

At Walmart, two boys asked me to help them find carpet cleaner – they had an all-purpose cleaner and asked me if that would suffice. They were both tall and gangly and looked older than I knew they were in their minds.

Cash told me just that morning how I activated the mother complex in men. He said they will look to me for nurturing, especially those without mothers to fill that void.

I scoured two aisles for them until we found one that would work. They were sweet and thankful. I was experiencing the mother archetype just like Cash said.

Omen, the black cat mother, cleaned herself next to me as we sat on the new chairs we got for our porch. We were millionaires but we lived in the hood. We were magicians but we were there to witness the end of the world: bad dressing, dull talking and mindless eating.

I pulled a tarot card that night to see if I was pregnant. The magician card: my other persona. The tarot was saying no – you're still a magician not a mother but the next morning I believed I could meld the two.

To be someone who uses tarot is a little bit embarrassing. Yes I inspired myself. Yes I was my own muse.

"I think you believe in a lot of New Age bullshit," Cash said to me when he came home that night.

He was in a bad mood and he was taking it out on me.

We debated yet again about the capacity of others. I believed anyone could tap into the magic if they knew how to pay attention. He thought it was an innate gift that only some people had – a select few. Few had Herculean capabilities in Cash's world. I thought the potential was in all, that everyone could be awakened. But Cash said hope was a waste of time.

I thought of time and how it might be distributed differently. How GOD might have eventually wondered whether each of his creations deserved to live out their whole life and experience their full potential. Maybe he thought that way at first but then saw not all humans could live that way. That it wasn't sustainable. That he couldn't make them like that every time. Or maybe it was about deserving.

Maybe he decided not everyone deserved to live to their highest potential and that dying younger would suffice. That man could get the picture or the point with less time, less years on the planet. Or he wouldn't and he'd have to repeat himself.

Maybe GOD got tired of wasting souls on bodies that didn't fight for infinity, for transcendence.

I was surrounded by broken souls without any nostalgia for the infinite or determination for a meaningful life, especially in Florida where most people were broken by opiates, alcohol, housing bubbles, and humidity. Cash said it was the stagnant air. The wind stopped blowing in summertime and the people got stuck.

"If there's a Hercules in every person then I have a soul mate in every girl," he said, trying to hurt me.

"And that means every guy I've dated was a Hercules too," I said, logically.

"Where is the magic in that? Fucking normie," he said.

I don't think he was used to being around people that tested his logic.

Everyone usually just listened to what he said. No one ever told him their thoughts, if they even had thoughts. Everyone just wanted to keep him happy, the golden boy.

He didn't like to live in the logos anyways. Neither did I but it came out of me anyways like a bad habit.

CHAPTER THIRTEEN: LEARNED HELPLESSNESS, AND THE SEVEN DEADLY CHAKRAS

Cash wanted to find a new girlfriend, the second wife. I was going to be the first wife now. I felt special but ideally I wanted it to be just us. But he told me from the start I would have to share him so I only struggled against myself; a silent battle with my own insecurity.

I liked the challenge, liked eating up and transcending my jealousy, my envy. I knew the experience would make me stronger. I was strong enough to be one of two lovers for Cash.

Since Mary was gone or, maybe since before she left, Cash was talking to a girl called Sommer. She was an addict and only nineteen. I didn't like that he was pursuing someone weak and vulnerable. But that was before I met her.

Sommer was not a normal girl, not a normie in any way, much less a normie than I was. And she definitely wasn't weak. As for vulnerable, hell, who wasn't?

He told me when he asked her to hang out the first time she texted that she didn't like conforming to time and that she couldn't make any promises. Ever. She was either really cool or really good at avoiding people.

Cash tried to have her meet up with us but she always slipped through his fingers. I think they had lunch a few times without me.

Cash went to lunch with lots of different girls, mostly young strippers. He wanted them to see true masculinity. He wanted to offer support and mentorship, hint at a different life, another way. He probably told them the same things he told me: he was a cult leader, wanted two wives, and was a GOD.

It made me laugh that he snagged me that way. But now I knew he had the power to back it up.

Cash, Dez, JT and I went to the Himalayan salt room downtown for our cult meeting. Sommer was supposed to meet us there but didn't. We all took shrooms. Lucci was late.

Cash was lying down on an amethyst table in the room when I crawled on top of him, in front of everyone. We went into our own world together, laughing and giggling.

We tried to match each of the seven chakras to each of

the seven deadly sins. Crown: pride, third eye: greed, throat: wrath, heart: envy, solar plexus: gluttony, sacral: lust, and root: sloth. It was just for fun but we went back and forth debating about which matched up with which and in the end he agreed with my choices. And in front of everyone, on the table, we were in our own world.

Lucci showed up and Cash offered him the table.

It was after Lucci's arrival that Dez announced, "I don't think I will ever fall in love again."

Everyone looked at her.

After no one said anything, she said, "Maria, would you leave the planet or would you stay on the earth if you had to make the choice?"

"What would be the circumstances?" I asked.

"No explanation. You have to make a choice."

I could feel Cash and her were in on something

"I'd stay on the planet. I love Earth. Everything is here."

"She's testing you," Cash said.

"I know. About what?"

"She's seeing if she can take you away with her and the rest of the aliens."

"Are you going?"

"I don't know yet."

"Well I changed my answer. I'd go wherever you're going."

"You can't change your answer," Dez said.

"Would you go with her?" I asked Cash.

"I'm probably going into the center of the earth."

"And taking me right?"

"Yes," Cash said but I felt anxious and hurt that Dez would take away my king.

Sommer texted Cash she was going to the event at Neenie's House that night. He sent an Uber for her since she didn't drive.

Art parties at Neenie's were fun. I was excited to see all the hippies and artists again in Fort Myers.

We parked across the street, walked to the entrance,

and then Cash went off to meet up with Sommer somewhere.

I had to stay with Dez and JT and Lucci outside the entrance. We all sat down at a picnic table. I was nervous and wanted to enter the event and dance and not think about Cash with Sommer but Dez wouldn't let me leave her side. This is what she was getting paid for.

Lucci told me to go bum a lighter off someone so we could all smoke JT's blunt.

I noticed Lucci would command me to do small tasks, like throw small pieces of trash away or fill up a glass of water. I knew Cash had been giving the boys stuff to read about masculinity. I found his attempts to tame my feminine chaos comical. But I felt that way about every man except Cash.

Dez was off the whole night, crying because Cash was being mean to her or she was frustrated that we didn't have a plan. But we never did. That was the point.

Cash told us earlier we were all going to Orlando that night to visit his grandpa. Everyone was going on this out of nowhere trip, obeying their cult leader. And now we sat waiting for him, being sort of rude to each other.

Finally, Cash came over to us. He was with Sommer. She had a puppy with her.

I was quiet. Cash told me later I was intimidating. But inside I felt queasy and sad.

We all went inside. Cash hung out with her almost the whole time we were there.

I ran around with the others, Dez always hovering around at my side.

Lucci and I took pictures in hats.

Dez and I were hit on by some guy while drinking wine.

I caught up with a few people I knew.

The owner of the place told me she thought Cash seemed like a Svengali type. I didn't know what a Svengali was but she talked to me in earnest like she was warning me.

"You're a very smart woman with a lot of charm. You can do whatever you want. Be kind and strong."

She must have talked to Leslie and Ashley about Cash

and the cult. They were all just jealous. Ashley had been jealous from the start, probably wanting Cash to fall for her during the eye gazing event. She complained a lot about being fat and getting overlooked.

The owner was a single old lady. She didn't know anything about true love.

Finally, Sommer was elsewhere and I got to be with Cash for a little bit. I sat in his lap while we listened to a tarot reader give Lucci a reading. But then Cash disappeared again.

JT disappeared too and Dez and I had to find him. He was sitting outside smoking his vape. He told us his brother had called and said he wanted to kill himself over the phone.

This had happened before. His brother was in a really bad relationship with an abusive girlfriend. JT rarely shared anything personal and never emotional. Whenever I asked him how he felt about anything, he'd just say, "I'm straight."

All three of them suffered from different anxieties; Dez, JT, and Lucci. Cash was good at managing them through their respective ghosts but I was apt to let them take over and run the show. I tried to be strong for Cash but I felt depleted with jealousy.

The event was ending and we were all waiting outside for Cash. He told us we were going to a kava bar and to meet him out front. It was midnight and we still needed to drive three hours to Orlando. He was off somewhere with Sommer.

Dez told me I needed to command Cash, as if it were that easy, to get home to pack and skip the kava bar.

I was complaining in Spanish to Lucci and JT, who could only understand part of what I was saying. I wanted to say ugly things that people couldn't understand.

Sommer was ugly, gangly, and grungy. Why would he pick her? I could never be attracted to someone like that. And she was so young.

I asked JT why I should be expected to be with someone like her.

"Man, I don't know your guys' deal. Don't try and make me part of it," he said.

Lucci said he was surprised to see me, normally beautiful and full of light showing so much ugliness.

"You have everything, Maria!" Dez said.

I looked at her, sort of shocked. I guess that was true. I tried to let the ugly emotions go away. But they didn't.

I asked for a sip of Dez's drink. She was drinking something out of a cup you get at a fast food restaurant with a straw and a lid.

She looked at me and made a face like she didn't want to give it to me but I took it from her. I laughed at her after I drank it. I thought it was going to be iced tea or lemonade. It was iced tea lemonade but it was spiked. So that was how she made it through.

Maybe that was why she cried so much. Maybe she was always sort of drunk. Like Mary. That's how they withstood Cash's severity.

He threatened to fire her all the time. Even when he did fire her once, she just kept showing up. Everyone always kept showing up in Cash's life. Everyone was so desperate to be with him.

Being with Cash I wondered if I hated myself since he was so strict and severe to me. But other people worked strict and severe jobs they didn't believe in, committing their lives to bureaucracy, to a protestant work ethic, to slavery.

I believed in Cash: the Saturnian father, the gangster priest, my cult leader. How could I consider what I was doing dangerous or wrong, when the world around me was so dangerous and wrong?

Finally, Cash came out of the party with Sommer and a couple of her friends. They were all tweakers.

"Cash, we need to go home and leave for Orlando. Everyone is too tired to go to kava," I said.

He agreed and told Lucci to help Sommer and her friends get to his house.

I was surprised how easy it was to get him to comply. Then I realized he was on more drugs. I couldn't tell which kind.

"Why are you sending Lucci with the tweakers? It's

not safe," I said.

"I'm the king. Don't argue with me," he growled.

I pushed too far.

Lucci called us from the car when we were driving back to Cash's.

"Hey these guys are tweaking out. Like, they are screaming their heads off at each other. They can't drive. We're going to get in an accident."

"See? You're putting Lucci in danger," I yelled at Cash.

Dez and JT stayed silent in the backseat.

"Stop disobeying me," Cash said.

When we got to the house, Cash went inside with Sommer and the tweakers and I stayed in the truck. Dez and Lucci tried to get me out of the truck.

"Will you just hit me?" I asked them.

Sommer was singing inside the house while Cash played guitar. She had a beautiful voice. She was singing Amy Winehouse.

Dez and Lucci wouldn't hit me.

Cash came outside and told me to pack.

"Why are you playing Amy Winehouse with her? That is mine." I said.

"Are you just going to be mad no matter what now?" Cash asked.

He was playful and giddy.

"You need to pack, little girl," he said.

So I went upstairs to pack. I was melancholy, singing sad songs with the three black cats hanging around as I threw random clothes into my duffle. They always hung around when I was sad.

I went back to the house and helped one of the tweakers get her phone out of the car. The tweaker that drove wasn't letting her into the car so I snatched the car keys from her. The other one thanked me profusely and then I gave her some advice.

"Don't let people fuck with you."

Lucci came outside to complain to me about how we

shouldn't be around such toxic people.

We were sitting on the front porch.

I lit a cigarette, turned to him and said, "We can't even deal with them for an hour. Think about what that says about us."

I went into the house again and Sommer asked me if I wanted to take a dab, the first time she spoke to me.

"Sure!" I said.

She took me to the car and gave me a dab.

"This is just what I needed," I said.

Sommer and the tweakers finally left. Dez, Lucci, JT, Cash and I finally went on our way to O-Town in Cash's meaningless blue truck.

Sommer left wearing Cash's Muay Thai boxers that he earned while training in Thailand. I had never even seen them before.

When we got to the Airbnb, I had to read the email the owners sent. I instructed Cash how to get inside the gate in a cold, calculating manner that he hated.

He slapped me on the face in front of everyone, telling me I needed to get right and stop disrespecting him.

When we got inside the apartment, he said he didn't want me to go on the late night swimming outing, that he didn't know if I was his soulmate.

I cried and cried. I begged him to take me with them. He refused. I sat on the stairs crying and waiting for him to return.

I wanted to say to him, "You really don't give a fuck, do you? You just fuck with us and we let you because you're rich and powerful and we love you."

But I couldn't say any of that to him, it would ruin the game. There was a fearful respect he had drawn out of me that I couldn't just turn off. He was extremely sensitive. You couldn't really talk about him or he'd turn the tables on you.

The next day I was most surprised to find that Cash was a tourist. He took us to gimmicky places. I figured that's just what happens to rich businessmen. All the gimmicks blend into the non-gimmicks and everything is just a gimmick when you have unlimited funds.

You're so used to spending money on people that you forget people might actually have a preference themselves on how they'd like to spend their time and your money.

If it costs money, the rich think, then it must have value and, therefore, be good. And if it's my money everyone must be having a good time.

Their money is like puppet strings upon the world.

Dance, monkey, dance.

In Orlando, Cash took us to this discovery museum for little kids. We all had to trail behind him. Dez pulled me along whenever I paused too long on my own at a display. He made me teach everyone yoga as we waited in line.

In Ocala, where his grandpa lived, Cash took us into the swamps on an airboat. And then we went to a restaurant and had fried frog legs and alligator.

We went to his grandpa's house and Cash was still angry at me. He wondered aloud whether he should introduce me or Dez as his girlfriend. My natural inclination was to shut down emotionally but instead, I stood up, walked inside, and introduced myself as his girlfriend before anything else could happen.

That night we stayed in Orlando at a resort with multiple pools and jacuzzis. It was like an adult water park. Cash gave everyone shrooms and then he and I went back to our hotel room and watched *Soul.* In the morning he bought me a new outfit.

On the drive home, Lucci talked about how bad he wanted a young wife.

"Why do you want a young wife?" I asked.

"Because learned helplessness is less likely to be a problem."

I had never heard of the concept of learned helplessness.

When I asked him to explain, he sighed and said, "Women who are older tend to blame external circumstances for their life outcome. The more bad stuff happens to them, the more bitter and angry they get."

Then he said he was too tired to explain more. He flicked my chin and told me not to worry, that his future wife was going to be my best friend.

Cash asked who would take ownership of all the drugs if we got pulled over. We all looked at each other. Cash said that I would since I didn't have anything at stake. Everyone else in the car had something at stake: kids, land, assets, probation.

I agreed solemnly. But we didn't get pulled over. Cash always drove the speed limit.

We only saw Sommer one more time after that and I got a chance to try again, to prove myself to be honey and milk, a good hostess, a good wife.

Late at night, out front of the house, she danced with her tiny skateboard in flow state, singing songs as Cash played guitar, but mostly complaining about her life.

For someone who was a tweaker, she was quite talented. She brought a few friends with her; one was a woman she had once been engaged to. The other was one of the tweakers who came over the first time. They were all using the tweaker for her car because her personality obviously sucked. Cash said she had a demon inside her.

Cash was tired of Sommer's complaining and lost interest in her after that. He stopped answering her phone calls. It seems she had already come down with a case of learned helplessness, only nineteen.

CHAPTER FOURTEEN: YACHTS, TARANTINO, AND THE HOOD

Cash and I looked at three yachts that week in an attempt to find our ark.

The first vessel we looked at was a beauty. And we met a true craftsman – a true boat genius. He was our people. We got more lives out of him in those short fifteen minutes under board then you can get out of most people ever.

He spoke with warnings edged in between brief but vivid descriptions of his life.

"The sea has one job and that's to kill you."

"When things go south I got three different buttons I can press."

"You got a lot to learn if you don't know what this button is."

"All she does is lull you into a false sense of security. I'm talking about the high seas, not my old lady."

The second vessel we saw we couldn't even go inside. The owner forgot to unlock it for the broker – a Catamaran. But when we saw "Shambhala" printed on the side we knew it was a sign we were on the right path.

Shambhala was where Cash said he was going to take me. That's where we had to go at just the right time. Cash said it was somewhere cold, somewhere in the middle of the ocean.

I finally googled "Shambhala," to see for myself where it was now that I knew how to spell it. I learned it was a transcendental concept in Buddhism for a state of mind.

But Cash assured me that wasn't all it was. Shambhala was a secret, hidden, actual place for souls like us.

The third vessel we looked at changed our lives: a bed and breakfast 80-footer called *Ocean Romance*. We'd never thought about having our own bed and breakfast before.

We spit balled excitedly; we could spread our love, our passion, our mythos to people who stayed on our boat. Cash's mom could make the food southern comfort style. We'd dress without a regard for time.

So we made an offer: 400 grand. They countered with 425k. So we countered with 410k on my phone in text messages to the broker, John King. They accepted and we pushed for time before we had to put down a 50k deposit.

We looked for yachts to escape the apocalypse on Monday. We got facials on Tuesday. And for the Wednesday cult meeting, we took the cult to a dinner show.

It was the one about the mafia kid, *A Bronx Tale*. Cash saw himself in the main character. A young boy gets picked up by way of friendship by the most powerful gangsters and becomes one himself. It was just like Cash's life.

Cash told me on our very first date about the scene in *A Bronx Tale* that inspired him to consider whether the women he dated were marriage material. They had to pass the "lock test."

If, when the man opens the car passenger door for their date, she reaches over and unlocks the door on the driver's side, then she's the one. If she doesn't, then she isn't.

I failed the test and Cash told me so and promptly informed me on our first date.

I never understood why I failed and thought the test was about unlocking the truck which was easy for him to do with the automatic clicker so I never picked up the behavior, even after he explained it to me and how he would like for me to perform said behavior. Behaving that way didn't make any sense to me at the time.

When I saw the play I understood it was coming from a time before cars had clickers. So then I understood how I could make it apply to the world of today and I started reaching over and pushing open his car door wide; an extra step that actually dissolved an action for him.

I thought it was stupid but he loved it.

There were a lot of behaviors he wanted out of me that felt stupid, like when he asked me for compliments and then got angry that he had to ask for them. So then I had to compliment him while he was angry which pissed me off. So then we were both angry.

Or when JT confessed his love for me. I felt like I got hit in an emotional hit and run. I was busy believing in the fairy tale, the mythos, the good in people, in our cult, when suddenly, out of nowhere, ulterior motives made their entrance.

Was I too focused on the prize? Or not focused enough on the prize? I kept forgetting I couldn't trust our followers just because I wanted to.

One afternoon JT typed out his confession of love for me in an unsent text message on his phone and showed it to me while I was putting groceries away one afternoon. Cash was paying him to do housework while he was working at the factory.

When I told Cash he was so upset he thought I should be comforting *him*. But I also wanted to be comforted. I once trusted JT and found myself feeling cheap and used. I guess that's how Cash and I felt. But he blamed me.

"You are like a mother to them because they lack maternal love. They didn't experience warm, unconditional, motherly love. But there is also a thin line that you can cross into inappropriateness. You have to be more aware."

He said the true cult leader is the woman.

I spent my days weathering storms of his moods. He missed his children. He had trust problems. He had high standards. His moods ran through me like electricity in a wire. I was so in tune with him already but he wanted to tune me up deeper so that I'd be hooked up to him like life support.

Cash got angry when I talked about my first book I wrote but didn't finish editing: *The Slut*. I thought he could help me add a strong male character presence in my book. But he would always get too upset to have any conversation around helping me write it. We couldn't even discuss it without fighting.

He didn't like how I knew all the rap songs that I grew up listening to in high school and junior high. But all those songs about womens' bare bottoms and pussies only made me think more about swim parties and slumber parties. Carefree, childish nudity. I'd never thought about how dark it was. All that sleaze at such a young age. There was so much more to life than sex. I already had enough hormones as a teenager. Who knows why I listened to Afroman anyways.

When Cash got irritated, he said he was going to drive

away in his truck with his three black cats. Well, that crushed me the most.

It was almost funny how badly you needed him and how little he needed you.

I wrote in my journal: *Why is a jealous boyfriend bad anyways?*

I stopped writing my dreams down. They only reminded me of ways I was inferior to Cash. They were dark, twisted, and desperate. I didn't want to acknowledge them. I didn't want to even think about what they were trying to tell me. By writing them down, by examining the details, they would get more powerful. Or would the power go away? Cash said writing them down would give them more power.

People talked about the summer heat starting up. I thought to myself, heat? What about the hell we're in? We could barely breathe from the smoke. The animosity, the scorn, the constant souring and churning, meanwhile, people were worried about the heat?! What about Cash's story? Cash's all-encompassing life?

Since I was in love with him, it was hard to go back to the way it was before, when he was just a cult leader and I was his little follower. He had made me larger than life through loving me; a queen. Now I had responsibilities in serving him, his family, and the cult.

There was something hungry about him. He orchestrated a very specific circle of people that depended on him. I wouldn't be surprised if he just disappeared at some point. He didn't owe anybody anything. Not even me. But he helped each follower in his circle in some necessary way. JT, Stephanie, and Stacey struggled with drug addictions, Mary with alcoholism, Dez with single motherhood, Lucci with friendship and women.

I was surrounded by people with real problems. It was funny how I used to wonder about them and now they were my friends. I used to live in the richest city with the smartest people trying to solve the problems of these people back in San Francisco. Those people in that big city, they're not that smart at all. They were just rich and didn't have any problems. They had no clue how hard most of the world laughed at them.

All my friends getting masters degrees suddenly looked so pathetic. People seemed so miserable going to grad school and working in social work. I wondered why they did it, though I had been inches close to going down the same path. Why would you ever do something you didn't enjoy?

Now I lived in the hood with my millionaire boyfriend. Cash and his mom laughed at me when I said I wanted to go to the park. I guess because of how hood it was. It was easy to forget because we were rich. He told us the church on the block would keep us protected but not to test it. I wasn't allowed to walk around the neighborhood.

"Plus, who's gonna fuck with us? We have three black cats. They take one look and say, nah not these fools."

He ran into the bathroom one morning when I was in the shower to tell me he found a hundred grand in cash.

"How?" I asked, pulling aside the shower curtain to look at him. He said something about his old Shopify account. Now we had enough spare cash for the yacht.

One day, I tried to explain to him how certain political commentary could be used as a tool – a necessary mechanism. Cash laughed and tossed away the leaky life vest I was using as a raft and pulled me aboard his ship, shaking his head, amused. And yes, even as I continued to listen regularly to the post leftist commentators I admired, I knew how absurdly pointless it all was.

The world was certainly in a bad way – what else could we do about it but continue griping? No – that was not *our* way – our way was to take to the seas. To abandon the world as it had abandoned us. *Ocean Romance*, island wedding, it all blended into single salvation.

Cash told me the political games were rigged and I knew he was right. I knew I needed him to show me the way and how to be more honest with myself. It was easy and enjoyable to fall into their games, their trap. I didn't want to be in anyone else's story except for Cash's.

Meanwhile, secretly, I was working on my rage. It was as if I had developed a secret technology that I couldn't share with anyone, one that had the capacity to get quite out of hand. I had no one to talk to about it. I placed a cold stone between Cash and myself to maintain a sense of control. But GOD didn't like stones.

Cash said he could see himself getting back together with Stacey one day. That tore a page out of my matrix. This woman lived as a vile creature in my mind. Sometimes Cash said she was bipolar, sometimes he said she was possessed. He told me when she took Ayahuasca, the goddess told her to kill herself. And yet he still considered her.

Many times I tried imagining this woman's positive qualities. Perhaps she told great jokes and stories, or maybe it was her high energy, her motivation to move, to make money, make shit, make drama. She must have a gargantuan personality. Cash loved a good story; it put all the twinkles in his eyes. But stability? Maybe he would never want stability.

From what she looked and sounded like on her Instagram and TikToks, I couldn't understand the attraction. She smeared her face with cakey orange makeup, pursed her lips like a duck in her selfies, and dressed like a rich bohemian-the most tasteless and inauthentic of styles. I'd likened her to a sort of ogress who kept her kids away from their father. But she wasn't ugly – it was my thinking that was ugly. Maybe that was my lesson and this was my test. I had to reclaim my light. I had to stop having these negative thoughts and stop being petty. Like Cash said, "Don't project your bad thoughts onto me." Sometimes he said he could feel me casting shadows on him.

When I told his mom I was writing his book, she said, "Like about all his trippy shit? All the drugs?"

Was he just a man who took his drug trips too seriously and too far? There were many literary heroes who did this and created an entire movement: Ken Kesey, Terence McKenna, Tao Lin, William Burroughs, Hunter S. Thompson. I thought Cash was a greater hero with more luminous goals than any of them. And yet... his own mother...

I felt unsettled by Stephanie's lack of appreciation for Cash's magnanimity. But then again, she spent all her time drinking, working for her son, and watching TV. She wavered in and out of the magic, sometimes playing into it with Cash's help, almost as good as Cash himself. But most of the time, she seemed unable to see at all.

"I don't want to cast judgment," he said when he had something to say about someone close to him, like when JT disappeared for hours to "go buy weed under the bridge" or when his mom slept in until 5 PM.

But they never hesitated to cast judgment on him.

CHAPTER FIFTEEN: STRIP CLUB, DEATH OF A BLACK CAT, AND CORTISONE

Cash came home with lipstick on his forehead one night. But I didn't see it until right before we went to bed.

He was the gallivanting type. I didn't completely mind. I wanted him to grow his power, his influence, his reach. I didn't want to keep his light away from all the people who might benefit, though I worried about the dystopian social scene of Fort Myers.

I knew there were artists and poets and entrepreneurs to be found but I watched him waste his time so easily with blacked-out tourists. Maybe I was too quick to judge. There could never be good finds without genuine interest at all times I suppose.

Cash had been a cult leader his entire life, he knew what he was doing. Yet followers were not so easily found. The low-functioning ran rampant, especially in Florida.

Lucci and Cash were out one night looking for a certain building owner to engage with about a business venture. Of course I wished them the best while I was stuck at home doing dishes. We were in a goddamn goldmine after all.

It was 1AM when he finally came home but for him that didn't matter. He still made a bonfire like he said he would.

"Where were you?"

"I was at the edge of a cliff. I saw lots of lost souls out there."

We spoke philosophically around the bonfire. His logic wasn't faulty or emotional but clear and clever and he enjoyed the discussion, didn't argue to persuade me as he usually did.

Later, much later, I saw the lipstick on his forehead. He admitted he went to a strip club with Lucci. I screamed at him for the first time that night. He was amused by my outrage, like it was something he was seeking all along. He told me he had a reason to be there.

In the morning I put myself in his shoes and told myself a story about his night at the strip club. And that night, when he came home early, he wrote his part. And we made our first story together. The main thing was to keep the main thing the main thing.

Cash's Night at the Strip Club

He said a prayer outside the strip club. And then he put his hand on the door handle, opened it slowly and stepped inside.

It was smoky, and unevenly lit; dark in some corners, bright in others. There was one small stage under a beam of orange light. The people sitting around the stage in couches and easy chairs were mostly overweight, all men, all over the age of 58.

But he was handsome, fit, clever-eyed, young, but older than he looked, something he had plenty of fun with. He lit a cigarette and strolled over to the bar.

"What can I get you honey?" The bartender, a brown, girlish young woman with one side purple, one side black curly ringlets asked.

"I'll take a club soda with lemon."

"What's your name?" he asked as she handed him the drink.

"Lex."

"Nice to meet you, Lex, my name's Cash," he said, in a soft, game show voice.

She smiled at him then went off to another customer. Cash took his drink to the stage, just in time to see the recently-turned 18-year-old girl he came to see.

His goal was not so much to embarrass her, though she did turn beet-red when she saw him, as it was to empower her, to dissuade her from the rough life through his presence at her tragic performance.

At Vixens every stripper dance was a tragedy happening in front of a lucky few that got to experience a mythological event in the middle of their drinking.

If they were really lucky, the stripper still had the semblance of awareness required to present herself in front of the gods.

All tragedy must involve both the almighty and the

aware.

And that was what Cash saw reflected in little Katie, the brand new stripper's eyes: the GOD of remorse, sitting right in the front row.

Incredible stuff, Cash thought, as he had long ago given up on pity, the pointless substance indulgent of ego as one must place oneself above another in order to look down upon them.

No, he nodded knowingly at the GOD of remorse's reflection in little Katie's eyes as she began to grind her ass crack up and down the pole, a simple move new strippers cling to.

Did she have the slightest clue of where she was playing? Did she know they both sat on the edge of darkness, that his soul hovered near the same abyss many a man had once faltered and fell into, never to see the light again? Under neon glow and trembling bass, he had risked much to show face at Hades' gate, like Orpheus traveling to the underworld to rescue his beloved, disguised. A saint must enter like a Trojan, the would-be brand of condom any ordinary man would use to penetrate our fallen angels' bodily depths. But he sought to enter the depths of her forgotten spirit, to plant simple seeds of remembrance that would take root and offer a sprout to bring her back from the pit of lost flesh dreams.

"Do you have the slightest clue of where you are playing?" He asked her.

"Well, they changed the name recently. Now it's called Vixens."

Victims, he thought grimly.

"Ah, yes. Classy place. It's kind of warm in here though."

"I'm fine when I'm moving but when I'm down and pulling I get cool."

"Ah, well come see me when you're down. I can't stay long. I might get spotted."

She tilted her head back and chuckled. "By who?"

"The red man himself."

He noticed her brow lowered and her body changed

dialects, suddenly aware his visit was a destined one, not fueled by the worship of a lesser deity. Sensing his gambit had been uncovered, he decided to mislead. He took a wad of her GOD and tossed it to the heavens and watched her face snap back to the illusion while Washington winked back.

He walked over to the bar and ordered an apple from the falling, winking gods, all $100 of them.

She kneeled before them and with an effective sweep, she piled them nicely.

He wondered if she thought the simple accuracy of this tidying normal or, if only she were aware, it might have something to do with her great mothers before her perfecting through years the art of practicing submission while the fathers went to war on their behalf.

That night Cash's girlfriend woke up to him jacking off in his sleep in the middle of the night. She woke him up.

"A demon must have jumped on my back!" He said. And then he told her of his journey.

I think I got pregnant on the same day one of the three black cats died. Maybe that's the soul that ended up in my womb, knowing it would be removed anyways.

Stephanie put the cat's body in the bathtub before we dug the hole in the backyard.

We discussed whether the mother cat, Omen, should be shown her son's dead body so that she would know to stop searching for him or whether that would be too shocking.

Later when we found his body missing, we figured she must have taken him out of the bathtub and gone off to bury him herself.

Earlier in the morning before we learned that the cat had been struck to its death, Cash and I were discussing the plight of the invasive reptile species we were observing imprisoned in a pen with a poor little turtle at the nature preserve in Cape Coral.

"I guess they're all reptiles but I can't imagine the iguana nor the Nile Monitor considers him as one of their own," I said, gesturing towards the other prisoners.

We looked at the incarcerated and pondered the meaning of their enslavement. Had their fates already been decided? Would their souls be declared innocent in the "great courts of law" of the United States of America? Or did they thrive in their high-cortisone, low-stress lifestyle?

Was happiness an achievable reality or was it only the outcome of maintaining hormones at levels that Big Pharma deemed normal? Neither Cash nor I trusted what Big Pharma had to say about our endocrine systems.

We could only reflect on their purpose under GOD. Were we wrong to lock them up? Was that the nature of our species or just another sign of the decaying times? Cash equated me to an argument that he did not agree with and he began to criticize me. He thought I still had inferior belief systems about the nature of happiness. He wanted to explore what I had long ago stopped believing in: the value of happiness.

"No one with a working mind could ever be satisfied," I told him. "As Seneca said, 'For if we could be satisfied with anything, we should have been satisfied long ago.' Chasing happiness was only for the mindless, the naïve, and the ignorant."

Someday soon I believed Cash would take me to the mythological waters and I'd never have to leave. But for now we struggled in swimming in between the logos and the mythos. The logical conditioning of our upbringing continued to rear its ugly head from our beautiful pool of the mythos like a hideous sea monster.

It was a problem that resulted in ugly feelings and words out of the both of us. Perhaps they were demons that attempted to prevent our transcendence, our fairy tale.

I didn't give up. I didn't give up on the love, the spirit, the muse, the angels that watched over us when we were in the moment, the mythos together; when we were one. I don't know if my angels joined up with his angels or if we had new angels show up but they sure did make beautiful music.

CHAPTER SIXTEEN: FULL MOON, ARCHETYPES, AND A BAPTISM

Cash and I were fighting a lot. Cash liked to get rises out of me to "see where I was at." I hated it.

"Do you really think we're soulmates? Do you think we are meant for each other?" He'd say.

"You're the one who's gonna fuck it up," I'd respond. "If anything, it's you who's gonna ruin it."

He said we shouldn't be away from each other at all, that we were supposed to always be together. We spent half the day apart at times.

"That's why we're fighting," he surmised. "People are messing with our magic."

After fighting, I usually drove to Walmart or Target. They were places I could go so he wouldn't get jealous that I was going somewhere without him, places I could be alone and think and write in the parking lot after buying something random like cleaning supplies or toothpicks.

When you hate the world or your life your only escape is writing about it; getting to the details. Somehow there is relief in the details.

I could remember that I'd already fallen in love with the world, with the mountains, with the ocean. My heart could break but nothing would ever break me. I had cast my soul on the sea, on crystal peaks, on trees. Good thing I had fallen in love with the adventure before him. Or maybe that was what was wrong with me.

We had just taken Stacey's car from her house and Cash felt terrible about it even though it was his car and she was just driving it. I was trying to lighten the mood by bringing the wine out. Cash drank a lot more of it than I did. I only meant for us to share a glass with dinner but he kept pouring himself glasses until it was gone.

We were making music together with the loop station. I was writing good lyrics and Cash was making good music but he was in a bad way. He decided to call his dad. He wanted masculine advice.

"I'm surrounded by all these women!"

We were in a play. Cash was the main character and we were his three supporting women: Stephanie, Dez, and me.

Stacey was the evil dragon. Mary was the wicked witch.

We had all sort of convinced him to take the car, to try to initiate some change in the situation so that he could get closer to seeing his kids. It was his car, after all, and we thought it made sense to take what was his when she wouldn't share what was theirs. We were desperate. Cash hadn't seen his kids for almost three months.

He let me listen to the conversation with his dad but gave me a sign to stay silent. He asked me what I thought afterwards.

"He's crazy," I said. "The good kind."

I was touched by Cash's dad's perspective. He saw spirits and felt energies as I had through sleep paralysis and meditation. He talked of the black box of Saturn, an energy I had also felt. And he spoke of spirituality in a way that resonated deeply with me. But like everything magical I encountered with Cash, it fell into place as just another part of our magic.

We started watching a movie in bed.

"Why do you think my dad is crazy?" Cash asked.

"I don't know. I can't explain it," I said, fixated on the movie.

"You don't know what you're talking about. I shouldn't have let you listen to us talk."

I went silent.

"You're just a little girl. Talk to me!"

I felt frozen. He became angrier.

The next thing I knew I was standing next to Cash's truck, leaning through the window begging him to stay as he sat in the driver's seat with the engine running.

"Is everything OK?" Stephanie came outside of the other house and asked.

"Yes, everything's fine," we said. She said something about being surprised to see us fighting. She went back inside.

"Maybe you're the reason all these bad things are happening to me, the reason why I can't see my daughters. Everyone is in the matrix trying to distract me and pull me into it. I just want to leave you all behind!"

I hated these moments when everyone became suspect, including me and I got blended into the mob of the people he placed in his life. I felt I would never be unique or special to him, would never be as high in his heart hierarchy as I had placed him in mine.

"I think I should go to Orlando alone. It will be good for me," Cash said.

"It will be good for us," I corrected.

"Yeah, sure," he said, sadly.

Cash had planned on taking me to Orlando with him to visit his sick grandfather again. I thought the time apart would do us some good, considering we'd never had any time apart before. But I was sad made the decision when we were fighting.

"I'm going to stop drinking. It's not worth risking our relationship. I was bogged down by the wine and didn't feel like explaining what I meant. The truth is I think your dad is brilliant and everything he said resonated with me deeply."

Secretly, I was excited to be alone finally.

Cash left for Orlando in his truck the next morning. His mom went off in her car to visit her mother. I was left with the house to myself for the first time.

The sun was burning through the fog. I thought it'd be a cool one outside. Not a chance. The heat was coming. People had warned me about it for so long.

Cash gave me a lot of tasks to do but I still made it out to the beach and went for a swim in some nearby springs. There were lots of Russians in the spring, even more than Floridians. I'd seen Russian enclaves in places like Thailand or Mexico but it was funny to see them in a place like Florida. It felt good to be alone with myself.

But the next morning Cash said he missed me too much. He needed to fly me out the next day. I didn't miss him but I said I did or else he would be upset.

On the phone he told me about a man he met the night before at a bar. He decided to call him Morpheus. Morpheus invited Cash back to his house to show him his apocalypse prep.

In one room he had multiple screens set up to monitor and track every single fire and flight in the country. In another room he had aquariums with various species of fish for breeding. In the garage he had a collection of ten or so guns he built himself.

"You don't need a license for the gun if you build it yourself," Morpheus said.

Cash was inspired.

"He's bloody brilliant! You should have been there, Maria! We gotta start our own."

I made a to-do list: study how to grow plants at sea, where to buy seeds, medicines, pills, and now fish. The end of the world was just the beginning of course.

I landed in Orlando and Cash picked me up. I was alone for only two nights. And then I was back with Cash. It was my lucky number day, May 21st, but we got into our worst fight yet.

"The Uber driver that took me to the airport was so funny. He told me all about herbalism, just like I want to study. I think he was trying to make connections with the people he drove. I gave him my Instagram in case you were interested in him."

"You gave him your Instagram?"

"Yeah. I mean, just my fake one," I lied.

"Why would you do that?"

"I thought you might be interested in him. I think he's looking for work. I thought he could be of value to you."

"What sort of value would a guy studying herbalism bring to me? You betrayed me!"

"No I didn't!"

"You are people pleasing again. You're deceiving me. You've crossed my line!"

"No! I would never cross your line!"

"You got me fucked up if you think I'm that stupid."

I cried and cried. We were supposed to go shopping but I couldn't get out of the car. I was so upset.

We left the mall and went to a park where he continued

trying to make me see how I had wronged him.

At one point he said, "I would never get someone else's number."

"That's not even true," I said. "You're looking for another girlfriend."

"I guess that's true," he said. "Not the best example," he added.

We sat at the park and he explained how I was always looking for attention. How I was needy, needing to please other people for validation. I stormed off.

I called my sister. I didn't tell her anything about what was going on though she probably knew something was up. Pretending everything was alright made everything feel alright and when Cash met me at the truck I wasn't emotional anymore. He was mad at me for leaving him.

"I don't know if I'm going to ask your dad to marry me," he said.

I felt like I was all the nightmares from his past, like he looked at me and could only see all the bad that had happened to him from past women that haunted him like ghosts.

He cut me out like a storybook character and put me on a different page in an entirely different book. But after confusion and crying and the end of the world, we made up and I found myself back inside his story.

"The way I acted mad with you is how I'm going to act around every other guy now."

We decided that once we got married and committed, everything would get better.

I balanced marriage on the crown of my skull, like a bucket of ocean. I could never lose sight of that dream: Cash and me forever.

I still felt bruised from these fights, from Cash saying, "he wasn't sure…" from the sheer pain of "crossing his line."

But I had no one to blame but my own ignorance, my own stupid, limited self. Maybe this was the accident I needed – like the Egyptians in their temples, how they created obstacles to undergo so they'd be stronger and less afraid during the real battles. Maybe something as stupid as exchanging information with my Uber driver was a lesson I needed to learn so I didn't mess up worse in the future. I could increase vigilance through vigilant elegance. I would consider Cash in every word, every thought. He was my North Star and if I could master following him we could master the world.

I looked at the green in the trees. Green must be the same color as the truth. Money is green. Money is power. Truth, power, nature: the holy trinity. We were well on our way into the fourth month together; we were going to see a lot more truth, a lot more green.

I took him out to a surprise play in Orlando. It was the Shakespearean version of Quentin Taratino's *Reservoir Dogs*. He was pleased.

After the show, we wandered around the city in slow motion, Cash-style. We stayed at a hotel in the city. The next day, on our way back south, we stopped for a night at the Ocala house.

In the pretty quiet of the country I had a melt-down. It was probably all the emotional tension, all the fighting.

I told him I was fighting an urge to run away. I told him it was a familiar feeling but I didn't want to feel that way. I told him how it was starting to sink in how stuck we were in Fort Myers, stuck for a long time. Neither of us even liked the place. I reminded him how he said the gulf was the toilet bowl of the United States and how the air was stagnant, and the people got stuck.

"I never live somewhere I don't like," I said.

I preferred to live somewhere I could at least surf. I'd always told myself that. It was a weird way to meltdown, to insist on a surfing lifestyle. But I thought since it was also his favorite thing to do, he would be on board with my mission.

"You're acting selfish," he said. "We're going to sailing school soon and there are all kinds of other watersports you can do in Fort Myers like kite boarding and paddle boarding."

Cash reminded me it was no longer all about me. I thought I had already understood that but I was learning that understanding a truth was different from living a truth. There was still a deeper realization, a greater self-undoing, and yet another ego-death.

He told me he could see different people in me: a playful, adventurous boy that was his best friend, an egotistical bitch know-it-all teacher's pet, and then a sweet, pretty little girl, whom he loved and adored the most.

I thought about all the people I'd seen in Cash: the charming, wild country boy who knew all the secret places, the blue-blooded country gentleman who quoted the bible and prayed every day, the sophisticated, posh Englishman who loved elegance and fine dining, the English hoodlum who could always find drugs in a snap, and the angry ghetto American who said things like "You got me fucked up."

We threw off the dredges of society so that we were left to simply be. No more woe and anxiety over the decay because we had renounced the world. But for now we lived in the ugliest of all cities.

I wondered where my brash unhappiness came from? Did I miss the world? Did I want to come up to the surface again? Cash said it was stress; the stress of unhappy things surrounding us like Cash's kids missing from our lives held ransom by Stacey.

He gave me two archetypes: the magician and the mother. What more could I possibly want? I would be a magic mother. He was the wizard, the king, the knight, the emperor, the pope.

Cash was checking his email on his MacBook in bed and I was planning our wedding under a Cancer moon and Sagittarius sun. He told me to watch him work and opened an email from his office manager. The email was about a logo for a new candle product. It was a cartoon wolf wearing a flower crown, with long eyelashes and purple eyeshadow in front of a full moon. He opened up Adobe Photoshop and used a tool to hide parts of the Cosmic Candles logo behind the wolf.

Then we started watching chocolateering videos on YouTube and he bought any materials he saw on Amazon

Prime. He bought a domain name. He was thinking about making chocolate for our next possible business venture. Chocolate was one of the underlying themes of our love. We met right after a cacao ceremony!

I pulled up our birth charts and Cash said I had his birth location wrong. He was born in Daytona Beach, not Salt Lake City. Cash loved telling people he was a triple Libra but the truth was he was a Scorpio rising.

"Of course you're a Scorpio rising!" I said. "That's why you love the ocean."

Cash was a little disconcerted.

"Don't worry. It's a good thing. I knew you couldn't be a Libra rising. They're so basic. Scorpios are the most powerful."

It was a rough patch in Ocala alright but nothing like the other fights and we got through it smoothly. We both stayed calm and it didn't feel like a fight; more like a turning point.

The next day we got into another fight.

We went back to the mall, and Cash asked me whether I needed him. I was detached, out of the mythos in an analytical, cerebral frame of mind and I said I didn't need him, technically. This time he was the one who shut down.

We were learning that a lot of anger occurred when one party attempted to enter the mythical realm without proper initiation out of the logos from the other party. We were still learning how to navigate our ship in between the two seas of logos and mythos.

In my journal I wrote, *I'm only now learning what causes the disconnection – my own over-analytical brain, the logos. Now – to marry the two: the logos and the mythos. Would that be mystic? Does the sum of logos and mythos equal the mystic?*

Cash wrote beneath my words: *The foundation of your logos must be transmuted.*

More fighting transpired on the night of the full moon.

We were having a barbeque at Lucci's for the Wednesday cult meeting. Lucci was grilling burgers as Cash,

Dez, and Mallory sipped wine outside.

I came outside and Cash was drawing Dez in the notebook that was supposed to be only drawings of me for my wedding day present.

"I thought you were only going to draw me!" I said.

"Just wait and see," Cash said.

He began to draw the other members of the cult.

As Lucci flipped the burgers, he looked at me over his shoulder and said, "You should feel lucky you're with a ten. There are so many girls walking around with total losers. Total tens with complete zeroes."

I looked at him and smiled coldly. Cash continued to draw. He asked me to get him the bottle of wine.

I refused.

Everyone looked at each other. No one had ever denied Cash before.

First Mallory then Dez jumped up to get the wine bottle but Cash told them to stop and said, "No, Maria will get it."

So I went inside the kitchen, grabbed the bottle, and poured him the wine.

At the dinner table, Mallory and Dez were already sitting on either side next to Cash's place at the head of the table. I sat down at the only space left, in between Dez and Lucci.

Cash sat down, glaring at me and said, "I guess I have a new girlfriend then."

After dinner, Cash said I was paying too much attention to Lucci, commented on how I made too much eye contact with him. He hinted that he might break up with me.

At the kava bar, he became angry when I spoke to Lucci and Dez more than him. He snapped at me.

So I left the kava bar and went to the truck, trying to decide what to do.

"Do you want to go home?" Cash asked, when he came outside.

"With you?"

"No. Alone."

I stammered.

He started walking away with his followers to another bar. I ran up to him.

"Are you going to submit?" He asked.

I said yes but only after giving it a few seconds' thought to leave forever, all of our fights over the past week hovering and stinking in the Florida summer humidity.

They went inside a bar.

I went to the fountain to cool off, secretly smoking a cigarette. I realized it was a magic fountain that I could throw a coin into and make a wish. I wished to be with Cash forever.

Later, I got him away from the cult and took him to the fountain to show him the magic. The top level granted three wishes, the second granted two, and the bottom granted one. Cash loved it and the night got rinsed clean.

Cash flicked a coin and made the top level no problem. We took everyone else to the fountain. Everyone made their wishes. No one else reached the top.

We all went to the 86 Room. Cash said it was his favorite bar. It was the bar I had seen all the way back in California on GoogleMaps and thought, "That bar will have interesting people."

"Don't you think you're being a little extra?" Cash asked, when I told him I was sad he hadn't taken me there yet.

I was wondering if he even loved me. It was a funny thing that set me off.

Lucci said, "The moon is making these women whacky."

Mallory was outrageous that night, dancing all over the town, pulling up her dress to show her thong, making blow job jokes.

Cash called Mallory, *leela*. He said the word like an incantation. I asked him why he called her that. He told me it was the word for the universal woman. I had to look it up to know he was using Sanskrit. *Leela* means divine play.

He said it in a way as if it would disarm her or reveal her demons. He wasn't speaking to Mallory but to the divine woman inside of her. He was talking to GOD.

I laughed at Lucci and Dez, who were overwhelmed by Mallory. Cash chided me for being entertained. But I thought she was a funny character, larger than life like we all should be. But by the end of that night, I was also overwhelmed by her.

She was Cash's little demon, his little *leela*. She went too far and she disgusted me, her blasphemous sermon about tossing a man's salad loudly and proudly at the bar, singing song after song on stage seductively. I was trying to get home and get to bed to make it home before midnight, Cash's rules.

But when we got home we had our worst fight of all.

"You disrespected me twice tonight!"

I went to lie in my car to create my own space, lighting sage and Palo Santo but then Cash pulled me out of it to discuss our problems, no, *my* problems, which I retorted were *his* problems, *his* trauma.

I wanted to enter his brain to find the part of him that loved me – the one that chose me, the one that saw me as *me* and not just as *leela*, the universal feminine.

"I'm just a ghost to you! Of all the terrible women you've been with and had in your life!" I yelled.

He told me he didn't want to marry me anymore.

"Well, I don't even know who you are," I said.

"What do you want?" He asked.

I asked him to baptize me. It was 4 AM. He told me to put on my bathing suit and get in the truck.

I put on a black dress over my bikini and waited in the passenger seat. He got into the truck wearing all white, sandals, and a big amber necklace.

We drove for an hour as the sun started waking up. He gave me a big mushroom to eat and he ate a smaller one. We got to a forested beach at a place called Punta Gorda.

He told me to find a smooth stone on the beach that would represent my heart. After I found it I would have to find him in the forest. He went into the forest and left me on the beach.

I searched for a few minutes until I found one. And

then I went down a long path in the woods along the beach, giggling my way through the maze until I reached him.

He had laid a blanket on the ground, the pale green Turkish cotton one he bought me at the farmer's market. He had me sit down and take my clothes off. He took his clothes off too.

Then he pulled me towards the water. We walked in up to our hips.

"Put the stone inside this bottle," he said, offering me a green glass bottle he must have found littered there. I put the stone inside the bottle and held it.

Then he took my wrists and closed his eyes.

"Thank you, cold lady for your protection and keeping Maria safe. We no longer need you anymore. Maria is protected now. Now tell her goodbye."

"Goodbye," I whispered to the stone inside of the bottle.

"Now throw the bottle as far as you can!"

I lugged the bottle twenty feet or so into the ocean.

"I can still hear the cold woman yelling," I said.

He tilted his head back and laughed a big belly laugh. I loved making him laugh more than anything in the world.

He dunked me under the water. I came up, we kissed, and then we walked to the shore and sat down on the blanket.

He wrapped a towel around me first and then another one around himself.

"Look at the dragonfly!" I said, pointing at a large dragonfly sitting atop a branch near our blanket.

"Is it wrong if I want to make love to you right now?" Cash asked.

"I don't think so," I said.

We made love on the blanket, right in front of the dragonfly. I could see his big, bulging dragonfly eyes watching us the whole time. We were both too nervous to come, so I faked an orgasm so we could stop.

Walking out of the forest after we got dressed, Cash sang,

When you were born you cried and the world laughed

Live your life so when you die
The world cries and you laugh

He sang it over and over again until I knew the words and could join in.

The sun was climbing into midmorning. We sat on some swings on the beach playground. Everything felt so good and back in place, back in order.

The funny thing was that we should have baptized Cash too. He had even darker demons.

So that was Thursday, the day before New Orleans, and we set about that day with a to-do list and we accomplished everything on it, even though we didn't even sleep.

Cash got a new lawyer and the new lawyer told him to give Stacey the car back. So that was one of the things we did.

And then the next day was Friday and we drove all morning to look at a boat in Fort Lauderdale and back. Then we left for New Orleans.

CHAPTER SEVENTEEN: NEW ORLEANS, XANAX, AND HEMINGWAY

On the drive to the airport, Cash texted his friends, "I'm on my way to New Orleans with two beautiful women and a $5000 refund from my attorney."

On the airplane to New Orleans, the intercom said it was now federal law to wear face masks. I hadn't been paying any attention to anything about the pandemic. It sounded insane.

New Orleans was a trip my sister and I planned that got turned into one her mother-in-law planned which then became a huge family ordeal where I had to beg my parents to allow Cash to come, which they did after they met him in Florida.

In the security line, Dez made a dirty joke.

"I always think of you when I put things in my mouth."

I asked Cash on the airplane whether he had ever gotten a blowjob from her.

"No," he said, looking pleased like he liked the idea.

The three of us were sharing a bed because it was Mary that was originally supposed to come. But that was before she got the boot. So Cash invited Dez to come in Mary's place.

When Stephanie found out Dez was coming, she invited herself along as well. She shared the surprise on Mother's Day with us that she and one of her alcoholic friends were coming via car.

And then there was the Xanax. Dez brought a bunch of Xanax that she and Cash popped throughout the whole trip.

Cash warned Dez and I that when he disappeared he would be at the Old Absinthe House. He said he might not return with us to Florida, might just end up lost in the city with a whole new crew of friends.

I felt anxious. I didn't want to lose him. I wanted to stay together and make our magic. But with Dez coming along, I knew our magic would be tainted.

We said some of the prettiest things flying somewhere above Louisiana, lighter up there in the sky, without Fort Myers' frequencies holding us down. I am at my most calm and peaceful on airplanes, trains, and buses. Oh, if only I had written down those sweet lines we exchanged up there in the sky over Louisiana, sweeter than the cocaine Cash liked to take when he had to run a really boring errand.

We talked about "the Swansons" as if we were outsiders observing another couple but the couple was really us; an improv game we made up and played. It started as something silly but I know there was greatness in there. The love we made in that conversation was so powerful that I can even snuggle up to it now.

I guess that's all love really is – it starts out as something silly then it turns into something great or you could swear there was something great about it but you never had any proof.

Cash thought people would feel something when they saw the three of us: a man with a woman on each side. I no longer believed it would amount to much in most people. Perhaps a glimmer or a ripple of intrigue, and then they'd go back into their steady stream of unconscious slavery. Cash overestimated our effect on people.

We got off the plane late and went straight to the streets of the Old French Quarter to meet up with Stephanie and her friend. My parents were already in for the night.

It definitely felt like the end of the world. It was a trashy time. The memorial three day weekend brought hundreds of people jam packed together like sardines that walked down the streets of New Orleans carrying large plastic tubes of alcohol, smoking blunts, looking around, glazed eyes, no one home. There were circles of people twerking and shaking their asses. One girl took her shirt off and shook her boobs around at onlookers on a balcony.

Cash hated trap music but I thought it the perfect soundtrack for the end of the world. The beat sounded like pages of sheet music getting tossed off a roof, one by one, with the notes slipping off the pages and bouncing off the ground.

Stephanie asked Cash if he wanted to go to a gentlemen's club. He didn't want to go and I didn't have to react. I probably would have disassociated anyway. I began to suspect Stephanie wasn't on my side anymore.

We kept on through the dismal repetition of faces – the seven deadly sins represented across multitudes – all backed by a dull, throbbing pain of existence.

It was distressing walking around that first night in the overpopulated ghost town of New Orleans. It was as haunting as a dreadful, bone-sweating nightmare. Crowds and crowds of the living dead.

On that first morning in New Orleans, Cash, Dez, Stephanie, and I got on a boat tour with my family and my sister's husband's family in the swamps of Louisiana. My sweet, simple, cookie-cutter family members laughed, joked, and behaved like tourists; playful spectators, half-assed critics. I had never felt satisfied by their life choices; simplicity, slow-cooked wealth, and socially acceptable dreams and fears. But on that trip their predictability was suddenly so appealing.

Cash talked about our mission and philosophized to me on the boat.

In hushed tones, I told Cash how exhausted I was. How afraid I was to fail, to not accomplish my mission. How exhausting life was. How tiring. How boring it was to be human and not limitless. He laughed at me.

"You go too deep sometimes. Everything is for enjoyment. It is just a dance."

He scribbled my portrait on a notepad.

"But what's the point of it all?"

"To fuck shit up!" He showed me his drawing. "Still haven't gotten your nose right…"

When he disappeared, as he said he would, I wanted to go directly to the Absinthe House where I knew he must be. But Dez wanted to go to the pool and didn't believe he was there. I suppose I gave too much power to her doubt. I suppose she was a control test.

I nurtured a belief in my own intuition by fighting through her doubt and poor oversight. But I could never tell if she was an idiot like Cash said or if she intended to weaken our love on purpose. Every time I was alone with her, she had something of an impairment to offer. She did it to Cash too but he knew how to deflect her deformities.

I told her we were going to the Absinthe House, not the pool, and to distract her from arguing with me, I asked her which of the deadly sins tempted her the most.

"Lust," she said.

I asked her who she would hook up with out of the cult if she had to but it couldn't be me and it couldn't be Cash.

She said she wouldn't hook up with any of the others because they were like family. They were like her brothers.

I was digging for information. I wanted to understand the sexual tension between her and Cash. But instead, I only revealed myself. Dez was empty-headed but pretty smart. She knew what I was doing. I knew what I was doing too, and it didn't feel good.

We found him at the Absinthe House, sitting on a stool, gazing around on some kind of drug. I could have been spending time with my family but instead I was following his instructions. Instead of complaining, I felt my brain rewiring towards a new function preparing for the Father Circuit. It was a gift though it felt like a curse when I was being solipsistic and wanted some time on my own to exercise or meditate.

That night, Cash went on the night fishing trip with my dad and the men in my brother-in-law's family.

I tried to take the ladies to the real New Orleans music scene while the men were gone, but the ladies wouldn't get out of their Uber when they saw where I was taking them.

We had only seen the touristy parts of New Orleans. I wanted to see the real scene and decide for myself whether or not New Orleans had a pulse. I forgot how afraid people were of the world – of danger and of dying. I never thought about dying unless I was wishing or longing for it.

The men were out late. Dez slipped me a Xanax and we fell asleep before he got home.

The next morning I woke up from a dream that Cash asked my dad to marry me. There were orchards of happiness and the whole dream was the color of dying leaves in fall.

But when I opened my eyes I saw that Cash might be getting his dick scrubbed by his assistant in bed. He always told me he wasn't attracted to Dez but, just as hers, his biggest temptation of the seven deadly sins was lust. I'd seen it work against him before.

I tried to leave to go work out in the gym but Cash wasn't having it.

"Come here!" He said. I lied down next to him. Dez started scratching his head. And then he started humping her.

I got up and went to write on the balcony. I wished he would let me go to work out at the gym and maybe then they could have sex and she could be our new girlfriend. And I could get a workout in. And she'd either sink or swim though I knew she'd sink and be one long flailing waste of time and space.

We took a bath together and Cash tried to connect with me. He told me about his night with the men. He knew he had to catch the most fish in the group and so he did. And then he asked my dad if he could marry me and my dad said yes.

I was unmoved.

He said demons drove him to want to have sex magic with Dez and me, that he thought it was fine because I asked about the blowjob on the plane and whether she was the second wife on Mother's Day. He always blamed his bad behavior on demons and me.

I stayed cold but as the day wore on I began to break. There was fire beneath the ice.

The three of us went searching for breakfast. Nobody would seat us. You were supposed to tip the host to get a seat, since it was Memorial Day weekend but Cash refused.

Him and Dez kept taking Xanax, getting more and more useless. I wasn't allowed to take anything because Cash thought I was pregnant. I didn't believe it until Dez said I wasn't. That's when I started thinking that I was. Dez was usually wrong.

We went to get foot massages. Dez sat in the chair next to Cash before I could and he said something about her being his new girlfriend. I sat boiling mad as my feet got massaged.

Dez chatted with Cash, and the masseuses, trying to lighten the mood like a Libra.

Once my massage finished, I stood up, yelled at Dez, "Never steal my seat again!" and left the salon. I walked to a bookstore.

Cash called me after his massage finished. He told me I needed to get back to them right away.

But I took too long and he called again, demanding to know where I was.

"I'm coming!"

I ran into him outside a casino.

"I just made $400!" He said to me, grinning.

"Well I don't care!" I yelled. I broke down sobbing.

Cash sent Dez home with his mom and her alcoholic friend in a car. I knew she had a long journey ahead of her. It was his fault but I blamed her since I couldn't blame him. He wouldn't have allowed me to blame him.

Once she was finally gone, I finally had Cash all to myself again. The air felt cleaner and purer when it was just us. Our magic could breathe again. He told me he would fire her. I told him he didn't have to. I didn't want to put a single mother out of a job.

We walked to my parents' hotel and said our goodbyes since they were leaving in a few hours. And then we were free to be.

We became the alter egos we made up for New Orleans weeks in advance: Frenchy and Maxine. I loved being Maxine because I got to talk back to Cash in a southern accent. I got away with saying sassy things I couldn't say as Maria, myself. We went to a park and got rewarded for our magic right away and found black tourmaline in the grass right next to the great Mississippi River. My first time at the first river I ever fell in love with reading adventure stories in great American literature as a little girl.

"This is just what we needed!" Cash exclaimed. To this day I don't know whether we really found it or not, whether Cash planted it there or pretended to find it. The gesture was nice either way.

I tried to guide my heart to forgiveness, to feather lightness. Cash often spoke about the importance of keeping the heart as light as a feather so that when you died and your heart was weighed against that of a feather, your heart would be lighter and you'd get to go to heaven.

We sat in our hotel room that night and wrote a song about the nasty city of New Orleans; all the ghosts, demons, degenerates, ratchets, and bad vibes. Cash said the Romans knew better than to build cities on swamps.

The next morning we finished Hemingway's *To Have and Have Not* in the park near our hotel. I loved the stern voice Cash used when he said the title aloud each time we opened the book, as if he himself was the weary sailor who narrated the tales of a life spent navigating crime, corruption, and poverty, "To have and have not!"

In the final pages of the last chapter, Hemingway wrote about the Estonian sailors called the Intrepid Voyagers. They sailed around the world and sent back articles about their adventures that were as popular in Estonia as the baseball or football programming in America.

We decided we would write adventure chronicles from our ark like the Intrepid Voyagers. Nothing and nobody was more important to me than the magic we would make, the magic we were making.

"There are a million ways to make money," Cash said as we walked around the arts district in New Orleans.

We went in and out of art galleries, rehashing the latest conversation with his business attorney. It looked like Stacey would be entitled to 49% of the crystal pyramid candle business after all.

He thought about selling the company and rebranding it, buying Stacey out or letting her buy him out. Sales were slowly plummeting and the latest attack involved Stacey's launch of her own version of the same business with the stolen Instagram account and all of their followers. Her candles sold out within the first few minutes. Cash's candles hadn't sold out since she started defaming him on social media. She also stole his latest product idea. Not to mention the most recent lies she spread about Cash on social media: his "narcissistic abuse" and taking advantage of her, since she was an "empath." Empaths seemed to be the most narcissistic of all.

At dinner that night, he said he didn't feel the need to be on the cover of Wired anymore- that he didn't need another wife anymore either. He was satisfied with just me. He said he had a vision when he went floating without me that he wouldn't be as powerful with me but he didn't care as much about power anymore.

"Really?" I asked.

"Finding your soulmate changes a lot of things," he said, spooning a glob of creme brulee in between his lips.

I waited a beat.

"We'll see," he said.

CHAPTER EIGHTEEN: HUMPHREY BOGART, CHOCOLATE, AND A PREGNANCY TEST

After a week in New Orleans, we went back to Florida. Cash was homesick. I wasn't.

Florida was still not my home, Cash was, but I did miss time traveling.

Florida never made it to the 2000s. I preferred any other time period than the rot of this millennium.

We got home and the mockingbird sang, the street lights turned on, and Cash lived in constant poetry, doing everything out of nowhere like handing me a topaz that looked like a jolly rancher.

Cash left within the hour to see Lucci. That's when I drove to CVS to get a pregnancy test.

When we were in New Orleans, there were a few times I wanted to go off and take one. It was always when I was upset, when we were fighting. Cash wouldn't let me. He wanted me to be happy, not angry when I checked. I just wanted a cigarette.

I had taken pregnancy tests before. They were always negative. This was the first one that came up positive. I didn't really feel anything, except a vague sense of accomplishment. What with all the industrial pollution, I doubted my ability to produce. But we did it.

I wondered how I should tell him.

I told him on the beach the next day. I wanted to come up with a good idea but the beach was fun and we hadn't fought about anything.

I asked him to guess what I had to tell him.

"Did you take one?" He asked.

He had prayed so many times to my womb while I had said my own secret prayers. We celebrated with ice cream.

But then, licking his ice cream cone, he said, "I wonder what Stacey will think."

My ice cream melted all over my hand.

A few days later, we were eating dinner at a restaurant on the beach. I was already sick and lethargic. He talked about having a threesome.

"With who?" I asked.

"Someone I find when I'm out at night at the bars.

What if I brought a girl home? Would you have sex with us?"

"Just some random?" I asked.

"Yeah," he said.

"Um, no. First of all, I'm pregnant. I have to protect my baby. I can't just have sex with anyone and risk the health of my baby."

He twisted his words around so that he didn't look so bad but they were still there. I still had to deal with them.

He wanted to drink so we went to a bar.

Sipping a cocktail, he looked at me with mean eyes and said, "Just because you're pregnant doesn't mean I have to stay with you."

Then he twisted his words around like a guilty little boy, but again, I still had to deal with them.

I started to hide my writings from Cash on my computer in a file titled, "Taxes_2019." Somehow he knew I was writing on my computer and he didn't like it. I told him he could access it whenever he wanted to but he didn't try.

I preached to Stephanie and her shit-talking friends on the backyard patio that maybe Cash and Stacey would work it all out on their own without the courts and that all we needed was to stay positive and willing to accept Stacey back into our lives with love no matter what. We needed to be ready to forgive her. But then the next day Stacey wouldn't let Cash see his kids on Father's Day though she had promised she would.

Cash disappeared and didn't answer my calls.

Stephanie and Dez went off to take Stacey's car again, as per Cash's instructions. An hour later, Cash called and told them, "Never mind, don't get the car," and they came home.

Cash finally showed up another hour later at sunset and we sat on the couch reading different books until he got upset at me. I wasn't comforting him enough. And then he broke up with me.

"What are you going to do with the pregnancy?" He asked.

"Kill it," I said, emotionlessly. I knew he wanted me to freak out and get upset but I had no emotions left to give him. I was all wrung out.

He took it back a few minutes later.

Through the window, I saw the light dripping off the pine trees, the needles leaking gold.

Foolhardily, clumsily, we went over our respective hurt feelings of the evening and how each event could have been prevented. We figured that, as individuals, Cash and I were each double times the sensitivity of a normal person. Together, as a couple, quadruple times. We were trying to learn how to handle one another with care. But as I got fatter, time got thinner.

I tried to study the distances between the edges, *the waves which have kept me from reaching you*. What was I putting between myself and Cash? What lurked in between us? Conditioning, fear, patterns. Cash was good, Cash was good, I told myself sometimes like a mantra.

We tried acting like things were normal, though they never had been. I got back into cinematic narratives as Cash got back into million-dollar ideas. I swooned over black and white Bogart and Bacall movies while Cash researched canning and bottling on his laptop.

I studied how Bacall served Bogart, lighting his cigarette before it had occurred to him to get a match, waiting on his every whim, as he served others. I saw Cash and me. I wanted to be like Bacall and serve Bogart with unflinching loyalty, like the wife in *Mosquito Coast*, who refused to abandon her morally-deteriorating husband, even as her children begged her in the name of survival. I'd go down with Cash in all his insanity.

We went looking for icons at the Lee County Fair one night, even though Cash was tired. We drove through paper trees, passed a cement factory, a golf course, went down Colonial Road with the Walmart and then we got on the 75.

I talked to him about how I'd been thinking a lot about wholesomeness and its power in a cynical, rotten, over-sexed world. He said he was too tired to think.

Cash told me many times never to correct him in front of other people. He got angry when I corrected him in front of his mom and Mallory that night. But he'd taken me to the fair when he was already exhausted; just to make me happy. He was good at making me happy. He just wasn't good at not making me sad.

Alcohol made Cash negative. Whenever he drank he started to see me as wrong and against him. He said that ever since I got pregnant I took him for granted. It felt like I was in the middle of a redneck cliché.

I worried because he said he didn't like to drink but he did, that he didn't like the bars, but he went to them anyways, and that he didn't like Fort Myers but he still wanted to be the king. These thoughts came floating up, ugly and revolting – like dead fish after a red tide. He also had ugly thoughts about me. That I didn't believe in him anymore.

It wasn't that I didn't believe in him. I was just trying to understand. But I continued to prove myself short sighted. I knew he had vision. He proved it so many times. He saw past the edges, saw the big picture. All I could see were the details, so many details.

"Trust the plan," he'd say.

The part I liked most about his magic was how he helped others like how he helped bring JT and Mallory together and helped them through their relationship issues.

But Stephanie told us one night that JT gave Mallory a venereal disease because he was fucking his ex-girlfriend on the side. Just like Cash did to me. The magic was rotting.

I started hating Florida. In the beginning, Cash transformed Florida for me. He made Florida feel like the sun shining through a window. I forgot to open the window and smell it for what it was: a steaming, stinking, humid shit hole. I was sinking it was so flat. The swampy greens made me sick. I dreamt about hiking in the mountains. I begged Cash to give me a clear answer on when we could leave but he couldn't give me one. He already had children there. We could be there for years.

But Cash really could play that guitar beautifully, another one of his magic tricks. I liked to lean my head on his shoulder as he played so I could watch his fingers move across the frets. I couldn't help but let my tears fall onto those strings.

CHAPTER NINETEEN: MILK & HONEY, PRIME RIB, AND VACCINES

I was nervous about going to Lucci's for the cult meeting that week. He invited a couple of his girlfriends to attend. I never knew when it was going to be the night that Cash fell in love with someone else.

In New Orleans he told me he didn't need another wife but he changed his mind when we got back to Florida. I think he was searching for her at the bars when he said he was out helping Lucci talk to women. I knew that my part at the end of the day was to remember I had no say.

"Don't I treat you well enough? Haven't I given you everything?"

I never felt guilty when he said things like that to me. He was just reminding me of the rules of the game.

Dez showed up with Cash's friend, Stone. She had started dating him to Cash's disapproval. I learned that she fucked a lot of his friends and employees. I was surprised she would go for Stone, who was grungy, dumb, and fat. I guess it was her lust. She told us that one night, after Stone took her and Rose out to dinner, Rose exclaimed, "There's just nothing there? There's really nothing going on under those jokes?"

I was sure Dez would fuck Cash when I left, if she hadn't already. Lately, he went to see her whenever I displeased him. He went to see lots of other women when I didn't respond in the precise way he wanted me to respond.

Maybe Dez was smarter than any of us gave her credit for. She stayed close to Cash but remained sexually liberated. She was still in her own power, though he verbally abused her at times. She got close to him but not too close where he completely destroyed her like he was destroying me. Cash sought to conquer his lovers. He wanted his wife to dissolve into him, have no cares besides his own happiness. I should have taken the assistant route.

I had always felt kindled by the darkness and thought nothing of it when I encountered it in the flesh. I thought darkness was a friend. I didn't know how it would feel to be destroyed by a powerful man. I didn't think about what destruction really meant. I just wanted to keep going but I was dissolving. It was fun being rich and not having to think about money. It was fun galloping around with a man who was so powerful. I just had to be pretty and sweet: milk and honey and give him my love. But I had a lot more than just milk and honey inside me. There were sparks, there was fire, there was GOD. Cash wanted it all of that gone. But I couldn't just will them out of me.

Cash had this masculinity complex. At first, I thought it was an inquiry, an experiment. Then, I saw a disorder. His obsession with a woman's adherence to increasingly specific and arbitrary standards was debilitating, not helpful, as I once thought it could be.

I believed the corrosion of womanhood was not the sexually objectifying clothing and appearance itself. I did not believe dressing poorly to be immoral. I believed the corrosion lied in the lack of capacity in young women to reflect upon their dressing choices. And that was what I was dismayed about: the mindlessness. I blamed the decay of society- no structure, only chaos. But it became clearer and clearer that Cash placed the blame on women not on the ways of the world.

"Only sluts wear Vans," he'd say. At first I thought it was a joke but then I realized he believed it.

It wasn't that he was worried he would dim my light. It was that he wanted to dim my light.

The latest bit in the cult was Cash's harkening to the followers of "milk and honey." He wrote a whole essay about it that day which he read to me in bed. He used an accent that sounded just like when he read the pervert's musings from *Against Nature*, a book I had picked up in New Orleans about a neurotic sociopath which inspired Oscar Wilde to write *The Picture of Dorian Gray*.

He read it aloud to the cult attendees at dinner.

When Cash read, it repulsed me. He sounded demonic with darkness dripping from his lips. He spoke like a posh Englishman, pompous and conceited. He loved the sound of his own voice. It grated against every cell in my body.

He read:

The feminine milk and honey, she delivers to me without cunning. Her being is owed, as is mine, to the great one. Her duty, without question, prescribed in blood by her honor, is to nourish – to provide her milk to her kin and to the one who holds the world together. Without this innate giving and recognition she simply ceases to be feminine, though that is not the common case. What is common is the honey, sweet honey. The honey is extra, it is.

From animal to goddess, endless samples of sweet honey could be tasted. But at its essence, or rather the spoon which carries it – is the ladle of gratitude. The curse of the dark ages in the realm of love within Lila is her lack of gratitude. I bet little boys learn manners- or even understand general appreciation much quicker than their counter. This may also explain why women are more susceptible to identifying with victimhood because their once beloved honey flows no more, they've lost their sweetness and now overly flaunt the base mode of a half glass of milk they can provide in the form of extravagantly kept vain beauty.

"Where is your honey, honey?"

I see your grace. I wink at it. Now feed me your nectar. After all, does thou not enjoy a pastry at dawn and a crème brulee at dusk? So it should be with your gestures of gratitude.

I, out of my longing for equality, will discuss the plagues of modernity to which men have fallen trap.

The most common terms while naturally lacking the poetic nature enjoyed by the woman still hold true. Man's duty is to <u>provide</u> and <u>protect</u> and that is by <u>any means necessary</u>.

Provide what? Hasn't the dark age sufficiently replaced the need for man's most base foundations? Isn't this the real reason men die earlier? They are replaced by artificial means under the illusion (*beep *beep) of safety?! ($500 fine!) NO. All that tech and convenience and illusion hidden behind Leviathan guarded social contracts does nothing more than make spiritual lesbians out of soccer moms and hands dad another beer! And this <u>truth</u> is what I, Cassius, the man inside all men, provides and protects you from. I systematically unravel your years of slavery so you can taste not freedom, but <u>earned</u> salvation and sovereignty through action.

Provide? Money? No. A house? No. These are further up the tree branches. It is spiritual nourishment I bring forth. It is prayer –

my ability to speak directly with GOD and gods and to command seas to part and to have the wisdom to offer fair judgment. Judgment that comes from laws – both handed down by the fathers and those gleaned in communion.

Only men in this age are gifted with prophecy – and that gift too is pushed out of our minds – taken back for abusing or not using its power with GOD's approval.

The beast of this world and others lurk in plain sight – at hospitals, at hotels, at bars. They smile at you and tell you you're pretty or smart and you even walk away saying things like, hey, they're alright!

But they call this the dark age for a reason, because when you close your outer eyes and open the middle one it's dark where it once was not. Only the chosen of the men whose hearts can lead others are granted access to this gnostic power – a dim lamp to which we see the true masters of puppets and the horns poking forth from the soothsayers and snake oiliest bald heads.

So my prescription to all men and women:

Men, you have innate gifts that must be uncovered – and this is done by initiation and seeking. Go to church – pray aloud – keep your word – set laws and follow them – discipline those who don't. Your instinct or gut feeling is 100x more reliable than asking the smartest woman you know what she thinks.

Women, milk and honey. It is your duty to serve man. Feed him. Dress his wounds both inside and out. Follow his law even if you don't yet agree for truth is revealed to all and will be revealed with time. Milk alone will never bring you joy. You need honey – love. Recognize the difficult load men must bear in this age. We are 5x more likely to kill ourselves, 5x more likely to abuse alcohol and drugs. We are attacked and mocked. This age hasn't been kind to us and we've fallen into traps just as you have. We need support, encouragement, <u>unwavering</u> devotion. Your devotional submission alone can transform a man into divinity. Just as we crave a sweet morsel, so too man craves a compliment, a gift, a surprise, a backrub, or even the cliché words of "I love you," will invigorate us so we can remember the whole point – how to love.

Everyone clapped.

Cash looked at me and smirked.

"Maria doesn't get it."

"No, I get it. I think it's good, I just think it could use some work to better demonstrate some of the arguments." Nobody was listening to me.

"I love it!" Dez said breathlessly like the words themselves had just finished ramming her.

I swear that night, Cash had Lucci in some sort of trance. As if someone put blinders on him like he was a horse at a race. Simple things I said went over his head. Cash had him marching to a very specific beat.

"What did you do to Lucci? What drugs did you give him?" I asked Cash later.

He just smiled. All his dark psychology books were not just toys to play with. He studied cult leaders, scientology, the occult. He understood the great service these entities provided. He knew people made up most of the magic in their own mind; he only had to play along, getting pieces of what sorts of magic they made when he didn't trip but watched them trip.

One of the women Lucci brought had short hair and was called Harper. She was very pretty without any makeup on, and had a grounding, earthy, sensual energy. The other woman was called Mandy and she had children and dreads.

I liked both of them and we all clicked quickly. They told me I was adorable and were intrigued by my ideas. But Cash wanted to remain the center focus.

Lucci told the girls that we like to call people "cabbage heads." I was surprised that my term was still being used. I had suggested it when I got tired of hearing the word "normie" so often and I guess it stuck. But even with cabbage heads I was bored of comparing myself to creatures as distinct from me as grains of sand to stars in the sky. I'd rather just ignore the normies and not think about them. But our cult was founded on being against normies.

We decided to go around the dinner table and say how many years we each thought the empire had left or how many years before everything went to shit.

"I say 5 to 7 years," Mandy, the one with children and dreads said.

"I like your optimism," Cash said, and I felt a pang of irritation. Whenever I heard him say something he said to me to someone else I felt possessive, cheap, replaceable. It made me think of how Mary must have hurt watching Cash use all of the same language he used with her on me. Words like *Soulmate*.

I think Mandy was the only one who actually answered the question.

"Well how do you know when it's coming?" she asked Cash.

"I don't. That's why I have her," he gestured at me. "My astrologer."

Cash asked everyone to go around the table and say something they were grateful for. When everyone finished, the girls wanted to know why I said I was grateful for my answer, which was diversity in thought.

I explained how I had recently begun investigating the nature of fascism, now that democracy had proven to be a sham. I was reexamining my predisposition towards seeing fascism as evil and trying to see what the potential benefit might be or what successes it had in the past.

"That's enough," Cash said.

I smiled at the girls.

There were chunks of unfinished prime rib lying around the room. Everything disgusted me at that point. The prime rib wrapped in bacon that he claimed was "my meal" though he was the one who picked the ingredients. I would never come up with such a despicable meal. All that meat. And the way he wouldn't let me speak.

"When I first met her, I thought she was a reporter," Cash went on. Was he outing me right now, in front of everyone? This had all been for the story, for the writing.

"She had that look of one, like she was hungry and looking for something to eat. I thought I could satisfy her. That we could all satisfy her. But we can't satisfy her. We can't satisfy a modern woman."

After dinner, we played a game that Harper suggested. Cash loved the idea of it. "Initiation, risk, trust... it's perfect," he said.

It was a game of dare that was dependent on whether the person daring the other said the same number between 1 and 10 at the same time as the person being dared.

I thought it was a fun game myself and made Lucci do exactly what he would never want to do: knock on a neighbor's door and invite them over for some tea.

"I don't want to open the door like that. You don't know what you're inviting in. They might keep coming back," he whined.

When Cash and Harper went, Cash cheated and said the number slightly after Harper. She protested but when she saw no one was on her side, she stopped. He dared her to do a naked cartwheel in the living room.

She completed her initiation gracefully. She looked like she was floating down from the sky as she cartwheeled across the doorway. She had a butt like a cute cherub.

I watched Cash watch her. He had the hungriest look on his face though he was the only one who had finished his dinner.

We went up to visit his grandpa again in Orlando.

I beat him in a swimming race at a hotel pool.

He looked me in the eyes and sneered, "You think you beat me? You think you could ever beat me?"

I didn't say anything but a little boy in the pool called out, "She beat you! She beat you!"

We went into the Jacuzzi and Cash told me a story. I knew he was trying to mess with my subconscious, one of those stories. He was doing weird things with his eyes and moving his body in ways that reminded me of Hindu dancing. I felt irritated.

That night Cash told me I was the only girl he'd ever met who really believed in GOD. He said it was because GOD had looked at me.

"Only those who have been looked at by GOD can truly believe in GOD," he said.

I couldn't tell him that he was breaking my connection to GOD. He would just deny it, blame me.

We stopped at the Ocala house again: cleaner air, brighter greens, nicer people. But I was so depressed I hardly went outside and lied around in bed instead. Cash told me to get out of dream world, to save it for later. But when I placed myself in dream world I was the only one who could get myself out of it. And I didn't want to leave.

Cash went outside to shoot guns during my online improv show because I didn't want him to watch after he got upset listening to my online audition earlier. He misheard me say, in character, that I was cheating on my boyfriend.

The shots were loud but I didn't dare ask him to stop shooting because I didn't want him to shoot me.

After my improv show was done, we sat outside eating dinner on the porch steps. We watched a cricket the size of my thumb crawl across the step.

"I'll pay you eight thousand dollars if you eat the head off that cricket," Cash said.

I couldn't even imagine myself touching the cricket. We stared at it.

"What would you do with the money?" He asked me.

"I'd live off of it," I said, accidentally revealing I still inhabited a reality without him.

"I wonder how long you're going to drag this out," he said.

He knew I was falling out of love with him. He knew it before I knew it though he still fought for me in the material realm, making me dinner, breakfast, bringing me exotic fruits, taking me on a hike to the springs.

He stopped on the hike to ask, "Do you even like being around me?"

I was feeling ill and disappointed to discover he was texting Mary again.

Cash liked to quote Charles Bukowski, "Beware the average man the average woman. Beware their love their love is average seeks average."

He quoted Bukowski more and more frequently.

That night Cash read Aleister Crowley's book, *The Rule of the Law* aloud. I faded in and out of sleep as Cash read in his normal reading voice. He just sounded like himself for once.

That night I had a dream about Charles Manson.

We were eating French fries at a diner I used to go to with my ex-boyfriend in Los Angeles.

"How come people don't know that you worked for the Beach Boys?" I asked Charles Manson. He looked a little like Edward Scissorhands.

"You know. Isn't that all that matters?" He had a gentle voice.

"I guess so. Hey, do you think they forgot about our milkshakes?" I looked around the diner which seemed empty.

"Maybe. You know, you need to leave him."

"Really?"

"Yeah. Find yourself a real cult leader. This guy's full of baloney."

"I know. Were you a real cult leader?"

"A real cult leader never calls himself a cult leader. Rule number one, girl."

"I see. But he's so powerful. I've never met a more powerful person."

"Hey, now."

"That's what Cash said when I said he wasn't that tall. I'm sorry. I just met you. I mean, I'm sure you're really powerful too. If we hang out again I'll probably see it."

"Look at your game, girl."

I woke up to Cash speaking in demonic voices. I couldn't make out what he was saying and I became so scared that I smacked him.

"Huh?" He woke up.

"You were possessed I think! There were some scary sounds coming out of your throat."

"There must be some dark energy attacking me."

"Or maybe it was the Aleister Crowley book."

"Yeah. It could have been that. We shouldn't be reading that sort of stuff."

We stopped in St. Pete's on our way back from Ocala. St. Petersburg looked like San Francisco. A cube of a city tucked into a crystal blue bay, however, on comparing the two on a map, they look more like Siamese twins torn apart in some Precambrian era. Maybe Florida was once a flexible foot that stretched down and all the way around the continent of South America to rest at California's lower back.

When I heard him talk about how everything was so feminine except parking spots I felt irritated and exhausted. As usual, he scapegoated feminism for everything wrong with the world.

One morning, he woke me up with a question, "Do you want to go hiking in the mountains all alone?"

"No," I said, groggy but knowing he was testing me.

I did want to go alone. But I passed his test with my lie and we didn't get into a big fight.

I was exhausted in the mornings and I slept until 1 or 2 pm. Cash stopped in to have sex with me for lunch. He usually went out to the bars in the evening and I tried to write.

One day we went to the Lasik center where Cash was going to have eye surgery so he didn't have to wear glasses anymore. The assistant was also a Libra and Cash chatted with her playfully. She talked about a new kind of procedure he could do which was partially laser and partially done by a doctor. I asked her about the difference in cost.

"I don't care about cost. I'm rich," Cash said to the assistant.

The assistant giggled a little bit. He flirted with her some more and then we left.

Cash said she would totally join the cult. I agreed without really thinking about it. I'd learned it was easier to just agree with Cash, especially when you didn't really care about what he was talking about. He didn't really care about your opinion if it didn't embellish his.

For the first time, Cash didn't want me to go to the cult meeting that week. He said he didn't want to be around my negativity, my doubt. He didn't want the others to be exposed to it either. I understood but I was hurt.

I didn't know what to do. I couldn't see him in the light anymore. I couldn't stop seeing that ugly part of him that humped his assistant next to me in bed the morning after he asked my dad to marry me. That part that dug to get emotional reactions out of me, that hurt me in order to "see where I was at," and made me cry uncontrollably. The man I didn't trust.

Cash was drunk, practically yelling a story in my ear after waking me up when he came home from the bars with the cult that night. The story was sweet but the smell of his breath was bad, reeked of alcohol, and I was so tired. When I told him so, he became incensed. And then we fought well into the early morning.

I woke up thinking about his snub nose. He talked of others' physiognomy, but never talked about his own.

He would point girls out at the bars, saying stuff like, "Look at the corners of her mouth. They're downturned. She suffers from dissatisfaction."

He said my broad forehead indicated intelligence and my defined nose, character. One time when he was mad he told me I had droopy eyes and big teeth but he didn't say what that meant. I wanted to use his weapon against him.

What's the physiognomy in a snub nose? I looked it up on google: attractive but immature, untrustworthy character.

I started making phone calls, talking to old friends.

I talked to an old friend from California. She was annoyed that I hadn't gotten and didn't plan to get the vaccine. I tried to tell her how in Florida we never locked ourselves up; it was a community effort. It was a shared understanding that we were all ready to die if that was the price of living in freedom. Nobody talked about the vaccines in Florida. We were never afraid of the virus in the first place. We had all accepted our fate whether through GOD or through fate but certainly not through western medical institutions.

Aren't you ready to die? I wanted to ask people, knowing I couldn't really ask that since death was still a taboo contemplation for a lot of people. They would think I was being depressive.

"People in Florida don't really talk about the vaccine," I tried to explain to my friend again.

"I mean, we all got our vaccines thinking it was for the good of everyone. You guys are like the person in the group project who didn't put in the effort."

"Did you just come up with that?" I asked, impressed by the metaphor.

"No, I saw it on a meme somewhere."

"Oh, right."

I thought it more proper to announce the source of a witticism prior to or at least after expressing it but I didn't chide her. And I didn't bother to point out that group projects in school were pointless exercises used to prepare young students to be good, obedient employees. She probably didn't even know the etymology of vaccine came from the word, "cow" since the first vaccine was invented by injecting people with cow pus.

Most people still saw academia to be some sort of worthwhile pursuit. As if college were not firstly a business at best and a scam at worst.

As I watched many of my friends continue on this path towards masters programs, towards repairing the broken system and therefore perpetuating it, I suffered in losing their minds.

I wanted to create a better, new world. That was what the cult was supposed to be about. But what had we done?

I was starting to see the cracks in Cash's theories. I couldn't even trust anyone in our cult. How could we create a new world together?

Talking to my friend I remembered how single-minded Californians are, how they latch onto new trends and forecasts and ideas with grit and greed, how ideas are like gold in the golden state and that they spread just like the California wildfires. I told Cash Californians were easiest to brainwash hence all their cults. Californians understood best the benefit of believing in something. And anyone who ended up in California had to believe in something at one point to get all that way west, even if it was just that they simply believed in California.

I started writing a story:

"You're one of the men we've been looking for, the man's man archetype, today's Humphrey Bogart, Hemingway sort. We've watched you acquire your skills and your power.

There will only be a select few people chosen to live forever. Only those who pass certain tests will be granted infinite life. What a dire mistake it would be to allow everyone a free pass forever. We have developed some questions to test you for the next phase of our search. For this new world without death, which philosophies would be best preserved? Which values would maintain the equilibrium of a society that could live forever?"

Cash and I argued about my story. We were lying in bed together. I'd been there all day; he had just gotten back from work.

He said that GOD and tradition was the only path.

"But," I said, "men are to blame for all wars, so why should they maintain dominance with their tradition?"

He shook his head. "When women are given predetermined roles defined by nature and ordained by GOD, the battle between sexes is abolished, anxieties quelled, and power struggles end."

"What about technology? Couldn't it change the human experience into an unforeseen dimension?" I asked.

"I've looked into that. It's not it."

"You are so limited!" I said.

Cash was sad I didn't believe in him anymore.

"Once you choose a path you are blinded!" I told him. "All ideology is toxic!"

When you commit to a belief, when you become certain, what do you lose and what do you gain? One loses their freedom, their virtue and therefore their connection to GOD. You lose everything. And for what? A false sense of security.

I once thought Cash was led by GOD; that he walked in the light. But suddenly all I could see was a pick-up artist, a con man. Or was I starting to see my true reflection mirrored back at me?

I began to despise Cash's masculine philosophies. Especially when he said women could only connect to GOD through men. I didn't, couldn't, wouldn't believe it; not after all my conversations with GOD. I could see the brokenness in his philosophy, the inherent harm.

Cash wasn't just down a rabbit hole; he was bombing the rabbit hole.

I started writing more of what Cash said verbatim. We argued in circles until he said, "GOD looked at me. I can do no wrong."

One morning, he gave me a cup of tea and I didn't drink it because I was afraid he had poisoned it. Or put something in it that would kill the baby.

Cash said he had a dream that we had a company called Wayward. He didn't know that the word "wayward" wasn't positive. We looked it up together and saw it was ominous.

Cash never saw the ending of *Mosquito Coast*. He fell asleep halfway through, right after Harrison Ford's character creates an ice machine on the remote Caribbean island he moved his family to in order to escape the evils of Western civilization. It's uncanny how much Harrison Ford looks like Cash in that movie. Cash never saw Ford destroy himself with his own ego, never saw the family narrowly escape their own ruin. Ford froze with his ice machine. He chose a position and stuck to it, ego attached like a parasite.

I wondered which movies I'd missed the endings to that hinted where I might be headed.

I soon found my answer.

I watched *The Wolf of Wall Street* and *Scarface* when Cash was out at the bars. I wanted to see the wedding dresses. I wanted to do a big gangster island 80s themed wedding to match my mom's big 80s wedding gown that I was going to wear. But Michelle Pfeifer and Margot Robbie lived lives of screaming and cocaine. The formerly pedestalled relegated to the background as neglected props. If I stayed, I'd become these women.

I read about Hortense Mancini, the socialite of King Louis XIV's royal court. I considered how I could remain in Cash's favor. All along I thought I could maintain a certain level of coolness and stay clever but I had lost my cool and I didn't feel clever when my unhappiness and blood supply swelled.

The women in Balzac's *Cousin Bette* haunted me: the wife and the mistress. The mistress was a vapid coquette who ran a salon out of her decadent apartment which was paid for by the husband of the wife. Through the novel's trajectory, she accumulated wealth and power but lost "character." And then there was the endlessly faithful and devoted wife who had no other aspirations aside from pleasing and caring for her husband who spent very little of his money on her. Throughout the novel, the wife lost wealth and power but supposedly gained greater "character." Who did I want to be? It wasn't so much who I *wanted* to be but who I *was*. I didn't have the patience nor the aptitude to be this doting, puerile, infinitely affectionate cloth of a woman though I tried. GOD knows I tried.

I wanted to do the right thing but I was born in an age when there was no "right thing" anymore. All we had were our own lights, our own paths. I almost gave mine away to Cash.

CHAPTER TWENTY: NEPTUNE RETROGRADE, CALIFORNIA, AND FULL MOON TRAVEL

Cash flew me out to California because I was so depressed. His moods were making it hard for me to move. Before I left he told me I was the only girl who gave him visions after sex. But I didn't believe anything he said anymore.

He was always on some joyride. All his words were tricks and charms meant to keep me in his grasp. He built up this whole beautiful, profound, and intricate illusion but when a tiny piece tore, the whole thing fell down.

Just like that, my perspective changed. It was like awakening from a strange dream. I was liberated and I wanted my soul back. I wondered if it was something in the sky, it felt so real, so material. And then I saw the shift – Neptune went retrograde. Or maybe it was the Zoloft that finally ran out of my body. So, no longer a somnambulist but awakened and homesick, I bought a round trip flight home on Cash's credit card.

"Did you know the moon is full tonight?" I asked my sister when she picked me up from the airport.

"Bad luck," she said.

"What? No, it's good luck to travel on the full moon," I said, as if my personal relationship with the moon, my individual matrix could make any meaning for anyone else.

Before the internet, street lamps, and cars, people probably traveled on full moons. I applied that sentiment to today, a time where we could easily travel on our whims without worrying about the moonlight. Was I timeless or nonsensical? I'd like to, at the very least, be poetic about everything. Or maybe I just wanted to be fucking normal.

Henry Miller once wrote to Anais Nin, "For me, cancer means the crab – the creature which could move in any direction. It is the sign in the zodiac for the poet – the halfway station in the round of realization. Opposite Cancer in the Zodiac is Capricorn, the house in which I am born, which is religious and represents renaissance in death. Cancer also means for me the disease of civilization, the extreme point of realization along the wrong path – hence the necessity to change one's course and begin all over again. Cancer then is the apogee of death in life, as Capricorn is of life in death."

And so, in the season of Cancer, I became ready to begin all over again. Over being dreary about society, I no longer wanted to plan for the apocalypse. I wanted to welcome a mass shift towards freedom, not survival. My experiment in tradition was over. I aimed to explore other realms.

The hummingbird from last summer showed up at my parents' house the morning after I arrived. We hung out in the garden and I wrote in my room. I looked at all my books and journals and simmered in all of the magic I left behind last year in this California headquarters of mine, before I gave up my freedom to follow a man, then a cause, then a different man.

That time I fell out of love with my cult leader.

I kept trying to call him and talk with him about everything but he never answered. I tried calling him on the way to the airport.

Finally he called me back as I waited in line for security.

"I think you should find someone else for the sailing class," I said, without pleasantries.

Our sailing class started the next day.

"What do you mean?" He asked, in a smiling voice.

"I mean I don't want to go with you anymore."

"You must go. You must submit to me," he said, his voice getting deeper, angrier.

"I don't want to submit to you anymore. I am not submitting." I said.

People were listening in the line. I thought about how weird I sounded.

"I am your king," he said.

"No. I don't submit."

"Okay, fine," he said and hung up.

His mom picked me up from the airport. She drove me to get donuts at Krispy Kreme.

"So what's going on with you and my son?" She asked, smoking a cigarette.

She smoked the cheapest brand you could buy from the drug store. Cash and I only smoked American Spirits.

"I've never seen him cry like that. And when I see my

son is hurting, I have to understand why," she continued. "And he told me you're pregnant. Is that true?"

"No," I said immediately.

"I don't know why he would lie about that."

"I think it's just something he wants. He just thinks I am," I said.

"Well what's going on? I thought you were all set to get married? What about the Hemingway house?"

I did not dig into my soul and give her any true information. My soul had sunk into an abyss I didn't have access to at the time. I gave her what pieces I had floating on the surface of my mind, similar snippets of what I said to my parents back home. I couldn't tell them what was really going on. They wouldn't understand why I had entered the relationship in the first place. I couldn't tell them I had joined a cult, that my boyfriend was the cult leader.

There had never been anyone to talk to about any of it, only me and the gods who only appeared once they decided to play their beautiful music or reveal pieces of what was behind the curtain of their hypnotic magic show.

As I chewed my Krispy Kreme donut, I told Cash's mom I wasn't ready to settle down. I was depressed in that house left all alone so often. I didn't think Cash was ready to settle down either.

When I got back to our little attic apartment I went to sleep on the couch. I didn't want to wake him up. He was disgusting to me. His phone was sitting on the coffee table. I picked it up and looked through it for the first time.

He already sent messages to all of his friends that I broke his heart. Scrolling further into the past I saw he was texting Mary about the sex they used to have, sending her old photos of them instead of answering my texts or calls over the weekend. Scrolling further I found multiple texts to anonymous phone numbers that were of photos of him and random women at the bars, similar to the photos he sent to me of us in the beginning.

I looked through his search history on Safari. He had multiple tabs open displaying his prior searches for "pick up artists strategies," "dark psychology," and "psychomagic." The last thing I looked at was his Twitter account. He followed profiles and liked posts that revolved around women submitting to men, the flaws and failures of modern women, and how to score with women.

He was a Florida man. He was just a player. He was the one you got away from. I would never want my child to have a father like him, to turn into a man like him.

Eventually Cash came out of bed and found me sleeping. He yelled at me and when I tried to leave he apologized. We lied down on the bed and held each other and cried. I cried at the destruction of the story, the terrible waste of what we did to each other. I stayed for three more days.

"I'm just trying to live a life worth writing about!" He kept saying. "I miscalculated. I got too caught up in the magic. I can fix anything."

He tried to get me to stay longer, said he'd change, that once we were married he'd commit to me. Maybe I would have stayed but then I finally saw him around his kids.

Since his baby mama was one of the people he told that I had broken his heart, she was allowing him to see his kids again. She thought I was out of the picture already.

"Never be afraid of anything," he said to his two-year-old the next evening.

She didn't want to hold the sparkler he was trying to hand her. They had just gotten back from an afternoon at Dave and Busters.

His mom told him his daughter was too tired.

He didn't seem like a real dad. More like he was acting like a dad. His mom did all of the work: the feeding, bathing, putting them to bed.

He became visually disappointed when his two-year-old didn't like the pink plastic unicorn guitar-shaped walkie-talkies he bought for her because she didn't understand how to use them or what they even were. I despised plastic toys. They made me think of Chinese slave labor.

"What about when you said you didn't know it could

be this easy? What about these five months of magic?" He asked.

He spent time away with me in his room until his mom called him on his phone to tell him his daughters were asking for him. He stayed a little bit longer with me, trying to convince me to stay when I was getting ready to leave. He had chosen me over them this whole time.

His children hovered silently around the house like sickly little phantoms in washed-out blonde shapes, with big, haunting blue eyes. I felt sorry for them.

He told me a story about him and Stacey one night. It made me sad, the way they treated each other. He told me it was supposed to be funny, that I should laugh. But all I could say was that I was sorry he had been in such a toxic relationship.

"Why do you want to change him? You shouldn't be with someone you want to change." His mom said to me when I was still at the house two days later.

I knew this was common sense that anyone could agree with but I didn't want to think like anyone in a common way. That was how normies thought. But it hooked into my skull like a parasite and dictated my behavior anyways.

His mom told me when he found out I was leaving him, he cried and asked her, "Why is GOD doing this to me?" A part of me wanted to use this against him, make him see that my leaving was a part of a test of our soulmate-ship, a test by GOD.

While he wanted to control so much, he was, at the same time, very controllable.

He could be thoughtless, allowing me to read his Facebook messages between him and Stacey when he wanted me to find evidence he could use against her in court. I read that she gave him a blowjob in March of 2020, though he had sworn they hadn't been intimate at that time.

Or maybe his love was so vivid he was blind to the details; thought our love was strong enough.

Maybe he really believed in me, in us. He was an innocent little boy playing a game he was serious about.

He never grew up but he was more powerful than all of us because of his belief in himself. We just wanted some of his light, some of that faith for ourselves. We played him as he played us yet we feigned innocence and pretended he was the bad guy. We wanted him to stop looking at himself so he could look at us.

"You knew about the two-wife thing," his mom said.

The two-wife thing wasn't even the problem. I wanted to tell her that I wanted to change him because she fucked him up. It was her fault that he was so traumatized and manipulative. But I didn't.

"He needs to spend his time with his children," she said, moving towards agreeing with my decision to leave.

He bought a yacht right before I left.

He offered to support me in Chicago. "I can rent us a chic little Chicago townhouse," he said.

No, this was exactly his motive. He controls people with his money, I thought.

"I'm going to go to Colombia. I want you to join me," he said next. I didn't even like that idea. There was nothing in it that I liked. What would we even do there? I couldn't imagine anything good about being around him, the con man, the pickup artist.

"The occult got us into this and the occult will get us out of this," I said, shuffling my tarot deck on the bed. We started pulling terrible cards together.

"Should we just give up now?" He asked me, trailing his finger on the card of Death.

He made me drive out to the Cape Coral Yacht Club to say goodbye. It was the place we first met. I was irritated he made me drive so far out of the way when I still had to drive four hours north to my friend's house in Leesburg.

We ate a pizza I picked up for us at a picnic table overlooking the gulf.

"Every princess needs a hero to rescue her," he said, watching me, already finished eating. He was still trying to get into my subconscious.

It reminded me of when I was a child and I used to

have daydreams of the boys from school rescuing me from a disaster I invented, a different one each time.

"So what did you learn from me?" I asked, still eating.

"Oh, you know, the liminal space, the gray area, writing, books, literature, the transcendent."

I waited, then asked, "Don't you want to know what I learned from you?"

"Sure," he said.

"You taught me how to be a winner," I said.

Walking back to my car we ran into one of his employees and her man. The man towered over Cash and I remembered how short Cash was, how Napoleonic.

We looked at each other, saying our goodbyes. Cash brushed away a tear.

"You're crying?" I asked.

"You don't know how much you mean to me," he said.

Then he pulled a gray hair off my head. We both looked at it, pinched between his fingers.

"A lightning bolt is going to strike you on your journey and you're gonna turn right back around."

"I don't think so."

I got into my Ford Escape and drove away.

To this day I don't know if the gray hair was planted. I haven't seen another one.

Mary moved into Cash's not even a week after I left. It was like I had picked up a whole town of toys, played with them for a little while, and when I left, I put everything back in its place as if nothing had happened, as if I had never been there.

CHAPTER TWENTY-ONE

There is a black path, a white path, and a red path. Cash walked the black path. I left him to walk the white path. He knew about cosmic consciousness; was guided by stars. But he chose darker paths. I don't know why. I guess he just wanted power.

We wanted to get pregnant. We were in love. We wanted to make it last forever, the faster the better. Enamored, we saw magic all around us, signs and symbols that we let tell us, that we made ourselves hear, *we were meant to be together*. We thought we could be anything. We thought we could write whatever we wanted and it would all come true.

I always had a hard time understanding that people say lots of things they don't mean. Especially passionate people. Especially people with big dreams and big brains and big egos. People like Cash and me.

I knew that in his world, with his logic, what I had done was unforgivable. But I also knew his logic wasn't clean, that he left cracks in between. Maybe I could still slip back inside one of those cracks, get back into liminal space where things were undecided and could still be undone.

The experience of abortion was like walking blindfolded, led somewhere unknown but I figured it had to be a better place than from where I started. I was wrong. It was a windowless prison of regret that I didn't know how long I'd be stuck inside of or if I'd ever get out.

Cash had said it was a gift from GOD. I had stopped believing in him by then. I didn't believe it was a gift from GOD. There were many gods, or at least I knew that Cash believed there were many gods. I knew that people like Cash and I used religion; we didn't let religion use us. I never blamed him though. It was trauma, it was his money, it was the way people moved for him.

It was an event. I whipped off the blindfold and found a tiny nine-week-old dead baby with blue diamond eyes the color of my wedding ring floating in the bathtub at a hotel in downtown Chicago. Before that I bled for hours on the bed, smoking a sativa weed vape and an indica weed vape, popping hydrocodone until it occured to me to take a bath.

I had wanted a water birth. It was the worst pain I ever felt.

I left the baby, fetus, abortion in Lake Michigan and prayed. I saw butterflies playing on the lake breeze and I walked back in the sand to my car smoking a cigarette. I started to pray every day.

For months I smoked a cigarette whenever I got into the car, whenever I walked somewhere, whenever my roommates were gone, whenever I took a phone call, whenever I made a phone call, and whenever I needed to leave a room.

It hit me later that I made it through a whole quarter of the pregnancy, made one-fourth of a baby. If I had known that before maybe I wouldn't have gone through with it.

Nine months later, I read on the internet that those who committed abortion would be reincarnated five hundred more times on earth. I was gonna be stuck here for the whole goddamn Kali Yuga.

CHAPTER TWENTY-TWO: THE END OF THE WORLD, CHICAGO, CLINICAL PSYCHOLOGY, AND AYAHUASCA

In the cult we used to say the circus was coming. Cash never liked for us to talk about the apocalypse in public so we made up a code word the same way we called normies cabbage heads. But I knew the circus was already here.

Downtown, late at night, a few blocks away from my hotel where I had the abortion I bummed a lighter off a couple of old men. They'd been playing golf in the sun all day. They invited me inside the bar, introduced me to their friends, and bought me a couple of Guinness's to drink with them.

I asked them if they were all vaccinated. They were. In order to perform improv I was supposed to get vaccinated. Nobody did a good job explaining why they got the vax. Only one of them said he understood why I didn't want to get it, why I was hesitant.

"But I never said I wasn't going to get it," I told them. "I'm just asking questions."

But the questioning made them think they needed to convince me to get it.

Nobody else I talked to after that had much of a thought process around why they got vaxxed. Most people I talked to got it, "because it's the right thing to do."

So the actual end of the world: more fires, more floods, less people. Was there really a battle going on between good and evil or was reality just mundane? Either way, once I was in Chicago I felt unprotected. Cash had a plan: the ark. What did I have? Just remnants of his engineering. I wondered about every person I met, every person I saw, whether they were a person or something else and if so what were they and did they have souls. I wondered if he was right about the end of the American empire being so near, that maybe I needed him and his ark just to survive. The seeds he planted in my brain were still being nourished by what I saw in the external world, even across half the country, all by myself. I could still feel him inside my head. In Chicago it certainly seemed like nonhumans ran the world and that most people didn't have souls; nonplayer characters. It made a lot more sense why things were so fucked up. That's probably why it stuck in my head. It sounded right.

A couple nights later, I realized I needed to get out of society after I called out all the people at the bar who were trying to get laid "low functioning." I was slut shaming. Then I slept in my car in a parking garage. I woke up the next morning and drove out of Chicago aimlessly. I had to readjust to the world after being in Cash's story for so long. I had to reinvent my perception of the world again.

In the middle of corn fields, Illinois, I went outside my Airbnb for a cigarette. I heard an orchestra of frogs and knew there were more frogs than people in that town. But the people probably thought they were more important.

Smoking, looking into the empty landscape, I wondered how I would go on. And then a wolf started howling. I decided I was brave and that I could go on being that way.

When I went back to Chicago, I stayed with a Peruvian PhD student named Luis who studied cancer cells in flies at the University of Chicago whom I met on the internet. Luis's mother was also an academic. When he was a child, she was out of his life earning academic accolades in foreign countries up until the age he turned 14 when she finished and returned to Peru. He owed his scholarly success to her sacrifices. She pursued high degrees so she could send him to the best schools. She sacrificed her time with him as a child so that he'd have the best education as an adult. The concept of his educated mother is what Cash despised, a woman prioritizing her career. Luis said his mom showed him how strong women can be.

But this poor PhD student was spending his life studying a disease that only existed because of a toxic society. His brilliance was wasted on the symptom instead of the actual problem. He'd do more if he helped dismantle the sick society by perhaps preventing the poisoning of our food, water, and air.

Luis said he understood why Dante's last ring of hell was for betrayers. When Luis was young, he cheated on his first girlfriend. Later, he was cheated on by someone else.

From the resulting pain and suffering he understood why Dante put betrayers in the worst rung of hell.

I wasn't sure who the betrayer was between Cash and I. He was explicit from the start, weaving me into his web of lies that weren't entirely untrue because their intention was mythos, not logos. In a hideous, defunct world I still admired his attempt to create his own world while I had been playing a role the whole time.

A month whipped by and I cried every day. Cash didn't talk to me.

I tapped into clinical normcore. Cash was spiritual bypassing. Cash was love bombing. Cash had a lack of object constancy. Cash was stonewalling me. I put him in the narcissist box, laughing at him in there like an overcoat hanging in the shower. But back in the land of normies, after seeing miles of mindless mediocrity, I wasn't sure narcissism was the worst thing anymore.

The clinical distorted reality into an ugly two-dimensional fiction. I felt like a cheap cardboard cutout when I described him to friends and family as a narcissist. It took months before I actually said the word but the descriptions I gave always warranted it. I undermined the nature of us. Narcissist. The word itself sounds like a snarl. Rarely, if ever, is the word employed as something other than as a blow to an opponent, like a hit in battleships.

But when the Gabby Pedito case was all over the news that summer, I wondered if I had narrowly escaped her fate. I watched the video with the cops who stopped her and her fiance, her eventual murderer, Brian Laundrie, in the middle of their road trip. Brian reminded me so much of Cash when he was performing; charismatic, light-hearted, chipper. It gave me flashbacks to the nights I stayed up late as a little girl, scared and worrying that my future boyfriend was going to kill me someday.

I wrote goodbye letters to him but didn't send them. I made videos of myself talking to him on my phone but didn't send them. I wrote love poems addressed to him. Then I readdressed them to GOD.

"He's a narcissist! You won't get closure!" My so-called friends said, "so-called" because when you lose your soulmate nobody is your friend. They didn't know he was magic, awake, powerful, brilliant. And what about relationships as mirrors? If I saw narcissism wasn't I seeing my own? If I saw brilliance wasn't the brilliance my own? In the forested pond, Narcissus saw a reflection after all.

I thought often of his favorite Hemingway quote:

"'Maybe...you'll fall in love with me all over again.'
'Hell,' I said, 'I love you enough now. What do you want to do? Ruin me?'
'Yes. I want to ruin you.'
'Good,' I said. 'That's what I want too.'

But Hemingway was more broken than me. I didn't have to suffer a destructive, chaotic love. I was enlightened, or at least aimed to be. I wanted to heal. I believed in the age of the awakening, the destruction of the dominator culture. We were in Kali Yuga, like Cash always said. But he scapegoated feminism and all of the liberations of women as the source of all our suffering. I remembered the women who had fought for my rights to be a free and respected member of society. Thanks to them, I didn't have to stay with an asshole. Their struggle gave me options. I didn't have to accept my fate. I could create it.

Women are stronger than men. We have endured rape, slavery, and other forms of oppression to a deeper, darker degree. Abortion is not horrible to us because we understand the importance of the life more than the pregnancy. We understand the nature of the life inside of us because it grows in our own body. It is a direct connection to GOD and closer than any man can ever get. What a woman decides to do is GOD's plan.

And yet, Hemingway had been on my mind for an entire year straight. The first house I moved into in Chicago was 2 miles away from his childhood home.

Cash was Bronze Age. I was New Age. I wanted a new world, he wanted a return to the old; to violence, to fighting, to tradition. I didn't think we could ever go backwards no matter how much we wanted to.

But he lived in the mythos! I could feel his glee, his power, his constant victory. Because he was a man that could only win, was forever correct and right and brave and true.

I wrote in my journal: *After you I will walk in endless myth, trying to find my way back to you. This break, this chasm, I needed it to work my way back to you. I had to lose you to understand you.*

Maybe the concept of soulmates was less about staying together forever and more about encountering each other over and over again across multiple lifetimes. A part of me thought my karma was dedicated to making it work with Cash. Maybe if I could figure out how our souls fit together, we wouldn't have to come back to earth again and we could float away into the great beyond, never to be separated again.

Or maybe enlightenment was about loving each individual like a lover, like GOD, to see GOD in every person and figure out where he was hiding. In what phrase, what action, what mood does each person contain GOD? Seeing Cash was to see what a person could be, what I could be. Maybe I was meeting myself in another life. Maybe that's what soulmates are. We even tend to love them more than ourselves in a grass is greener mentality. You love yourself when it's on another side, in another body more than you love yourself now, in your current body.

"You'll never find another man like me," he would say. I wanted to be magnanimous too. I wanted to go all out in his way, with eyes flashing, chin high, ready to look anyone and everyone straight in the eye. Like a GOD. Maybe I could be a GOD too. Maybe we went against the gods and that's why we suffered.

Some nights I missed him so bad I pleaded to him in my journal: *How could you leave behind your own creation? Please scoop me back up before I am gone from you forever, before I find someone who will treat me right and respectfully. I'd prefer being disrespected in your honor.*

I imagined myself arguing with him that our angel was still there, still waiting for us to pull him out of the ether. We would cry together, rolling around in bed for days, healing, learning to forgive each other for the illusions we had thrust upon each other.

Many days I had to convince myself that once I finished this book he would talk to me again. Writing the book was an act that saved me when I didn't have him anymore, after I threw everything away. After I finished the book I could return to him and that drove me to finish it.

Sometimes I saw Cash as if he were right beside me, walking with me and the guys I hung around in Chicago. I thought about his dominance, his grabbing, his scowling when I wasn't loving on him hard enough – tugging me, pulling on me constantly; his demanding masculinity – how I adored and missed that energy.

"Look at them, they're rich enough to have yachts," one of the boys I was with said, gesturing to the marina. I thought of them as boys because I doubted they would ever become men. Now I knew the world was teeming with boys and lacking men, a terrible truth I didn't learn until Cash.

Would I ever recover from being with one of the last men? Did I worship him simply because he demanded it of me? I wondered if he ever really loved me or if it was just my submission and then I wondered whether I ever really loved him or if it was just his power. Was it the way he made his decisions, with the precision and the seriousness of a scalpel? Was it just the way he was in all his actions; dead serious? He never made a move before he set his decision at a hundred percent and then he moved into that reality. And if he changed his mind he was dead serious too.

His brilliance still hummed, the wavelength we had been on still vibrated. I let my cult leader cut my mound of moon on my left hand. In palmistry that's the future hand. Did he cut into my future? Was I attached forever?

One night, dozing off, I felt him in my head. *You're here?* I exclaimed, ecstatic. He was an orb of bliss, of happiness, pure joy. Or maybe it was GOD himself. I always got my men mixed up with GOD.

I felt urged to send him bible quotes, especially Job

42:5-6, "My ears had heard of you but now my eyes have seen you. Therefore I despise myself and repent in dust and ashes." But then I remembered Mary used to send him bible quotes so I resisted the urge.

I felt like a traitor to the universe, like I had broken a sacred contract. I asked for what I wanted and then I threw it away once I had it. Maybe I really was a heartbreaker, going after a man I didn't trust. I left and Mary went back. How could she? Maybe that was true love. Maybe I was bitter that I couldn't go that deep – that I left before I tasted the truth. I chose "me" over "us."

I left him because I thought he was more wrong than right. But back among the masses with their stench of mindlessness and ignorant sin, he became more right than wrong. My life became meaningless again without him, every face had holes for eyes, smoke for brains, and I did not understand their words. How could so many be so aimless and pleased by knowing nothing? No one had the burning desire for the truth, not like Cash and I did. How scary everything was. How wrong everyone was. How I just wanted to be in the arms of the dangerous man that I loved.

Scenes of him flashed through my head; some dreams, some memories.

"Why do you just leave without telling me?" He asked, coming outside to sit beside me on the balcony at our hotel.

I didn't say anything. I smiled. Inside I felt irritated but I hid it.

"You are too independent, too selfish. You should ask me to come outside with you when you come out here."

"Welcome to the sunset," I said, in a cheerful, antidepressant way.

Maybe I was not woman enough, not caring enough, too cold to entertain this hot beast of a man, with emotions as ferocious as his ambition. Looking back on these moments I wished I had replied with more milk and honey. I resented my coldness.

As modern women our roles were undefined. We hadn't been instructed how to be good women and for that I was broken. I was never taught how to treat a man. Only how he should treat me. And even that wasn't very clear.

I thought about the music video Cash showed me on our first date; of the woman who looked in the mirror and saw both angel and devil. If both the evil and goodness came from within, perhaps it was all just a dance after all, beautiful and meaningless. The devil wanted to continue creating, having a blast, fucking shit up. The angel sought to transcend everything, fly high into a different state, into enlightenment, and achieve the mission. The devil simply wanted to prolong the fun. There is the human drama and the angelic return; to prolong the suffering or to become the rapture. Was I a rebel, a sinner, or a saint?

When I went to delete him from my Instagram, I noticed he had 666 followers. When I unfollowed him, the number became 665. Or was I the devil?

In mirrors, I noticed my still swollen breasts prepared for nursing. It reminded me of when I used to take birth control. I used to be one of those teenagers walking around stuffed with hormone pills that tricked our bodies into thinking we were pregnant and made our boobs big and plump. I did twelve years of faking out my body and then, three years later, terminated my first pregnancy that I had asked for, had prayed for.

Three different people told me about their experiences dating narcissists once I was in Chicago. Everyone used that fucking word.

Three different strangers approached me in public and asked if I wanted to hear about the end of times.

I kept meeting Libran men.

When the universal hits, it slaps. You are confronted. Your "you" is just a pattern in "us," in "we," in "GOD." That's what the mythos was all about. And now the ancient myths were illuminated, blossoming up into the modern era. I didn't need Cash to live in the mythos. The mythos was already happening, uniting with reality whether we liked it or not.

Soon there would be no reality, only the psychic. The

more tapped in you are to your psyche, the closer you are to your own truth, your own power, your own story. You'll see your guides, your symbols, your meaning – the more connected you are to yourself the more connected you are to the world.

In my journal I wrote: *We're all tuning into each other's frequencies. Are you in? Are you on the right frequency where you're ready to share everything with everyone? Have you danced with your shadow? Make your insides beautiful enough to show everyone, beautiful enough that people will want to look at them. Because everything is rising, everything is vibrating higher. We will all know one another's deepest darkest secrets sooner than later.*

As theories changed faster, as people thought deeper, as we continued to fluctuate and change, we moved upwards. The material realm became more meaningless. Except for those conditioned by the matrix to obsess over material identity.

There was a war. And it was for souls. You either saw what was happening or you didn't.

I believed a lot of people were waking up. I concentrated on finding others like me who were committed to self-empowerment and building the new world.

I thought all this before I met my first dear friend in Chicago, Daniel, the psychonaut. He told me the planet was entering a whole new stage of enlightenment. He told me many things that aligned with what Cash spoke about: different tribes of alien species living on earth and embedded into our DNA, Rothschild, Rockefeller and pedophilia, the sexual dance of Shakti and the passivity of Shiva, Jungian archetypes, and the age of Kali Yuga.

I started going to ayahuasca ceremonies. Daniel wanted me to decide for myself if it was a cult. I knew right away that it wasn't. It wasn't for power, it was for love. The shaman radiated like the moon with her Kundalini energy, using her powers for healing not for control. She told me meditating for twenty minutes during Kali Yuga made as much progress as meditating for twenty years.

Daniel thought the vaccine was like an IQ test. He

said the universe was moving into a higher vibration and that the people who died were not able to make it into the passing over of higher energies. I didn't know about that but I made a fake vaccine card so I could get where I wanted to go and buy myself more time.

Cash's remaining followers began to reach out to me one by one as summer wound down. They said it was bad and getting worse. Cash was beating Mary, trying to impregnate other girls, fucked then fired Dez, and was giving Lucci the silent treatment.

"He chewed her up and spit her out," Lucci said about Cash and a 21-year-old he was trying to impregnate.

It was worse than I could have imagined.

"How's the MK Ultra operation going?"

"MK what?"

"Never mind. What about the cult?"

"I hate when he does cult stuff. I just pretend he's not doing it. He's got this new kid all wrapped up in it. Yeah, you know, I just completely ignore anything about the cult. Whenever he gets like that. I just pretend it's not even happening."

"You sound so much like him."

"How did we all fall under his spell?" Lucci asked me, ignoring my statement. I didn't want to tell him I wasn't sure we could ever escape it. How if he was still hanging around Cash he was probably not going to be able to get out. How I still didn't feel completely out of it myself. I told him that Ayahuasca helped.

Lucci told me that one night when they were out Cash asked him if he had any money. Lucci had 300 dollars in cash. He handed the wad over to him. Cash took it, counted it, and then threw it at some girls who were being bitchy to them. Then he walked away.

But Lucci began to sound like he was gathering information from me, kept asking about the book, called me on days that were too coincidental to not connect back to Cash so I stopped answering his calls.

Dez said she didn't blame me for leaving one bit and that,

"you made the right choice." Everyone said that when I told them the story. I still felt like I made the wrong one.

"Am I on speaker phone?" They always asked.

"Yes, because I'm driving," I'd say.

In a way, I felt responsible. I was the only one who could command a semblance of respect out of him, some coherence. He was like a shooting star that only I had the power to catch. He needed me, needed our connection. But he kept searching for it in the wrong people. But from my clinical normcore studies, that was just my own narcissism.

In October, he finally responded to a happy birthday email I sent him with a happy birthday email to me. We sent tortured love poetry back and forth for a few weeks until I erupted in pain and fury and then he erupted in pain and fury. Then there was more silence from him.

A year after I left Florida, I finally finished writing *The Cult Leader*. My agent said I had to get Cash to sign off on the use of his name and reputation.

My hair was long by then and wavy, all the way down my spine. I dyed it black, packed all black, and flew to Florida. I'd go to all the old places, all his favorite bars until he saw me. I would seduce him all over again, fresh start. I'd call myself Felicity, his good luck girl. And this time, I'd be in charge.

9 781088 281284